THE
ASTROV
LEGACY

BY CONSTANCE HEAVEN

Constance Heaven

THE
ASTROV
LEGACY

COWARD, McCANN & GEOGHEGAN, INC.

NEW YORK

F
HEA

For DAVID and VIVIEN

We hold these truths to be sacred and undeniable; that all men are created equal and independent, that from that equal creation they derive rights inherent and inalienable, among which are the preservation of life, and liberty, and the pursuit of happiness.

Thomas Jefferson

Chapter 1

It seems strange to me now when I love it so deeply, but I had never wanted to come to Russia, never once. It was four years since my sister had married a certain Count Andrei Kuragin and gone to live in that far-off barbarous country. Again and again Rilla had written urging me to make my home with them, but always I had refused, finding a dozen excuses. Yet there I was, against my will, in the huge creaking travelling carriage with its six horses, jerking and jolting over the deeply rutted road until I felt that every separate bone in my body was bruised and aching.

How many more miles to Moscow, I said to myself wearily, and the tune I used to sing to my little brothers when I put them to bed went dancing through my mind—

> How many miles to Babylon?
> Three score miles and ten.
> Can I get there by candlelight?
> Yes and back again. . . .

Well, we wouldn't be in Moscow by candlelight at this rate or by cockcrow either. Not that I cared a row of pins how long it took. I wished it were Babylon or China or Timbuktoo, anywhere but Russia and living on Count Andrei's charity, even if he was my sister's husband. . . .

A long musical snore broke into my thoughts and I glanced at my two companions. The stout elderly lady beside me was sleeping peacefully, double chin gently bobbing up and down on the satin and lace at her throat. She was so enveloped in shawls, scarves and furs that she took up more than three-quarters of the seat so that I was wedged tightly into the corner. Opposite me the French maid sat bolt upright as if her backbone had been starched, her eyes closed, her pinched nose disdainful, her thin lips compressed in a sour line of disapproval. Even in sleep, her black-gloved hands clutched at my lady's jewel case as

1

though at any moment some robber was threatening to snatch it out of her grasp.

After weeks of journeying across Europe in the uncertain weather of February, I was heartily weary of my companions, not that Madame Lubova had been anything but kind to me. Luckily she did not realize I had overheard the violent protest she had raised when a high-ranking official at the Russian Embassy in London had asked her if she would be good enough to escort the little English Miss to Moscow.

'What! That dowdy little thing!' she had exclaimed in her penetrating voice. The poor man had looked horribly embarrassed when he introduced us though Madame was honeysweet. She did not know then that I spoke fluent French and even a little German though she had made good use of me since at halts and posting stations.

I longed to open a window but did not dare. At the merest breath of fresh air Madame would shriek and declare herself ready to die of congestion of the lungs. No doubt it was freezing outside, but inside the carriage it was stifling, what with being packed so closely together, the stale smell of the many picnic meals we had eaten and the reek of the brandy Madame Lubova liked to sip at intervals, to say nothing of the musky perfume she sprinkled vigorously around her, and the powerful odour of the two spoiled and petted little spaniels. The overfed Togo on my lap snuffled noisily in his sleep and Mitzi curled up on the opposite seat, who was always being stuffed with chocolates, had been travel-sick more than once. I was rapidly building up a violent dislike of Russia and all things Russian, and yet when this last pressing invitation from Rilla had come to our drab little house in Fulham, it had seemed like a marvellous escape from the dull monotony of my life and the wretchedness of a broken heart.

'Of course you must go,' Mamma had said at once. 'Just think of it, Sophie, a whole year with your sister. It will be a new life. Think of all the pretty things she will be able to give you now she has married so well. You will see Moscow and St Petersburg ... there will be balls and parties, all the fun you've missed, my darling, all you might have had if only dear Papa had lived. You know how often you've grumbled at having to teach those wretched children for a mere pittance.

2

You have been looking tired out for weeks. It makes me so happy to think that now you can put all that behind you.'

She did not know about Edward, no one did. That was something locked in my own heart and confided to nobody. Edward, those hateful children's elder brother, just down from Oxford, who had come so often to the schoolroom to talk and laugh with me ... Edward with his charming manners and gay smile whom I had loved with all the agony, all the torment and passion of my eighteen years ... Edward, who had walked with me in the park and taken me to Ranelagh and one hot unforgettable afternoon had kissed me in the shade of the giant palms in the great conservatory.

The carriage was slithering and sliding through snow and ice. I sighed and pushed aside the leather curtain to peer through the misty mud-splashed window. Outside it was not yet quite dusk and the miles and miles of flat snow-covered fields were not encouraging. Hurt pride and misery still burned in my heart. It had been so easy to believe in Edward's promises and so painful when I realized how little they meant. Even now the recollection was like a new-healed wound that you fear to touch. How could I forget that October morning wild with wind and flying leaves and the announcement of his engagement in *The Times*, pushed in front of my nose by those horrible sharp-eyed children giggling at the shocked dismay that try as I would I could not hide.

And when the long day ended at last, Edward had come hurrying after me as I walked home, taking my arm, trying to explain, saying it made no difference, while the rain splashed down on us through the trees like the tears I refused to shed. He put his arms round me, whispering we could still be friends, trying to reach my lips with his deceitful kisses until I thrust him away from me and ran ... ran all the way home from Chelsea to Fulham to shut myself in my room, burying my face in the pillow, hating him because I knew now how easy he must have thought me, hating myself because in spite of everything I still wanted him, and desperately unhappy.

Deliberately I tried to turn my mind away from the bitter memory. Poor dear Mamma had had such a hard struggle to bring up six fatherless children on a tiny income, it was no wonder that she had been so delighted when her eldest daughter had married a wealthy Russian who had come into our simple homely lives like a thunderbolt, like a being from another planet, and had snatched my beloved sister away from us. Mamma had long been forced to pocket her pride and accept what charity she could for the sake of the little ones, but I was different. I still burned with angry resentment. How dare he come bursting into our existence to take Rilla away from us as if by right! Did he think the monthly remittances that came through his London lawyer were any compensation? I would have liked to fling his gold back in his face if it had not been for Rilla. . . .

A violent lurch of the carriage threw me forward on to my knees. The little dog gave a yelp of anguish as he hit the floor. The carriage was plunging and rocking like a ship in a violent storm. Madame Lubova woke up and began to scream at the top of her powerful lungs.

Madame fancied herself as a tragedienne. She had entranced audiences at the Alexandrinsky Theatre before she married the elderly Monsieur Lubov, killed him off in a year and became an immensely wealthy widow. At moments of crisis the old love revived. I had never seen a play but I was quite sure that Sarah Siddons had nothing on Madame Lubova in a rage.

'God have mercy on us!' she screeched, one hand clutching dramatically at her ample bosom. 'What has happened? Are we going to be killed? Sophie . . . Colette . . . is it an accident? Is it robbers? Are we to be murdered?'

The bandboxes, the hand luggage were all tumbled together on the floor. I was rubbing my bruised knees and desperately trying to keep my balance as the carriage came to a shuddering halt, leaning heavily to one side so that I was forced to hold myself upright by gripping the handle of the door.

'Sophie, for heaven's sake pick up poor little Togo,' shrieked Madame. 'My God, he must be dying, the noise he is making!'

In the midst of the pandemonium the head of our coachman muffled to the eyes against the cold appeared at the tilted window and behind him the prim impassive face of Madame's English footman. He cut across the Russian's mumbled apologies.

'Do not be afraid, Madame,' he said calmly. 'It is merely the axle that has given way, that is all. It's a wonder it's not happened before on this vile road. It can be mended if only we can get help to lift the carriage. They say there is an inn not

4

a quarter of a mile ahead of us. If you and the young ladies care to step down, I will lead the way with one of the carriage lamps and you can wait there in comfort until we get it repaired.'

Thank goodness for Phillips, I thought gratefully, as we clambered out of the door and I was lifted to the ground from the dizzy angle at which the carriage had fallen. It took a great deal of hauling and pushing to get Madame through the same opening and her language in mingled French and Russian had to be heard to be believed, but at last we were all in the road. I resolutely picked up my small travelling bag and with one of the fur rugs over my arm and the two small dogs tugging at their leashes, we set out after the footman with his flickering light.

We floundered in glue-like mud, skidded on patches of ice and felt the freezing snow penetrate our thin kid boots, but in a very short time we were picking our way across a stone-flagged courtyard and in the doorway the innkeeper was bowing down to the ground at sight of Madame. Then we were inside a huge stone-walled room furnished with rough chairs and tables and a gigantic iron stove sending out billowing waves of welcome heat.

Madame of course was demanding a private room and boiling tea immediately.

'Certainly, your honour, certainly,' said the innkeeper respectfully and took up one of the iron candlesticks.

'Come, Sophie,' said Madame imperiously as she mounted the creaking wooden staircase after him.

'No, I would prefer to wait here.' I don't know why I suddenly rebelled. Perhaps it was the days and days of being boxed up all together in the carriage.

Colette looked round with haughty disapproval. 'You are very bold, Mademoiselle. The public room of an inn is hardly the place for a young lady.'

'What is wrong with it?' I said coolly. 'The dogs are soaking wet and very muddy. They can dry here by the stove.'

'Oh leave her,' exlaimed Madame irritably. 'My head is bursting already. The English are all mad. You ought to know that by now. Mind you see Togo does not take cold, Sophie. He is very delicate and subject to chills on the liver. Ask for some warm milk for him.'

'Very well, Madame.'

I made a little face behind her back. Not a word of concern

5

for me and my chilled feet. I could drop dead so long as Togo had his comforts. All the same I sighed with relief. It was the first moment during all the weeks of travelling when I could be alone for a few minutes and I welcomed it. The furthest I had been from home in all my twenty years had been a trip to Bath with those two unruly and detestable children and now I had come through so many countries, heard so many foreign tongues, eaten so many strange foods, that I felt dizzy.

The inn seemed a poor enough place but as I looked round the unfamiliar room with its stained walls and dirty stone floor, I felt a little thrill of excitement and interest. It was already dark and shadowy except for the pools of yellow light round the candles guttering in their iron holders. In one corner a man lay asleep on the floor, a shapeless filthy bundle in a rough un-dressed sheepskin coat. His head with its mop of greasy black hair was pillowed on his pedlar's pack.

The only other travellers sat close together by the shuttered window. One of them looked curiously out of place in his green uniform embroidered with gold oak leaves, the scarlet fur-lined cloak thrown carelessly back from broad shoulders. He had risen politely when we entered, now he sat down again, talking quietly. I had never imagined Russians could look like that. Rilla's husband was dark, unmistakably foreign, but this young officer had hair tawny as a lion. It fell across his forehead and the flickering light caught gleams of bronze as he tossed it back. He was leaning towards his companion speaking in French, earnestly, vehemently, I caught the word 'liberté' as he brought down his fist on the table with an angry violence. It was 1825, almost thirty-six years since the French revolution and Napoleon had come and gone since then. This seemed a strange subject to be discussing so fiercely in the common room of an inn. They looked like conspirators planning some dark deed, I thought to myself, and then laughed at the absurd fantasy. I pulled a stool close to the stove, throwing back the white silk shawl from my head and unhooking my cloak. I shook out the fur rug I had brought from the carriage and spread it on the floor for the little dogs.

The fierce heat after the bitter cold outside made me drowsy. I think I must have slept a little because the very next thing I knew was a ferocious barking and I opened my eyes to see a huge grey dog, big as a wolf, chasing a terrified Togo round

6

the room while Mitzi cowered under my stool. The following few moments were sheer pandemonium with a mop-headed maidservant screeching at the top of her voice, the young officer trying to grab the yard dog's collar and the grubby pedlar sitting up shaking his fist and shouting incomprehensible curses at me and the dogs.

The wolfhound had picked Togo up and was shaking him like a rat. I screamed and the young man at great risk to himself seized the dog's head, forced open its jaws and released the spaniel. With a powerful movement he hurled the great dog through the door.

'See that he is chained up in future. The brute's dangerous,' he said curtly to the terrified serving girl. She bobbed a curtsey and bolted from the room slamming the door. He came back to where I was on my knees examining the shivering whining Togo.

'Is the little creature hurt? Let me see,' and he took the dog from me.

I scrambled to my feet. 'I am most grateful to you, Monsieur. Without you I don't know what might have happened.'

He was feeling Togo carefully with gentle probing fingers. 'I think he is more frightened than anything else,' he said as he put him back in my arms and, startled, I saw the blood on his wrist.

'You are hurt,' I exclaimed.

'It is nothing.' Grey eyes under straight dark brows were frowning down at me disapprovingly.

'You should take more care of your charges, Mademoiselle. That beast outside is half wolf. He could have killed the little dogs. I would strongly advise you to join your mistress upstairs without delay.'

Before I could gather my wits for an indignant reply, he had clicked his heels, bowed, thrown a piece of money to the pedlar, still grumbling as he gathered up his pack scattered all across the floor, nodded to his companion and strode out of the room.

Greatly irritated by his peremptory tone, I was just beginning to wonder whether I had been a little rash in trying to show my independence when the second traveller who had remained in the background taking no part in the uproar said quietly, 'Forgive me, Mademoiselle, but do you realize your coffee will soon be ice-cold.'

'Coffee?'

'The girl brought it a few minutes ago and our savage friend came in with her. Allow me to pour it for you.'

'Thank you.'

The man who came out of the shadows was tall and very thin. I was looking at a pale face seemingly chiselled out of marble with dark brown hair, a thin line of moustache and heavily-lidded eyes that for some odd reason when they met mine both fascinated and repelled me. He was the very embodiment of all the doomed heroes in the forbidden novels I had devoured under the blankets when I was a schoolgirl. How fantastic that there actually were men who looked like that!

'Are you sure you are feeling quite well, Mademoiselle?'

The dry ironic tone brought me back to earth. Really, I was behaving like an absolute idiot!

'I am perfectly well,' I answered quickly.

'Drink your coffee then. It will restore you,' said the stranger and handed me the cup and sat down on the bench at the other side of the stove. Sipping the coffee, I noticed that his black riding coat fitted him to perfection as did the buff breeches and polished boots. The lace at his throat and wrists was immaculate but I, who knew all about the struggle to keep up appearances on little or no money, saw at once that though his dress was scrupulously neat, it was also well worn. There was about him none of the careless elegance of the very rich.

'Are you on your way to Moscow, Mademoiselle?' he asked casually.

'Yes, Monsieur. Madame Lubova was kind enough to allow me to travel with her.'

'As her companion, no doubt, or are you perhaps going to teach English in one of the schools?'

'How did you guess I was English?'

He shrugged his shoulders. 'It is not difficult. The English have a certain something which is quite unmistakable. Besides Madame did say something of the sort.'

I felt myself blush. He must have been very observant to have noticed so much. Both he and the young officer had made the same mistake and I supposed I did look rather like a governess or a schoolteacher in my plain dark woollen dress with its neat lace collar. It was not that I did not like pretty clothes as much as anyone but the bank draft which Rilla had sent to buy new dresses for my trip lay untouched at the bottom of my leather trunk. All the same I raised my head with a touch of pride.

'It so happens that I am going to stay with my sister.'

'Indeed.'

Those strange eyes were turned on me with such an intent look that involuntarily I turned away my head. I felt his searching gaze examine me from head to foot and was horribly conscious of my untidy hair, my crumpled dress and grubby hands. Then he said suddenly, 'Is your sister by any chance a Mademoiselle Weston?'

I stared at him in astonishment. 'Yes, she is, but how could you possibly know that?'

'No magic, Mademoiselle, I assure you, merely a lucky guess. I once met your sister and there is a certain likeness. Then of course there is the name on your travelling bag.'

'But it is so strange. To think that you should have known her and that we should meet here by chance. . . .'

'Not so strange. I am returning to Russia after some years in Europe. There are not many travellers at this time of the year and this is the direct route.'

'Yes, I suppose so. My sister is married now. She is the Countess Kuragina.'

There was no mistaking the sharp intake of his breath or the flash in his eyes. The words came out in a hissing whisper.

'So . . . then Dmitri still lives.'

'But of course, why should he not?' I was puzzled by his tone. 'My sister is not married to him. She is the wife of his brother, Andrei Kuragin.'

'Andrei . . . is it possible? I never thought of that, not after what happened. . . .'

The stranger seemed curiously agitated though he had not moved. His eyes bored into me. 'And Paul? What of Paul?'

'Paul? Oh you mean Andrei's nephew? He is ten now. In her last letter to me my sister said how pleased they were that he had grown so much stronger.'

'I see.'

With an abrupt movement the stranger got up, pushing back the bench with a clatter and moving away from me. His reaction had been so unexpected that I hesitated before I said, 'Do you then know the Kuragins, Monsieur?'

'Do I know them?' He swung round on me with a gesture that had something menacing in it. 'Andrei Kuragin is . . .' Then he stopped. All the emotion died out of his face. He said coldly, 'Forgive me, Mademoiselle. I have been more than three years away from Russia and your news took me by surprise. I was once on intimate terms with the Kuragins, extremely intimate, but much has happened since then. I hope I have not disturbed you.'

'No, of course not, but I don't understand.' My own dislike of my brother-in-law and an eager curiosity to know more drove out good manners. I leaned forward. 'But what happened? Did you quarrel with Count Andrei? Did he do you some injury?'

The answer came so swift and ferocious that it was frightening. 'He destroyed the one thing that made my life worth living . . . only he failed to destroy me.' His words seemed to hang in the air, heavy with threat. Then his manner changed. 'What happened between us is in the past, Mademoiselle. It need cause you no concern.'

The icy chill in his tone rebuffed me and before I could apologize or say anything further, he had nodded briefly, picked up his cloak and turned to the door calling for the landlord to settle his account.

I stared after him. Who was he? What memories had my thoughtless remarks stirred up? What secret was hidden in his bitter anger at the very mention of Andrei Kuragin? All the distrust I had felt for my sister's husband came surging up in me with redoubled force.

Togo was whining and pawing at my skirts. I poured the rest of the milk into a saucer and put it down for the dogs, crumbling up the sweet biscuits for them, but my thoughts were far away. I was back in England four years ago now almost to the day. Mama and I had come home from the market, struggling through the snow with our loaded baskets, to find a stranger in our shabby little front parlour, a tall well-dressed stranger, who had not waited for introductions but had seized both Mamma's hands, raised them gallantly to his lips and said gravely, 'I am a thief, Madame, a robber, for I have come to steal your daughter.'

It had been a disturbing day with the younger children

wildly excited, Mamma dazzled and bewildered and Rilla going
about in a dream, her eyes shining like stars. Count Andrei had
succeeded in charming everyone, even down to Tabby, the
maid-of-all-work, who kept leaving the kitchen to come and
peer at him as if she expected him to disappear in a puff of
smoke. I seemed to be the only one unimpressed. I kept
remembering what everyone else appeared to have forgotten.
It was barely three months since my sister had come back from
her year as a governess in Russia, looking so white, strained
and unhappy that we had feared for her health. She had never
said a word of what had happened on the great estate of
Arachino where the Kuragins lived, and we had not pressed
questions on her, but Rilla and I had always been so close, I
had sensed her misery and suffered with her. And who had been
the cause of it but the all-conquering stranger who now sat in
one of our faded armchairs, smiling, reaching up to pull Rilla
down beside him and commanding the household as if by right.

It made me angry though I could not show it. It had been
like that all my life. Other people used to think me shy and
timid. 'What a quiet little thing your second daughter is,' they
said to Mamma, 'with hardly a word to say for herself.' They
didn't know how fiercely I felt about everything, only my
sister knew that. We had always shared every secret though there
were five years between us and no one, not even Mamma, had
guessed how desperately I had missed her and how wretchedly
lonely I had been during the year she had gone away to Russia.
Then she had come back and just when we seemed to be
settling back into our quiet happy life together, this foreigner
had come and I had to lose her all over again.

Always as far back as I could remember I had been fiercely
independent. Even as a baby I had hated people to help me.
I wanted to do everything for myself. Perhaps that comes from
being the second child with an elder sister so much more
beautiful and clever than I was and a brother just a year
younger who was the first boy and Mamma's darling. When I
began to grow up and realized how poor we were, I would have
gone out and cleaned steps rather than accept charity. I hated
Andrei's generosity, I resented the gifts he showered on the
children, I quarrelled with Rilla over the necklace of amethysts
he bought me as a bridesmaid's present.

'I chose it particularly. They are the colour of your eyes,

11

violets in an English wood,' he said in his charming way, smiling and tilting up my chin to look at him because he was so tall and I so small. I had jerked my head away. I would have liked to hurl the necklace back at him and only wore it at the wedding because Rilla had begged me to do so almost with tears.

He had rushed my sister into marriage in no time at all. Goodness knows what strings he was able to pull but there was scarcely time to buy even a wedding gown. As for a trousseau, he dismissed it with a wave of his hand. 'We will buy what is needed in Paris on our return journey.'

The unfamiliar church was fantastic with corkscrew pillars like sticks of barley sugar inlaid with a mosaic of coloured stone. I knew nothing of Byzantine art and was determined not to like what I saw. It was all too theatrical, too unreal, I thought, when I followed my sister up the aisle. The painted walls gleaming with dim gilded figures, the fretted golden screen that hid the altar. The priest in his jewel-embroidered cope, his tall mitre-like hat and long hair looked like someone out of an eastern painting. I stood stiff as a statue while the singing surged and eddied round me in a language I could not understand. I refused to respond, despising the ritual, unwilling to admit that I was impressed in spite of myself when the pages held the gold crowns above the heads of the bride and bridegroom, when they both drank wine from the same cup and the priest bound their wrists together with a white silk scarf and led them three times round the altar to signify that henceforward they would walk through life side by side.

I was aware too that Andrei guessed at my dislike and lightly dismissed it. I had passed an open door one day and heard him speaking to Rilla. Guiltily I stopped to listen.

'Your little sister bears me a grudge,' I heard him say and Rilla answered quickly, 'Nonsense, Andrei, how could anyone dislike you?'

'A great many people, my pet, as you know only too well.'

'Don't speak of the past. It is over and done with.'

'I thank God every day for it and for you, but one has to live with it and he still does exist somewhere. . . .'

I had hurried on, angry with him for no reason, angry with myself for listening, but now crouched by the stove I remembered it and wondered. Did the man I had just seen play some part in the past that had to be forgotten?

Rilla had written often in the last four years asking me to visit them in Russia and always I had found some reason that made it impossible. Mamma could not spare me or I had found a new situation with people I liked or one of the children had measles or mumps or whooping cough. Then there had been Edward. If Rilla had been there I would have told her everything, but it was too precious, too much locked in my heart to put in letters. I thought I wanted to die when he jilted me and yet with my wretchedness there was something else, something that made it all the more bitter. He had thrown me aside for the daughter of a banker. Not for love, not for birth—my father might have been a prodigal waster but he was a gentleman born and bred—but simply for money and I despised him for it.

Then this winter there had been the birth of Rilla's baby son. We had waited and waited for news and when it came we could scarcely believe it. The baby was born and dead within a few bleak months. The sadness had overshadowed our Christmas. How could I refuse to go to my sister now when she wrote again with a pleading urgency?

'Andrei is kind and loving as always but I do so long for someone from home.'

With a start I realized that I must have been sitting there for two hours or more. The stove needed more wood. The room was growing colder and I shivered even in my thick cloak. The pedlar in his corner grunted and turned over noisily in his sleep. I was just beginning to wonder if I ought to look for the landlord and ask what news there was of the carriage when a terrific commotion broke out in the yard. There was the clatter of horses, then shouts, yells and the lumbering sound of wheels on stone cobbles. The little spaniels woke up and began a frenzied barking. I had a sudden panic in case the big dog broke loose again. Togo shot across the room and I was just hurrying after him when the door opened and Phillips appeared, still calm despite the snow all down his greatcoat and thick on his boots. He shook his head in answer to my question.

'It's no good, Miss. Those blockheads out there couldn't mend a child's go-cart, let alone an English carriage,' he said contemptuously. 'We shall have to wait till the morning. There's a smith in the next village, the innkeeper says, who was once employed in the imperial stables.' He looked at me with his thin smile. 'Shall I tell the mistress or will you, Miss?'

13

Both of us knew what could happen when Madame flew into a rage.

'I will if you like, Phillips. She'll be angry but it can't be helped. I had better go up now, I suppose, no good putting it off.'

I could not spend the rest of the night in the public room of an inn, that was certain. I must find out something about accommodation. I called the little dogs and went up the dark creaking staircase. Only one door faced me on the landing and I knocked gently.

'Who is it?' Colette opened it a crack. 'Oh it's you, Mademoiselle Sophie. You had better come in.'

'The carriage cannot be mended till morning,' I whispered. 'Phillips has just come to tell me.'

'Ssh . . . Madame has just dozed off.'

It was a big bare room with only one candle burning on a small table where the samovar still simmered. Madame lay sprawled on the bed, a fur rug over her, sleeping heavily. Obviously she had enjoyed the rest of the brandy in the silver flasks. One of the bags was half unpacked and combs, brushes, mirrors, creams, perfumes, half-eaten chocolates, sugared biscuits were scattered everywhere in an untidy muddle. Despite Colette, Madame went through rooms like a hurricane, I thought with distaste. Mamma had brought us up to despise disorderly living.

'It is not worth waking her,' I said quietly to Colette. 'She will only be upset. The morning is soon enough for that. We'll manage how we can.'

There was only one bed, a hard sofa and an upright wooden chair. It looked like being an uncomfortable night. I argued with Colette and at last persuaded her to lie down on the sofa. The dogs had jumped on the bed and snuggled against their mistress. I wrapped myself in one of the rugs and settled down as best I could in the chair. I thought as I snuffed out the candle that it would be impossible to sleep a wink. I stared at the faint glow of the stove in the corner, all the events of the evening jumbled up in my mind, and suddenly I did not know anything more until I woke up, stiff and aching, to see Colette already lighting the samovar. I swallowed the hot fragrant tea gratefully, nibbling a biscuit, still only half awake.

I must have been dreaming, I thought confusedly when I dipped my face in the bowl of freezing water, a muddled dream which I could not quite remember but strangely enough it was not Edward's face or that of the dark stranger which had hovered teasingly before me all night, but the tawny hair and frowning grey eyes of the young officer whom I had completely forgotten.

I hardly even had time to run a comb through my tangled hair before Madame was sitting up and demanding immediate attention.

'Tea, child, for the love of God!' she was exclaiming. 'What a terrible night! I've not closed my eyes for a single instant and my mouth is dry as a sandpit.'

I exchanged a quick grin with Colette before I knelt down to fasten the leashes on the little dogs.

'I will take them out while you finish dressing,' I offered, glad to escape from the stuffy overheated room.

In the courtyard I found a miraculous change in the weather. The grey slush had vanished. It was colder but the sun shone on a fresh fall of snow, turning everything to a dazzling purity. The air was like splinters of ice but I breathed deeply feeling my spirits rise. In a few hours I would be with my sister. There would be so much to talk about. The gloomy thoughts of the night before vanished with the weariness of the journey.

When at last we were safely in the coach, Madame leaned over to pinch my cheek.

'Well, Miss Sophie, whom did you meet downstairs last night? Oh to be twenty again! You don't know how fortunate you are, my child. Who has put the sparkle into your eyes this morning, eh?'

'There was no one,' I said happily while the horses gathered speed and the carriage rolled on its way to Moscow. 'No one of any importance at all,' and believed I was speaking the simple truth.

15

The carriage stopped outside a tall narrow house painted blue with cream wooden shutters in what Madame Lubova said was one of the most fashionable streets in Moscow. While Phillips and the coachman were carrying the leather trunk up the steps, she enveloped me in a soft scented embrace, kissing me on both cheeks.

'Give my respects to Count Andrei, my dear, and to your sister also of course, and don't forget your old friend,' she said warmly. 'I shall always be happy to see you and so will Togo and Mitzi. Say goodbye to Sophie, my darlings,' and I had to hug and kiss both little dogs before I was allowed to step down from the carriage.

I thought I would be glad to part company with my tiresome travelling companions but it was with a curious feeling of loss that I watched the horses pull away before I raised my hand to the brass knocker. A footman opened the door and left me in a stiffly furnished anteroom like a stranger. I felt just as I had done when applying for a new position in England, very shy and quite certain they would dislike me on the spot. I almost did not recognize my sister when she came hurrying in; her red hair was so fashionably dressed and she looked so elegant in a morning gown of fine blue wool trimmed with squirrel. I thought of all the times we had huddled before the nursery fire toasting buns or scorching our fingers on a few cheap chestnuts.

But I needn't have worried. Rilla was just the same. She flung her arms round my neck regardless of her finery and for a few minutes we were laughing and crying together, questions and answers tumbling over one another. Then she held me at arms' length, the Rilla I had always loved so much.

'How pale you look, darling,' she said, 'and I'm not surprised. What a time you must have had. We expected you yesterday and I was half out of my mind with anxiety when you did not come. Was Madame Lubova very terrible? Andrei calls her a damned old witch but there was no one else he could think of and you could not travel all those miles alone.'

'She was really very kind,' I said, 'if it hadn't been for the dogs and the brandy and her tantrums. When she really got into her stride, she was every tragedy queen rolled into one,' and I stalked round the room giving a fair imitation of one of her rages just as I used to do of all the people we met in the old days and we went into helpless giggles because we were so happy to be together again.

Presently Rilla took me up to my bedroom. 'Do you like it?' she asked anxiously. 'I furnished it to please you. Andrei said I could do just as I liked.'

Rilla had always had perfect taste. She had bought French furniture, a little bow-fronted chest in rosewood, a fine gilt mirror, an Aubusson carpet in rose pink and cream. I suddenly felt so happy to be there with her after all the months of wretchedness that I wanted to dance and sing. I twirled all round the room in sheer delight and then caught sight of myself in the long pier glass and gave a shriek of pure horror.

'How awful I look! What a fright! No wonder your footman stared at me. He must have thought I was someone applying for a post in the kitchens!'

I could see myself, the dark dress creased and spotted from nursing the dogs, the lace collar rumpled, my hair in rats-tails, my face pale and smudged with dust. I had always envied Rilla's fire-red curls and green eyes. She was twenty-five, tall and slim with grace and poise, whereas I was so small and had never seen any beauty in my mousy fair hair and violet eyes except during those ecstatic months with Edward that were all a lie. Rilla put her hands round my waist drawing me back against her.

'What happened to the money I sent you, Sophie? Wasn't it enough or did you give it to Mamma instead of spending it on yourself?'

'I didn't touch any of it. It's here in my trunk.'

'But why on earth. . . ?'

'I don't want your husband's money,' I said with quick pride. 'Isn't it bad enough that he provides for Mamma? He does not need to keep me as well. I prefer not to be under an obligation to anyone.'

'Still the same old Sophie! Do you remember what Papa used

17

to say? "Sophie's proud as the devil, not like me who'd take money from a blind beggar if he offered it!" '

I said nothing. Papa had shot himself when I was only ten, but I had still been old enough to envy the bond that had always existed between him and my sister.

Rilla smiled and pulled me down to sit beside her on the bed. 'Listen, Sophie, if it makes you feel any better about it, the money is not Andrei's but mine. He gives me an allowance and never asks how I spend it. Can't I give my own sister a few pretty dresses if I like?'

Put like that I began to see how foolish and petty I had been, standing on my dignity and thinking myself very grand for that reason.

Rilla said suddenly, 'Shall we go shopping now, this afternoon? Stefan shall take us in the sleigh . . . or are you too tired?'

Tired! All my weariness seemed to disappear like magic. For the first time in months I felt light-hearted.

'Do you remember,' went on Rilla, 'how we used to plan what we would do if we won a lottery or if some aunt or cousin or godparent left us a legacy? Well, now you can pretend it has all come true.'

'But what about your husband?' I asked doubtfully. 'Will he mind?'

Rilla laughed. 'Of course he won't. In any case Andrei is out at some meeting or other, he will not be back till evening. Wash your face, my pet, and I'll finish dressing. Then we will have a quick luncheon and off we will go.'

Rilla had a sleigh for her own use painted a gay scarlet with blue leather harness. Stefan was a strapping young peasant looking enormous in his padded winter overcoat reaching to his feet. The silver bells tinkled joyously as the steel runners went skimming over the packed ice of the road. Dry freezing air nipped my cheeks but we were warm and cosy under the bearskin rugs and I was far too excited to feel cold.

It had never once occurred to me that anything in Russia could be beautiful, but as we rounded a corner and the street widened, I caught my breath at sight of the battlemented walls notched into the shape of swallows' tails enclosing a forest of golden domes and towers glittering in the frosty sun. Beyond there was something so startling that I could scarcely believe my eyes. What was it? A church . . . or a heap of children's toys

18

fallen from the sky? Domes and minarets shaped like pine-apples, like turbans, like pumpkins, heaped like exotic fruit, gold, blue, red, yellow and green, each one surmounted by its cross.

'What is it?' I whispered and Rilla smiled at my look of wonder.

'Everyone gasps at their first glimpse of the Kremlin and St Basil's Cathedral,' she said teasingly. 'Andrei says this is the very heart of Russia and even though the Tsar lives mainly in Petersburg, they have all been crowned here right back to the first Prince of Muscovy.'

It was a wonderful afternoon. I could not take my eyes from the pavements, crowded not with dull poverty-stricken people as I had imagined but with elegantly dressed women in fabulous furs and tall men in striking uniforms, scarlet, black and green like the young officer at the inn, their gold epaulettes glittering, their long fur-lined cloaks sweeping the snowy ground. There were strange outlandish figures in shapeless padded garments looking as broad as they were long, peasants in undressed sheep-skins, beggars in tattered rags, men with tall hats and hooked noses, with almond eyes and yellow skins, Kalmucks, Tartars, Cossacks.

'From the Caucasus, from Bokhara, Siberia, Samarkand,' said Rilla in answer to my questions. For the first time I realized what a vast country Russia was.

In the shop on Tverskaya Street rolls of exotic materials were spread out for our choice, silks and velvets, organzas and damasks. The Countess Kuragina was an important customer. We pored over Parisian fashion plates and dressmakers hovered around me with tape measures, jabbering together in Russian, their mouths full of pins, draping me with lengths of material as if I were a dummy until I protested.

'It is too many, Rilla. You must not be so extravagant.'

But my sister only smiled. We came home with bandboxes filled with expensive trifles, scarves, cobweb silk stockings and a new bonnet in pink velvet with grey ostrich feathers that I could not resist and a muff to go with it of silver fox. I had never owned anything so exquisite or so costly.

It was four o'clock but already dark when we came out of the shop and shivered in the icy cold. I was glad when Stefan drew up smartly at the blue door, snow spraying up from the runners and the horses' breath like jets of steam, and I was not sorry to hurry into the warmth and comfort of the house.

When I had washed and changed into my best dress, a lilac merino with bands of blue braid which Mamma had made for me, I took out the bonnet and could not resist trying it on. I tied the pink ribbons under my chin and then impulsively picked up the muff and went racing down the stairs and headlong into the drawing room.

'Look, Rilla,' I exclaimed. 'Aren't they fabulous together?' and then I stopped, feeling foolish, for my sister was not there and someone else had got up lazily from one of the deep armchairs and stood, glass in hand, looking me up and down critically.

'Absolutely ravishing, especially the muff. So that's what you and Rilla have been doing all the afternoon. I hope to God you have not ruined me.'

For four years I had been nursing a hateful picture of Andrei Kuragin in my mind and now, seeing him standing before me, he was both as I had imagined him and yet utterly different. He must be about thirty-seven by now, I thought, not handsome but striking certainly with his dark hair and light blue eyes and the high cheek bones that gave him such a foreign look. Taken by surprise I could find no words and he put down his glass and came towards me.

'So, little sister, you've found your way to us at last, have you? It has taken long enough.'

He took my hand and was about to raise it to his lips when he changed his mind. Instead he reached out, drew me to him and kissed me lightly on both cheeks. For some reason that I could never explain, a tiny shiver ran through me at his touch and he sensed it immediately. He raised his eyebrows.

'Am I such an ogre? We shall have to teach you, Rilla and I, that all Russians are not barbarians.'

He was teasing me of course, just as if I were a foolish child. 'I have never thought such a thing for a moment, Count Kuragin,' I replied with dignity.

'Haven't you? I certainly gained that impression, and pray don't take off that delectable bonnet,' he went on as I began to untie the ribbons. 'You can create a new fashion by coming to supper in it.'

'Now you are being absurd.'

20

'If you say so,' he moved away from me to the side table where glasses and decanters had been set out. 'Will you drink something while we wait for Rilla ... lemonade, ratafia, peppermint. ...'

Some devil inside me prompted me to say provocatively, 'Thank you, no. I would prefer vodka,' though I had not the faintest notion what it tasted like.

He turned and looked at me consideringly, then shook his head. 'No, my child, I think not. You are not like my Rilla. You haven't the head for it.'

Why did everything he said always make me feel so angry?

'Very well, then I will take nothing,' I said coolly and went past him to sit on the sofa. A huge dog lay stretched in front of the handsome porcelain stove, his coat of chestnut and cream the same colour as the silky rug.

'Take care. Malika is not accustomed to strangers,' said Andrei.

'I am not afraid. I like dogs.'

'Good, but I should warn you that he is a Borzoi, Russian to the very backbone.' He had turned back to the table and was refilling his own glass. Then he swung round and faced me, his manner changed, the light jesting tone quite vanished. He said abruptly, 'Tell me, Sophie, do you think it was very kind to refuse all Rilla's invitations over the last four years? Did it never once strike you that your sister might be lonely here in Russia with neither family nor friends nor anyone close to her?'

I was so taken aback that I could not answer immediately. I had never thought of myself as selfish in my stubborn refusal. I said lamely, 'But she had you.'

'Yes, she had me,' he replied dryly, 'and there is Dmitri who is often sick and Paul who is a child and a whole house full of serfs, but it's hardly the same as a sister. Don't think that Rilla has ever breathed a word against you. She is a very remarkable person, your sister, did you realize that? Probably not, families never do. But I know that there were times when she must have longed for one of her own kin and not even I could make up for it and I had thought someone so close to her, someone she loved as much as she loves you, would have had more understanding of her needs.'

It was so unexpected, so different from what I had imagined. In a flash I saw myself as he did, selfishly occupied with my own

21

loneliness, filled with resentment because my sister was so happy, but he did not know everything.

'I don't know what you mean,' I said quickly. 'There were so many other things to be thought of ... my mother, the children, the work I had to do. ...' Then I fell silent because his eyes were scanning my face, contemptuously, I felt, and the next moment Rilla came in and he turned at once to her with such obvious pleasure that a pang of envy shot through me. Between these two there seemed to be something so close and warm that I felt shut out.

'Why does he say she needs me when it is so clear that he is all she could ever want?' I thought to myself.

Conversation at supper was mostly about people and events of which I as yet knew nothing. Andrei's mood had changed. He was charmingly attentive, asking questions about Mamma and the children, but all his remarks were tinged with an ironic humour that irritated me. Between him and Rilla was a light teasing banter that I was too young to understand, too ignorant of men like him to realize how much deep feeling it concealed.

We had already reached the dessert when he said suddenly, 'I saw Leon today, Rilla. He and his sister are in Moscow with their grandfather.'

'I thought Leon was in Petersburg with the regiment,' said Rilla.

'He is on leave. His grandfather has had another heart attack, a serious one. Irina is overjoyed he is here. The silly child adores her brother.'

'Why silly?' I objected. 'It seems to me only natural for a sister to be fond of her brother.'

'Quite so, but then you don't know Leon. His mind is set on other things,' said Andrei lightly. 'There's a challenge for you, Sophie. Set that enchanting bonnet of yours at Prince Leonid Astrov and see what happens. I'll wager a hundred roubles that you'll have him eating out of your hand in no time.'

'Andrei, you're being outrageous,' interrupted Rilla. 'Whatever will Sophie think of you?'

'No worse than she does already, isn't that so, Sophie?' He leaned back in his chair. 'What do you say? Are you going to accept my challenge?'

I did not know how to answer his teasing and Rilla said

quickly, 'Don't be ridiculous, Andrei. As far as I am concerned, I would prefer us to see as little of Leon as possible.'

'You see how your sister commands my life,' remarked Andrei with a wave of his hand.

'Don't believe him. He pays not the slightest heed to me and does just as he pleases.' There was a faint edge to Rilla's voice that surprised me. 'In any case,' she went on, 'Prince Astrov has made up his mind about his grandson's marriage. Everyone in Moscow is talking about it.'

'I don't doubt it and Leon will fight him over it tooth and nail. Why do you dislike him so much, my pet?'

'I don't dislike him,' answered Rilla coolly. 'But Leon is perpetually in scrapes and more often than not involving you in them. Last year in Petersburg it was gambling, then it was horse racing. Heaven knows where he finds the money. He seems to enjoy shocking everyone. I tremble to think what he will do here in Moscow.'

'Well, you reformed me, perhaps Sophie can do the same for Leon,' said Andrei and smiled. It was astonishing how it lit the dark face so that for an instant I glimpsed the charm that had swept my sister off her feet. 'I think I know him better then you, my dear,' he was saying. 'His grandfather keeps him on too tight a rein. He is like one of my thoroughbreds. Keep him shut up and he will kick his stall to pieces. Leon is for ever in rebellion.'

'What does he rebel against?' I asked curiously.

'Oh everything ... his grandfather, his commanding officer, even the Tsar ... he wants to change the whole world and he still thinks he can. Maybe you're right, Rilla. Your little sister is too young for Leon.'

'Do you have to speak of me as if I were still at school, Count Kuragin?' I protested indignantly.

'You look so enchantingly young, I really can't help it, and you don't need to address me as if we were at a public meeting. I'm quite human, you know.'

'Andrei, don't tease her.'

'I'm not teasing. I am perfectly serious.'

It was ridiculous but I made up my mind there and then to dislike Prince Leonid and his sister, which only goes to show how stupidly wrong you can be if you allow prejudice to sway judgment.

23

I heard my sister say a little sharply, 'What was the meeting you had to attend today? You didn't tell me when you hurried off so early this morning.'

'Didn't I?' Andrei was cracking walnuts. He put one on my plate and then held out the other to his wife. 'Open your mouth, my dear, these are quite delicious. It was nothing important. Just a few old friends lunching together at the English Club.'

Rilla frowned but said nothing more and it was odd that I, who knew him so little, felt absolutely sure that he was avoiding a direct answer to the question. I wondered why.

I excused myself after supper. I felt exhausted. So much had happened that it seemed days rather than hours since the night at the inn. Rilla kissed me good night and I watched her go arm in arm with Andrei into the drawing room.

While I brushed my hair, fifty strokes as Mamma had always taught us, it occurred to me that for the first time for months a day had gone by and I had scarcely spared a thought for Edward. For a long time, nearly two years, I had lived in a dream, a fool's paradise, and then it had shattered. Perhaps it was just as well. I stared into the mirror and even managed to smile at myself. I might as well realize once and for all that no dashing hero was ever likely to look twice at my ordinary little face.

When I climbed into bed, I suddenly remembered the stranger and the feeling of unease that he had somehow conjured up. I wondered if Rilla would know who he was if I described him to her. I could imagine Andrei's comment, mocking, contemptuous, dismissing my reaction as a childish fancy. It would be pleasant, I thought, as I snuggled into the warmed sweet-scented sheets to bring him down a peg or two, to make him feel he owed me something instead of the other way round. I forgot that life has more tricks in store than one bargains for and that little fantasies sometimes have a way of turning into painful reality.

Chapter 3

I had always been so busy drilling French verbs into those detestable children and helping Mamma in the house that I thought the hours would drag when I had nothing to do but enjoy myself, but they simply flew by. Rilla had such a wide circle of friends and acquaintances that we were always calling on someone or receiving visitors; there were tea parties, charity bazaars and drawing-room concerts. I found myself moving in the very highest society and I sometimes thought the aristocratic Princesses and Countesses were inclined to look down their high-bred noses at Rilla, the young Englishwoman who had come to Russia as a mere governess and had married her employer's brother . . . to say nothing of the little sister who looked so plain, poor thing! I had actually heard someone say that one day when we took off our wraps in our hostess's bedroom and the same speaker went on with a spiteful look at Rilla.

'Andrei Kuragin was always a fool about women. What on earth did he see in her? She fusses over the peasant brats at Arachino and hasn't even given him a son!'

I saw the look of pain that crossed my sister's face and my blood boiled at their malice. Rilla was worth a hundred of them.

Perhaps it was because our days were always so occupied that we did not confide in one another as we used to do. I never told my sister about Edward though sometimes I longed to do so; and I discovered that Rilla would not speak of her baby. Once when we were in her bedroom and she asked me to fetch her something from the dressing table, I saw a baby's rattle lying there, a pretty thing in the shape of a silver bear, and thoughtlessly I picked it up and shook it.

Rilla snatched it out of my hand. 'I forgot to put it away with everything else,' she said and dropped it into a drawer, slamming it shut. I wanted to ask questions but the closed look on my sister's face forbade it.

There was something else too. She and Andrei slept in different rooms. Perhaps it wasn't so strange, I thought. I had never lived in society like this before. Perhaps it was the custom in Russia amongst those with wealth enough to share large luxurious houses and yet I wondered. They were so fond of one another but occasionally I was aware of a feeling of tension. It was not that they quarrelled or even spoke sharply to one another, but sometimes Rilla had a fine-drawn look. She seemed almost feverishly determined to fill every moment of her life and Andrei was often away.

'He is not like so many other Russians,' she explained one morning when we sat late over our coffee and rolls. 'They leave everything to a steward or a factory manager and live here or in Petersburg, but Andrei likes to oversee everything himself. You will understand what I mean when we go to Arachino. There are the birch forests where the timber is cut and the factories and the horses he has begun to breed. There are other estates too. He likes to visit them personally. Do you know that we own more than four thousand serfs?'

'Own them? You can't own people.'

'Yes, you can, body and soul, men, women and children, just like the black slaves we used to read about in America,' said Rilla dryly. 'It has taken me a long time to grow used to the idea. Some people buy and sell them just like horses or cattle, except that they take more care of their animals; they are more valuable. You even see advertisements in the news sheets . . . one able-bodied male, two females and a healthy child.'

'How horrible. Do you do that?'

Rilla smiled. 'No, Andrei would not permit it though some of his neighbours think he is out of his mind. They say he is too indulgent because he takes care that his peasants are decently housed and cared for if they are sick. He had a terrible quarrel once with Leon's grandfather over it. He has an estate about twenty miles from Arachino.'

'What happened?' I asked curiously.

'It was Leon's fault really. He opposes everything Prince Astrov does and sometimes Andrei encourages him. He has always liked him from a boy. He was a cadet when Andrei was a major in the Guards.'

It was strange how Leon's name kept cropping up. Everywhere we went, we heard gossip about him, his debts, his mistresses, his quarrels with his grandfather. I began to be very curious. I had already met Irina and to my surprise liked her immensely. She was a dark-haired brown-eyed girl, a year younger than me and she had welcomed me at once into her own circle of young people. But though she often spoke of her adored brother, he never accompanied her. He had his own apartments in the Astrov palace and lived his own life.

Rilla had begun to put cups and plates together with quick nervous fingers. 'Perhaps Leon is not entirely to blame for the way he behaves,' she said thoughtfully. 'The old man is a tyrant, he really is, and Leon was only fourteen when his father was killed fighting against Napoleon at Borodino, and his mother died when Irina was born. It was their grandfather who brought them up. He is over eighty now and rules everyone around him with a rod of iron.'

And Irina hated him. I knew that already and had guessed how unhappy she was at home. What was the use of being a Princess, rich and well-born, without affection or love? I thought how miserable I would have been without Mamma and the children.

'So you see, darling,' Rilla was saying, 'things are not always so easy for Andrei. You know that Dmitri was almost killed by one of his own serfs, a crazy boy who had an imaginary grievance, and he has never fully recovered. He depends on Andrei for everything.'

It was all so different from what I had imagined. I began to be a little ashamed of my hasty judgment grown out of prejudice and resentment.

Rilla had lifted the tray and stood looking down at it for a moment, her face troubled. 'Sometimes it makes me afraid.'

'Afraid? But why?'

'It's so difficult to put into words, but Russians are unpredictable. You never know quite what they will do, even the peasants. Hold them down and they grow sullen. Set them free to do as they wish and they hate you because you own land and possessions and they have none ... there are other things too.'

'What sort of things?'

But Rilla shook her head. 'Nothing you need worry your head about, darling. I'm being fanciful as Andrei says sometimes. Call Katya for me, will you? And you must hurry if you are to lunch with Irina.'

The Astrov palace was a huge gloomy house and Irina's sitting room was dark with heavy furniture that nothing could make look cheerful. She had a governess companion who was supposed to go everywhere with her. 'The Ogre' we called her and she was a German, sullen-faced and humourless. Irina spent her time trying to escape from her.

'Grandfather calls Fraülein into his room every morning and makes her give an account of all I have done the previous day,' she confessed to me over lunch. 'It's awful. It's worse than being at the Convent. At least I used to have fun with the other girls and wasn't spied on all the time.'

'Does your brother feel the same?'

'Oh yes, but it's easier for Leon. He can do what he likes when he is with the regiment except that he is dependent on grandfather for every rouble. It makes him furious. After all he is twenty-six now and the estates will all be his one day, but grandfather will not let him have any say in the running of them. He still treats him as if he was an irresponsible schoolboy.' Irina grinned at me. 'I have been telling him all about you. You will meet him tomorrow. He has promised to come with us when we go skating in the Petrovsky Park.'

There was to be quite a party of us. There had been some doubt expressed as to whether the ice still held. In early March there had been days of half thaw, but for the last week, a hard frost had returned and I was looking forward to it. Skating was a pastime we had often enjoyed at home simply because it cost so little, no more than a few shillings for a secondhand pair of skates.

Rilla was to have accompanied us but at the last moment she developed a bad throat and Andrei who happened to be at home that afternoon offered to take me. He drove the sleigh himself, his long whip lightly flicking the ears of the high-stepping thoroughbreds with their long silky manes and tails, Stefan perched on the step at the back.

Irina met us on the edge of the lake with Michael Federov. He was a Lieutenant in her brother's regiment whom I had met already and suspected of being in love with her. Irina looked flushed and defiant.

'Grandfather forbade me to come because Fraülein has a

migraine but I just walked out of the house. He will be so angry when I go home.'

'Why isn't Leon with you?' asked Andrei.

'He sends his apologies,' put in young Federov quickly. 'The Grand Duke Nicholas has arrived in Moscow and has sent for him.' He smiled down at Irina's troubled face. 'Don't worry, Ira, I will take you back to the palace. Prince Astrov will not say anything to me.'

'Well, now that's settled,' said Andrei cheerfully, 'let's get on the ice. Sophie is going to show us how to skate.'

I was struggling with the white boots Rilla had lent me and wished as I did a hundred times that he would not always tease me. Michael Federov's excuse had sounded a great deal too glib. Obviously Prince Leonid just could not be bothered even to be courteous to his sister's friends. I tugged so irritably at the lace that it broke and I fumbled with it. My hands even in the fur gloves were numbed with the cold.

'Allow me,' said Andrei and knelt to knot and lace my boots with strong capable fingers.

It was already growing dusk but flares blazed all round the lake and lanterns glowed, pink, blue and gold, in the frosted trees. A peasant orchestra was playing gay gypsy music and every now and again one of them would sing a verse of some ballad, hauntingly sweet and melancholy. The ice was crowded with skaters, some gliding with linked hands like lovers, some moving precisely with folded arms and frowning at the merry groups who flew all over the place, shrieking with merriment when their feet suddenly shot from under them and down they went. There was even one impeccably dressed gentleman solemnly propelling a chair with runners in which lolled a pale beauty wrapped in exquisite furs. Nothing could have been less like our humble little parties on Hampstead Heath with our home-knitted mittens and woollen mufflers.

Soon we too were gliding across the ice, Michael with Irina and Andrei with me. It was marvellously exhilarating. My secret fear that my old skill would have deserted me soon vanished. The main lake was crowded but beyond there were vast empty spaces.

'Can't we go on to where there are fewer skaters?' I asked, but Andrei shook his head, saying something I did not catch above the roar of people and music.

I was growing more and more confident. Last winter I had gone skating with Edward more than once, a secret joy that no one knew of, and he had taught me all kinds of new steps. With a sudden daring I pulled myself away from Andrei and went spinning off on my own. I saw them watching me and it went to my head. I ventured on more and more difficult turns. Irina was clapping her hands. I saw Andrei's ironical smile and it spurred me on. I intended to end with a showy spin like a ballet dancer but I overreached myself, my feet swung from under me, I teetered ridiculously for an instant and then sat down with an undignified bump on the ice.

I was totally unprepared for the gale of laughter that greeted my mishap. I tried to scramble to my feet and only made myself look more ludicrous. Laughter, even if it is good-natured, is hard to bear when you are young and sensitive and I could have wept with sheer mortification.

Andrei came to my aid. He hauled me unceremoniously to my feet while Irina hovered around, still giggling.

'I'm glad I caused you and your friends so much cheap entertainment,' I said stiffly.

Irina stopped laughing, looking hurt and bewildered. Andrei said coolly, 'Everyone falls on the ice sooner or later.' There was still a hint of amusement in the blue eyes and I would have liked to stalk away in indignation but it is impossible to do than on the ice when you are still unsteady on your feet, and he had a firm hold of my arm.

'Oh come, Sophie, you don't mind a little fun, do you?' and he gave me a shake as if I were a silly child. 'We all make fools of ourselves at some time. Come and have something to eat.' He was propelling me towards the bank where stalls were set up, selling every imaginable kind of food.

'What would you like?' Andrei was saying. 'The *kulich* are very good or there are sausages or *blini* stuffed with herring or do you prefer sweet cakes?'

I was bruised and quite unreasonably angry. 'Nothing, thank you,' I replied with freezing dignity.

'Nonsense. You'll feel much better with something inside you. Rilla is just the same. She is always bad-tempered when she is hungry.'

He was pushing something wrapped in silver paper into my gloved fingers. It smelled delicious. I hadn't realized how the frosty air had sharpened my appetite and the *kulich*, a sort of brioche filled with savoury meat, was the most appetizing thing I had ever tasted. The hot tea flavoured with mint was marvellously refreshing.

'That's better,' remarked Andrei gaily. 'You're looking a little more human already.'

'Are you sure you're not hurt?' asked Irina anxiously.

'No, I'm perfectly all right.'

'You don't mind if Michael and I go on skating?'

'Of course not.'

They glided away together in perfect unison. Irina was a great deal more expert than I was. All I had done was to make myself look very foolish. It was stupid to feel tears prick at my eyes over so silly and trivial an incident.

A great many people came up to greet Andrei. He would have included me in their conversation but I hung back. I knew I was behaving badly and I didn't care. After a little while he gave me a quick glance.

'Do you mind being left for a few minutes, Sophie? I've just seen someone I want to have a word with.'

I shook my head. 'Please don't worry about me.'

'I shall not be long.' He touched my cheek lightly. 'Now don't sulk and don't do anything rash while I am gone, will you?'

I watched him skate swiftly across the ice, tall and graceful in his long fur-lined cloak. I sipped my tea and waited but he did not come back and it grew colder and colder. Quite unreasonably I began to feel neglected. After all I was not a child. I did not have to do as I was told. I thought rebelliously that I would make one more circuit of the lake and then come back to where Stefan waited with the sleigh. Already some of the skaters were driving away.

I moved out from the bank and skimmed to the end of the pond where it closed into a narrow neck and then opened out again to a further stretch. It was deserted and exactly suited my mood. The day that had started so well was all spoiled. I felt sure that Andrei despised me just as Edward had done. A wave of black depression swept over me and I skated on thoughtlessly, scarcely noticing where I was going.

It was very quiet. The music had faded into the distance. There were no more flares, no more lanterns, only a young slip of a moon casting a greenish light. I was not far from the bank when I heard the cracking. With a sharp touch of fear I realized that the surface was thin and dangerous. I could see dark patches where the ice floes were splitting. I felt the freezing water lap over my boots. In another moment I would be plunged into the green depths. I screamed and threw out my arms in panic and someone grabbed at me. Someone was dragging me backwards. I stumbled and the grip tightened. A voice said, 'Don't fight, little fool. Let yourself go,' and then I was being pulled up the bank through the stiff frozen rushes. Someone was steadying me against the trunk of a tree.

'What in God's name are you thinking of?' said my rescuer in an irritated tone. 'Are you trying to commit suicide? Didn't you see the warning? It is in big enough letters.'

I had seen a board but the Russian characters had meant nothing to me and foolishly I had taken no notice of it.

'Thank you for your help,' I said unsteadily. 'I don't know what I should have done if. . . .'

It had all happened so suddenly. I was still shuddering, my teeth chattering with cold and nerves. I hunted for a handkerchief and pushed back my white fur hood. I could see little of the man who stood beside me except that he was tall and dressed in black, but I did notice that he was not wearing skates. He must have been walking along the overgrown path at the edge of the lake.

'I don't know how I am to get you back,' he said in annoyance. He turned towards me and I gasped because for an instant it might have been Andrei looking at me, then I realized my mistake. It was just a trick of the uncertain light.

'Mon Dieu, we do seem to meet in odd circumstances. First a broken axle and now when you are on the point of drowning. I congratulate you, Mademoiselle Weston. Is this how you occupy yourself in Moscow?'

It was the stranger of the inn and in the half darkness he was like a dark apparition coming out of nowhere.

'You need not concern yourself with me, Monsieur. My friends are probably looking for me already.'

He was watching me with the same brooding look that had made me feel uneasy before. I would have moved away but he held me by the arm.

'One moment, Mademoiselle. There is something you can tell me. Is Andrei Kuragin back in Moscow?'

32

'Yes, he is here,' I answered shortly. 'Surely you must know that.'

'Not in the circles I move in nowadays,' he answered dryly. He still held me fast. 'And the child, Paul, is he here too?'

'No, he is at Arachino.'

'Ah, he remains with his crazy father.'

I stared at him. 'I don't understand you. Count Dmitri is not out of his mind.'

'No? Rumour says otherwise, my dear young lady.'

He still held me in a firm grip but his eyes were not on me but on the misty darkness of the lake.

'So ... Andrei has lost his son.' He smiled but there was nothing pleasant about it. 'It is enough to make me believe that there is still a God somewhere.'

He frightened me and I tried to pull away. He released my arm, but under his black otterskin cap, his eyes remained cold and watchful. In a strange way there was an attraction about him, the attraction of a proud and savage animal, never at peace, never tamed. Somewhere in my father's library there had been a copy of *Paradise Lost*. I used to steal in and take it down from the shelves fascinated by the pictures. The proud head of the fallen Lucifer might have been that of the stranger looking down at me.

'Not so handsome as your sister, but you have something more mysterious,' he murmured, 'silver-gilt hair and eyes like amethysts.' He laughed softly. 'Did they never tell you of the Rusalki?'

'The what?'

'They are water sprites with skins like pale moonlight. They live in lonely lakes and lure young men to drown themselves in the black depths. The Rusalki are always dangerous.'

With a sudden movement he bent his head and kissed me full on the mouth. His lips were cold as ice and I shuddered. The crazy thought went racing through my mind that this is how witches must feel when kissed by the devil. The next moment he had drawn back.

'Keep to the path for a little, then strike out to the centre of the lake, it is safe enough there,' he said curtly.

I edged along the bank groping with difficulty through the reeds and I had not gone far when I heard Andrei calling me and I could not help wondering if the stranger had seen him and was deliberately avoiding him.

'Wherever have you been?' Andrei reached my side, his voice sharp with anxiety. 'Irina and I have been hunting everywhere. I warned you that it could be dangerous away from the big lake.'

'I didn't hear you,' I said wearily, 'and it doesn't matter. I was perfectly safe.'

He was looking past me into the woods. 'Who was that with you?'

'No one.'

'No one? Don't lie. I saw him as I came up. Is it someone you have met before?'

'If you must know,' I replied quickly, 'he saved me from going through the ice, and I don't have to answer to you for everything I do.'

'Did I sound as bad as that? I beg your pardon.' He smiled and took my arm. 'But what would Rilla say if I allowed anything to happen to you?' He bent and peered into my face. 'You look upset and I'm not surprised. I think I had better take you home as soon as possible. You're not so accustomed to the cold as we are.'

I might have told him then about my two meetings with the man whose name I still did not know, but Andrei's manner had made me angry and afterwards it all seemed rather foolish and not worth mentioning. After all he was probably only a man who bore an imaginary grudge and liked to make himself mysterious. There are plenty of people who enjoy making spiteful remarks about others more successful than themselves. Even I, with my limited experience, had met men and women just like that and despised them. I made up my mind to think no more about him.

Chapter 4

The gilt-edged invitation arrived the following week. Andrei threw it on the breakfast table with an exclamation.

'A ball at the Astrov palace! Whatever is the old man thinking of! It's the first for years.'

Rilla picked up the card. 'We are all invited, you too, Sophie. That must be Irina's doing.'

'Must we go?' Andrei was slitting open the rest of his letters with a pearl-handled knife.

'Of course we must. Besides, Sophie will enjoy it,' and Rilla smiled at me. 'Everyone who is anyone will be there.'

'That's what I mean,' said Andrei wryly. 'I shall be ex-cruciatingly bored and forced to dance with a number of extremely frivolous young women without an idea between them ... unless Sophie takes pity on me.' He leaned across the table putting a finger under my chin. 'Will you let me fill up your card here and now and save me from a fate worse than death?'

'Andrei,' said Rilla sharply, 'don't be absurd. You confuse Sophie with your teasing.'

'Nonsense, Sophie knows very well what I think of her.' He rose, bundling his correspondence together. 'I'll leave you to the delightful discussion of the creations in which you are going to dazzle our Muscovite society.'

Sometimes I wished I did know what he thought of me. He could be charming but I was never quite sure. However, just then it was a good deal more exciting to go upstairs with Rilla and look through the new gowns which had arrived from the dressmaker and decide which of them I was going to wear.

One of them was in palest pink velvet with cream lace foaming round my bare shoulders and caught up in flounces round the skirt with knots of flowers. When I looked in the mirror on the night of the ball, I blushed a little at myself. I had never before worn anything cut so daringly low. Rilla's hair-dresser had piled my hair in curls high on my head with a cluster of roses and ribbon. I stared at the unfamiliar image in the glass and for an instant knew a feeling of panic as if somehow I was stepping into the unknown, a queer certainty that tonight I was going forward into something from which there would be no drawing back. I shivered and then told myself sternly not to be foolish. 'A goose walked over your grave' we used to say at home at any such silly tremors. I heard Rilla calling me, snatched up my fur wrap and went hurrying down the stairs.

In the hall Andrei was waiting for us. It was the first time I had seen him in full evening dress and he looked so distinguished in his dark blue coat, the cross of St George at his neck, his cloak lined with black fox, that I fully understood Rilla's pride in her husband. For once he did not make his usual ironic comment. Instead he looked me up and down, smiling, and took the two bouquets of camellias Katya was holding, pink for me and white for Rilla.

'Andrei! They must have cost a fortune at this time of the year,' my sister exclaimed.

'They did,' he answered dryly, 'but it is not every day that I have the privilege of escorting the two loveliest young women in Moscow.'

He rarely paid compliments and I was sure he did not mean it or if he did, he intended it only for Rilla who looked absolutely beautiful in deep moss green with diamonds glittering in her red hair, but all the same I felt tremendously happy, shy and excited at the prospect of my first real ball.

The air was like ice as the sleigh glided swiftly past the park, the trees like black tracery against a pale sky. But when we reached the palace and discarded our shawls and cloaks, the hall scented by great pillars of flowers and hung with tapestries in a faded rose and blue, was warm as a luxuriant winter garden.

We went up a marble staircase with a gilded handrail amidst a crowd of guests. I felt lost among so many magnificent gowns, so many heads crowned with tiaras, feathers and flowers, so many tall men in every imaginable kind of uniform. At the top Prince Astrov waited to receive his guests. He was not a big man and he was plainly dressed in a dark old-fashioned uniform embroidered with gold, the brilliant scarlet sash of some foreign order across his breast, but I could not take my eyes from his face. For some reason he reminded me of the eagle Irina and I had watched one day in the Zoological Gardens. The same thick thatch of white hair, small glittering eyes under fiercely jutting eyebrows, brown leathery skin and stern unrelenting mouth. No wonder Irina was terrified of him.

He did not look any too pleased even now when he was greeting his guests. He shook hands with Andrei, bowed stiffly to Rilla and I was quite sure he did not even see me at all as I dropped my curtsey. His eyes were roving over the crowded staircase as if he were looking impatiently for someone else and who that was soon became obvious. Beside him stood Irina looking pale and unhappy as if she had been crying. She pressed my hand with a desperate whisper behind her fan.

'It is Leon. He is not here.' There was no time to say more with the other guests pressing on behind us.

Beyond Irina stood another couple, an elderly lady magnificently dressed and a young girl.

'Madame Leskova,' murmured Rilla, 'how do you do? And Olga too. How charming you look, my dear.'

This was the young woman the Moscow gossips had linked with Prince Leon. I looked at her with curiosity. Like her mother she was elaborately dressed. She was taller than I with a fine figure and her dark brown hair was threaded with pearls. She had a proud sullen look and scarcely glanced at me when Rilla introduced us. For no reason at all I decided I did not like her.

Then we had passed on into the ballroom and I caught my breath in wonder. It was all white and gold with slender pillars of green malachite and crystal chandeliers lighting a gilded frieze of flowers and fruit. On red velvet chairs along the walls sat Irina's governess with the other elderly ladies gossiping and whispering behind their black lace fans. I was conscious of their eyes scanning every newcomer.

My agonized fear that my sister would be swallowed up in the glittering throng leaving me alone, a wallflower, unremarked and forgotten, disappeared after the first few minutes. The young men who came to speak to Andrei and kiss Rilla's hand were very soon filling up my card. After a little I forgot my shyness and began to enjoy myself. An hour flew by and it was almost midnight when Irina sought me out and flushed and breathless, we sat together in a corner for a moment, sipping iced lemonade and exchanging confidences.

'Grandfather is so angry with Leon,' whispered Irina. 'They quarrelled this morning dreadfully. I heard them right across the hall. You see, Sophie, tonight is terribly important. It has not been announced but the Grand Duke Nicholas will be here by the time we go to supper. It is a great honour and Leon is a Captain in his regiment so he will expect him to be present.'

The Grand Duke was the younger brother of Tsar Alexander, that much I knew. 'Perhaps your brother has been detained somewhere,' I said consolingly. 'After all it can happen.'

'You don't know Leon. He has done this deliberately and I know why. It is because . . .' she looked away, 'because of Olga. . . .'

'What do you mean?'

'Grandfather intends Leon to marry her. He wanted to announce their engagement this evening. That is what they were arguing about. . . .'

Poor Olga! No wonder she looked sullen. How dreadful to wait and wait for a selfish young man who disliked you too much even to show ordinary courtesy.

Irina was seized by her governess and went with her reluctantly. Then Michael Federov claimed me and dancing far too energetically in the mazurka, he caught his silver spur in one of my lace flounces and ripped it from the hem. He was so upset and so profuse with his scarlet-faced apologies that despite my annoyance I had to forgive him. Rilla was nowhere to be seen so I retreated to one of the anterooms holding the lace frill in my hand and an obliging maidservant fetched needle and thread and made a hasty repair.

I came back to the ballroom and stood for an instant in one of the deep curtained window embrasures. Through the frosty glass I could see an inner courtyard of the great house, still and peaceful, the leafless trees casting queer twisted shadows. Behind me was music and laughter and in front of me only the silvery quiet and moonlight on the statue of a young girl slender and naked holding an urn above her head. In summer it must be a fountain.

'Pretty, isn't she? Are you running away too?' said a voice so close to me that I started and my ivory fan slipped to the floor. The young officer behind me stooped to pick it up and as he straightened himself, I recognized him with a shock of surprise. I saw him frown. Then a look of recognition sprang into his eyes.

'What on earth are you doing here?' he exclaimed, then caught himself up with a little smile. 'I beg your pardon, but I never imagined that Prince Astrov counted Madame Lubova among his acquaintances.'

'Do you know her then?'

'We all know her, here and in Petersburg. The stakes are high at her gaming tables.'

'Do you mean you gamble?'

'Sometimes . . . but I've not seen you there.'

'No.'

It was on the tip of my tongue to tell him who I was and then something in the way he spoke, the touch of condescension in his manner, changed my mind. It might be amusing to let him go on thinking me the humble companion of the old actress.

'How are the little dogs?' he asked.

'Togo and Mitzi are very well,' I answered primly.

'No more dog fights, I trust?'

'None. And your wrist? You suffered no ill effects from the bite, I hope?'

'Obviously not since I am still alive.'

I caught his eye and then we were both laughing. He pushed aside the velvet curtain so that a shaft of light fell across the alcove and I read the surprise in his face at my altered looks.

'Your mistress must be very good to you.'

'Oh she is. She gave me this dress.'

'It was not the dress I was thinking of.'

'What else then?'

'As if you didn't know. How many men this evening have told you how lovely you are?'

I wanted to say, 'None but you,' but the words stuck in my throat because he had taken my hand. No one since Edward had ever said such a thing and I had sworn never to be trusting again.

The orchestra was playing a sweet haunting melody and he lifted his head. 'That will be the supper waltz,' he said abruptly. 'Will you do me the honour?'

I had promised to join Rilla and Andrei at the buffet table

but I had forgotten about that for the moment and I let him lead me among the dancing couples.

No unmarried girl in England would have dreamed of waltzing with a stranger. I could feel his gloved hand burning through the lace of my gown. I was so small I barely reached his shoulder but as we swung round in the dance, I could see his white dress uniform stiff with gold braid and catch a glimpse of the fine-boned face with something tense and strained about it, the tawny hair brushed forward so that it fell across his forehead, the grey eyes with long dark lashes that any woman might have envied.

I had been chatting quite gaily with my other partners, now for some reason I could think of nothing to say. I knew he was smiling down at me.

'Do you know,' he was murmuring, 'your hair shines like silver? It is fine and soft as thistledown and smells of summer. It reminds me of days in the country when I was a boy.'

It was the loveliest thing anyone had ever said to me and I gave myself up to a dreamy delight, floating round and round in his arms with closed eyes till I was deliciously giddy. When quite suddenly the music stopped, I could scarcely keep my feet and he put his arm round me.

I opened my eyes to see that we were close to one of the great inlaid mahogany doors. The orchestra burst into a polonaise, the door swung open and Prince Astrov came in accompanied by a good-looking man in a splendid uniform with two or three officers at his heels.

This must be the Grand Duke, I thought, and watched him, dazzled and curious. Those people nearest the door were already bowing and curtseying. Nicholas stopped to say a word here and there, extending his hand graciously. Then he looked up, said something to the Prince and came directly across the room to us.

'Well, Leon, my boy,' he said jovially, 'I hear I must congratulate you. The Prince tells me that you are shortly to be betrothed and this no doubt is the fortunate young lady of your choice. Pray present her to me.'

I might have guessed that this was Irina's brother, and yet how could I have known? The whole situation burst on me in one dizzying flash. His reluctance to attend the ball because his grandfather was forcing his hand, and now. . . . Oh God, what on earth was I to do? Passionately I wished the ground would open and swallow me up! Only of course it did nothing of the kind and Leon was not looking in the least disconcerted.

He said calmly, 'You are mistaken, sir. I am not marrying anyone. This lady is a dear friend of mine from England.'

'Indeed.' Nicholas raised an eyeglass and surveyed me through it as I sank into a deep curtsey. Then a mischievous smile lightened his rather heavy features. 'Charming, my dear boy, she's quite charming. What a devil of a lad you are to be sure!' Then the smile vanished. He drew himself up, his voice stern. 'All the same, some things are not done; they are simply not done. You had better see me in the morning,' and he walked on, his gentlemen following after him, openly grinning at one another, their raking glances sending the blood surging into my cheeks.

Prince Astrov had paused by his grandson, his face hard as stone. 'You choose to be insolent, sir,' he said and the icy whisper made me shiver. 'How dare you bring this young woman into my house and insult my guests, to say nothing of his Imperial Highness. You bring shame on an honourable name,' and the old man hurried after his royal guest leaving us isolated.

'Damnation!' The exclamation burst out of him, then Leon shrugged his shoulders. 'I apologize for my grandfather. It is I who am to blame.'

'It doesn't matter.'

'It matters a great deal. However there's no help for it now. We will have to face it out. Let me take you to supper.'

All round me I could see people staring, their faces curious and without pity. I saw Olga standing quite alone, her eyes fixed on me, two spots of colour burning in her pale cheeks. I would have liked to run from the room but I was not going to act the coward. Let them think what they please. I held up my head and took Leon's arm.

The supper room opened out of the ballroom and few people were there as yet. They were still crowding around the Grand Duke. Leon took two glasses of champagne from a hovering waiter and handed one to me. He had a most engaging grin when he was not frowning. It made him look younger, almost boyish.

'To hell with grandfather and his Imperial Highness,' he said and raised his glass. 'To us.'

41

I had never tasted champagne before. It ran through my veins like cold fire. 'What will happen?' I asked.

'Oh, grandfather will rage and Nicholas will have men on the carpet, talking about the honour of the regiment. He can be very strait-laced.'

The wine was taking its effect. Suddenly the whole incident seemed no more than a splendid joke. I saw Andrei and Rilla come through the door and waved to them gaily, but my brother-in-law was not smiling. He came purposefully towards us, putting me aside and confronting Leon.

'This young lady happens to be my wife's sister,' he said and though he spoke quietly, there was a cold edge to his voice. 'I have the strongest possible objection to a member of my family being treated by you or your grandfather or by the Grand Duke for that matter as if she were one of your fancy women.'

Leon looked from him to me with bewilderment. 'You are quite wrong. Believe me, Andrei, I had no idea . . . I never thought. . . .'

'I can scarcely believe that. Surely Irina must have told you.'

'Yes, she did, but how could I know that the Sophie she spoke of was the same person as . . . as. . . .'

'It is my fault,' I broke in. 'You see we had met before and I thought . . . I mean he thought I was with Madame Lubova and. . . .' I was floundering in helpless explanation and Andrei cut me short.

'Kindly leave this to me. Whatever you thought or Sophie led you to believe, Leon, I still don't care to see anyone used as a catspaw to spite your grandfather or to humiliate that unfortunate young woman, Olga Leskova. It is not the conduct of a gentleman.'

Leon flushed. 'I don't permit you or anyone to teach me how to behave.'

'Then behave decently,' was Andrei's curt reply, 'and don't insult a lady under my protection.'

'I've told you already, I did not know who she was. If she had told me. . . .'

'Don't try and hide behind a child like Sophie.'

Leon bit his lip. 'Are you calling me a liar, because in that case. . . .'

'In that case, you will defend your honour by sending me a challenge, I presume,' said Andrei contemptuously. 'You can spare yourself the trouble. I have no intention of shooting you for the pleasure of every scandalmonger in Moscow. Come, my dear,' he took Rilla's arm as he turned away, 'you too, Sophie. I think it best that we should leave this house.'

'One moment.' Leon put a hand on his shoulder and swung him back. 'Grandfather can say what he pleases but not you. Perhaps this will change your mind,' and deliberately he flicked his glove across Andrei's cheek.

Rilla gasped. The guests crowding round the buffet tables looked up startled, scenting scandal, their eyes alight with a malicious interest. A public quarrel with the Grand Duke likely to enter the room at any moment was unthinkable. It all seemed to have blown up out of nothing and now the two tall men faced one another angrily and my heart beat so violently I thought it would jump into my throat.

The silence lasted seconds and seemed an hour. Then Andrei said quietly, 'You damned young fool! If that is what you want, you can have it,' and he turned on his heel and walked straight out of the room. With a worried look Rilla hurried after him, taking me along with her.

In the sleigh driving home, no one spoke until Rilla said hesitantly, 'We ought not to have left before the Grand Duke. He will be offended.'

'The Grand Duke be hanged! This is my affair,' said Andrei shortly. 'You must allow me to deal with it in my own way.'

Rilla said nothing more and, huddled in my corner, I was upset, bewildered and resentful all at once. How could I possibly know that all this would arise from such a simple thing as not telling Leon who I was? And if I had, would it have stopped him? I doubted it. Andrei was probably right. He had used me as a handy weapon in his battle with his grandfather and I didn't know why the thought made me feel so miserable.

When we entered the hall of the house, Andrei bade us a curt goodnight and went to his own room.

Rilla said, 'You had better go to bed, Sophie. I will fetch us something to drink.'

When she came into my room with two glasses of hot milk and some biscuits on a tray, I was already in my dressing gown, the pink dress which I had put on so joyfully a few hours before thrown untidily across the bed.

We sipped the milk in silence for a minute or two, then I

looked anxiously at my sister. 'They won't really fight, will they? They couldn't . . . not over so stupid a thing.'

'How can I tell? Andrei is no fire-eater, but Leon insulted him publicly and he is a proud man.' Rilla put down her glass and turned on me. 'Whatever made you behave in such an idiotic manner?'

'But I didn't know . . . I never realized. . . .'

'Where did you meet him? Why did you never tell us?'

'It was at the inn. . . .'

'The inn . . . how strange. . . .' For an instant Rilla's expression softened and she smiled.

'What do you mean?'

'Nothing . . . only the first time I saw Andrei was at an inn . . . in Finland. . . .'

There was a moment of silence, then she went on quickly, 'What happened? Did he speak to you?'

'Not really . . . it was just accidental. He saved Togo from being killed and then I never thought about it again until tonight when he spoke to me . . . it was just a joke,' I ended lamely.

'It's so like Leon. No thought for anyone but himself.'

'I think he must be very unhappy.'

'If he is, it's his own fault,' said Rilla sharply. 'Andrei has been good to him and this is the thanks he gets. Oh how I hate these stupid duels! Why on earth do men want to kill one another over nothing? It is not the first time for Leon either. I don't like him, Sophie. It would be far better to have nothing to do with him even if he is Irina's brother.'

'I am not likely to, am I . . . not now.'

Rilla had put the glasses together on the tray. She leaned forward and kissed my cheek.

'Don't worry too much about it, darling. Perhaps it will work out. I'll try and talk to Andrei in the morning. He will have cooled down by then.'

'Rilla. . . .'

'Yes. What is it?'

'Rilla, is everything all right between you and Andrei?'

I didn't quite know what made me ask the question that had lain at the back of my mind.

Rilla moved away from me. 'Yes, of course it is. I don't know what you mean.'

'It's just that sometimes I've wondered . . . I mean . . .

44

well. . . .' I didn't know how to put it and in the end I just blurted it out. 'You don't even sleep in the same room.'

'Why should we? Don't be absurd. You know nothing about such things, Sophie.'

'Is it . . . is it because of the baby?'

'No, no, no! Why must you go on and on?' was Rilla's sharp answer. 'You're imagining things, Sophie. We don't always agree about everything . . . why should we? But there is nothing wrong between Andrei and me, nothing at all. Now go to sleep and don't forget what I said about Leon.'

But when I blew out the candles and climbed into bed, sleep was very far away. Rilla had not convinced me and why was she so much against Leon? It was not like her—she was always so kind, so tolerant. All I could see when I closed my eyes was the pale proud face with the unquiet grey eyes and Andrei facing him, two men who had been good friends and were now deadly enemies because of my stupidity.

'Please God,' I prayed as I had done when I was very young and everything had gone wrong, 'please God, let it all come right and don't let anything happen to them because of me.'

Only somehow, here in this alien country, the simple homely God of my childhood seemed very far away.

Chapter 5

It was late when I woke and I felt heavy and languid after a restless night. I peered at my watch on the table beside the bed. It said eleven o'clock already and I rang the silver bell. In next to no time Katya had come bustling in with coffee, crisp rolls and a dish of peach conserve.

Katya was a rosy-cheeked, merry-eyed peasant girl no older than myself. 'The Countess said I was not to bring your tray till you rang, Mademoiselle,' she said cheerfully, 'and to tell you she has to go out but will be back for luncheon.'

She settled the tray comfortably on my knees and went to swing back the curtains so that brilliant sunshine flooded the room.

'It's a lovely morning. Count Andrei was out of the house soon after eight.' She came back to the bed, hands on hips, eyes sparkling with curiosity. Katya had been educated in the school Andrei had installed at Arachino and spoke excellent French. 'Did you enjoy the ball, Mademoiselle Sophie? Stefan says the Grand Duke was there but the Master insisted on leaving long before the end.'

No doubt the servants had been gossiping already but I did not want to talk about it. I said wearily, 'Please Katya, I have a headache. I'll ring when I want you.'

Katya grinned sympathetically. She tucked a warm fleecy shawl round my shoulders. 'Don't you worry, Mademoiselle,' she said. 'You ring when you please. I'll be waiting.'

The hot coffee revived me. It was no use brooding over last night. I would just have to wait and see what happened. The bright morning tempted me. I thought that as soon as I was up, I would take Malika walking in the park. I had become good friends with the big dog and the fresh air would do my headache good. I began to feel more cheerful.

I had scarcely finished dressing when Katya was back again, radiating excitement.

'There's someone asking for you, Mademoiselle, and you'll

never guess who.' She paused dramatically. 'It is Prince Astrov.'

'Prince Astrov! It can't be. You must be mistaken.'

'Oh not the old gentleman, the young Captain. Prince Leon himself.'

'Oh no!'

I was taken aback. I was quite sure I ought not to receive him, not after the quarrel with Andrei and especially as Rilla had been so very insistent, and yet ... I took a hasty glance at myself in the mirror. The new dove-grey walking dress and matching fur-trimmed jacket fitted me to perfection. After all I was my own mistress. Why shouldn't I do as I pleased? I made up my mind.

'Tell him I'm just about to go out, but I can spare him a moment, Katya,' I said firmly. There could not possibly be any harm in that.

'With pleasure, Mademoiselle.' The girl grinned and disappeared.

Deliberately I brought out my pink velvet bonnet with the ostrich feathers, hunted for gloves and muff, summoned all my dignity and went down the stairs.

He was waiting for me in the drawing room, standing by the window, not in uniform but in a dark green many-caped coat with a sporting cut, his hat and gloves in his hand.

'I have come to apologize for Ira,' he said immediately without any polite preliminaries. 'It appears that you and she had planned a shopping expedition, but she danced so much at the ball, she is not feeling well this morning.'

I could well imagine what had taken place when the guests had departed. It was not dancing that had upset Irina but it was true about the shopping. The events of the previous night had driven it clean out of my mind.

'It is very kind of you to take so much trouble. It is nothing serious, I hope.'

'I think not.'

There was an awkward moment of silence. I could think of nothing to say and was very conscious of his eyes on me. Then we both spoke together.

'I beg your pardon,' he said.

'Please go on.'

'I was about to say that I am afraid I am no substitute for Ira. I am no expert on the choosing of bonnets, but if you care

47

to drive with me, Mademoiselle Sophie, I have a new team and was intending to try out their paces in the Sparrow Hills.'

The audacity of such a suggestion in the circumstances quite took my breath away. I ought to refuse at once of course. What on earth would Andrei say ... or Rilla ... but it was so very intriguing and I had never gone driving with a young man like him before.

'I shan't let them run away with you,' he said dryly while I hesitated and that settled it for me. There was a challenging spark in the grey eyes that I could not resist whatever the consequences.

'I never imagined you would,' I answered coolly. 'Thank you. It would be delightful.'

If he was surprised, he did not show it. We went together down the steps watched by a curious Katya and he handed me up into the high seat of the troika, wrapping the fur rugs closely around me. Then he leaped up beside me taking the reins from his groom and dismissing him with a gesture.

The troika was a gay sporting affair, painted in blue and silver with the three horses harnessed abreast, the leader in the shafts, while the other two galloped at its sides, free and spirited, with only a single strap linking them with the shafts.

Leon skilfully weaved his way in and out of the city streets. Then we left the houses behind us and were climbing up into the hills. As soon as we reached an open stretch, he gave them their heads and we leaped forward. The light carriage rocked from side to side. It was wildly exhilarating and quite terrifying. Leon was looking straight ahead, his face intent, the reins in one gloved hand, his whip in the other. Faster and faster we went while I held on, grimly determined to die rather than show the slightest tremor.

'Had enough?' he said at one moment when we rounded a corner and the troika lurched so violently I made a desperate clutch at his arm.

'Not if you haven't,' I retorted breathlessly. He laughed and stood up, legs apart, bracing himself against the wind. The long whip curled again around the leader's ears.

We were following the slope of a hill, the forest coming down close to the road on one side and on the other a sheer drop into the valley below. At the next bend I saw ahead one of the lumbering ox carts driven by the peasants. The man shouted and pulled his beasts as near as he could to the bank of the forest. The space between the cart and the edge was so narrow that I shut my eyes. He must stop, he must! But Leon was smiling, his head flung back. Through a rushing in my ears I heard him shout, 'Hold on to me!' and I reached up putting both arms round his waist, clinging with all my strength. I never knew exactly what happened. I had a notion that as we swung past, it was only by some miraculous link between Leon and his horses that he kept the carriage steady. I knew a moment of absolute terror and then he was saying, 'It's all over. We've done it!' with a note of pure exaltation in his voice.

He was slowing down now. I opened my eyes to see him looking down at me with his engaging grin.

'Scared?' I shook my head, quite unable to speak. 'There's an inn at the top of the hill,' he went on, 'we'll stop, rest the horses and see what the landlord can find for us.'

A few minutes later we were driving into a stone-paved courtyard. Stable boys came running to the horses' heads and Leon lifted me down. The inn stood high up in the hills with a little walled garden at its side. While Leon gave his orders, I walked unsteadily along the path so that I could see over the parapet across the dark forest of larch and spruce to where the Moskva river curved in a silver streak towards the city. Though snow still encrusted the ground and hung in the trees, there was a mysterious softness in the pine-scented air, a faint taste of spring, a smell of new earth and rising sap.

'Are you cold?' asked Leon behind me. 'Would you prefer to go inside?'

'Not yet.'

'I often come here,' he said, leaning on the stone wall beside me. 'It's a good place to be alone. Up here you can forget what's going on down in the city.'

'Do you dislike people so much?'

'Very often, but not just at this moment.'

I stole a glance at him. He looked different this morning, relaxed, almost happy.

'Why not at this moment?'

'Do you really want to know?'

'Of course.'

'I surprised myself. Always up to now I have preferred to drive alone.'

'Then why did you ask me?'

He shrugged his shoulders. 'I never expected you to come with me.'

'What a shock it must have been! Is that why you drove so recklessly? Who was it you were testing? Yourself or me?'

'Both of us perhaps. I may say you came through with flying colours.'

'I didn't feel like it,' I confessed ruefully. 'I kept seeing a horrible picture of us both lying dead at the bottom of the valley.'

'What a brute I am,' he said repentantly. 'My grandfather is right. He told me this morning I ought to be horse-whipped.'

In a moment it seemed the gaiety had vanished. We were back to last night, to the anger and bitterness like a cold wind blowing off the snow. I shivered.

'You're freezing,' he said quickly. 'We'll go inside. Our coffee should be ready by now.'

In the inn we sat by the window and Leon stirred the black brew moodily. I wanted to ask him what had happened between him and Andrei. Surely Rilla must be wrong. Surely they could not meet and shoot at one another over a few foolish words spoken in the heat of the moment. I was plucking up courage to say what I thought when he looked up meeting my eyes squarely.

'I owe you an apology ... and an explanation.'

'I think I know it already. Prince Astrov wishes you to marry Olga and you do not love her.'

'It is not as simple as that. I wish it were.'

He was crumbling one of the sweet biscuits in his fingers. He had unusual hands, slender but muscular. Their strength on the reins that morning had saved us from disaster. He leaned back in his chair as if he had made up his mind.

'What do you know about us?'

'What is there to know?'

He smiled bitterly. 'The Astrovs have a house in Moscow and another in Petersburg, estates in the country and God knows how many serfs, I've lost count—and yet they own nothing. They're paupers living on memories and an ancient name.'

'I don't understand you.'

'It's all mortgaged. Every stick and stone in the hands of money-lenders and Olga Leskova has a great fortune. Her father

50

was one of the richest merchants in Moscow and her mother married beneath her. She would give it all, every miserable rouble, to hang the Astrov title round her daughter's neck. Now do you understand?'

How horrible! A woman who was willing to sell her child into a loveless marriage just for an aristocratic name and a place in society. And he? I thought of Edward and was filled with a passionate contempt. Were all men alike?

'What about Olga?' I asked. 'Does she care for you?'

Leon shrugged his shoulders. 'Why should she?'

I could not help remembering that young girl with the sullen black eyes, waiting for him, hurt and rejected. A great many women had broken their hearts over him if rumours were true.

'Why has everything been lost?' I persisted. 'My sister says that Arachino was once like that but Andrei has pulled it back on its feet.'

'Andrei is not an Astrov and he has a free hand. Dmitri leaves everything to him. He is not one of a long line of princely wasters growing fat on the life blood of others until now there is nothing left but empty husks.'

All my independence rose up in fierce rebellion against his hopeless attitude. I said, 'It is foolish to talk like that. You could change it if you wished.'

'Could I? I'm one of them, that's the worst part of it. The same blood runs in my veins.' Leon was staring down into his coffee cup with a wry twisted smile. 'As a matter of fact I have been asking myself that ever since grandfather nearly died a couple of months ago. If the Jews close in on him, it will kill him. The family honour—it's all he lives for and if I marry Olga, our inheritance will be safe. Do you think I want his death on my conscience for the rest of my life?'

I had not seen it like that and my anger faded. Nothing is simple and it is so easy to judge others. 'I'm sorry,' I said. Impulsively I stretched my hand across the table and he clasped it.

'Are you?'

I think perhaps that up until then he had been speaking as much to himself as to me, but now his eyes were on my face.

'Do you know something?' he said dreamily. 'I would like to paint you, just as you are now with the sun touching your hair and that absurd little bonnet.'

51

'Paint me?' I repeated, bewildered.

'Ridiculous, isn't it? An Astrov put brush to canvas like some beggarly serf starving in a stinking garret!' Leon's imitation of his grandfather's rasping tone was unmistakable. Then abruptly he got up. 'But that's another story and you have already heard far too much about me. Come, we ought to be returning. It's late.'

Leon drove back swiftly, saying little. I remembered the question I had wanted to ask but when I looked up at the aloof disdainful profile beside me, it was difficult to find the right words. Outside the house, he gave me no time. He handed me down from the carriage, thanking me formally for the pleasure of my company as if there had never been those brief moments of intimacy on the hill top.

I said, 'Please tell Ira that I hope she will soon be better.'

'Of course.' He bowed and kissed my hand. Then he had leaped up again into the troika and whipped up the horses.

Vassily the footman opened the door and I was slipping up the stairs when Rilla came out of the dining room.

'Sophie, will you come in here for a moment?' she said. 'I must speak to you.'

She had not raised her voice but I knew the look on her face. I had faced it years ago when I had defied my elder sister and was due for punishment. I came down into the hall again reluctantly.

'What is it?' I said when the door was safely closed behind me.

'How could you do such a thing?' Rilla rounded on me. 'Have you no thought at all for Andrei or even for me?'

'Why? What have I done that is so disgraceful?'

'Don't stand there trying to look innocent. I told you last night. I asked you not to see Leon.'

I had been angry with him, yet now I defended him passionately.

'I remembered what you told me and I didn't mean to ... but he came here ... and he is not at all like you said, Rilla. He is terribly unhappy and he explained everything ... he apologized. ...'

'And charmed you just as he does every other young woman he meets! How could you be so foolish!'

'You're being unfair. I won't listen to you.' I would have

moved towards the door but Rilla put out a hand and pulled me back.

'You will listen. He came with apologies, you say. Do you know what happened before that? This morning before you were up, his Lieutenant was here with a message for Andrei. Everyone is talking about it already. Tomorrow morning they will be facing one another in the Petrovsky Park with loaded pistols and all on account of a silly little girl who goes romping off with the first man who troubles to pay her a few empty compliments. Do you think you can drive through the streets of Moscow with a young man of his reputation without all the world knowing about it?'

'I don't believe it. It's not true. It can't be true,' I said fiercely. 'Leon wouldn't do such a thing, not after what he said.'

'Oh yes he would. He's like all the Astrovs, handsome, charming and utterly selfish, without a particle of feeling for anyone but themselves. Oh God, it makes me sick to think of it ... if anything happens to Andrei. ...' and Rilla sank down in one of the chairs burying her face in her hands.

'Oh Rilla darling, it won't, it can't,' I ran to kneel beside her, putting my arms round her waist. 'Can't we do something? Can't we stop it? I'll go to Leon. I'll make him see how wicked it is.'

'You're such a child, Sophie.' Rilla cupped my face in her two hands. 'It's just a game to you, isn't it? I'm not blaming you, not really. How could you understand? You've never met anyone like Leon before. Nothing like this ever happened at Fulham.' She looked away from me. 'Andrei would never forgive me if I interfered. Men are such fools about what they call their honour.'

'I used to read about such things in novels,' I said despairingly, sitting back on my heels. 'I never thought they happened in real life, not to people like us.'

'Neither did I,' said Rilla dryly. 'Four years in Russia have taught me differently.' She got up wearily. 'And now we had better eat something. It's long past lunch time.'

'I don't want anything.'

'Of course you do. It won't help if you start fainting from hunger.'

But when the food came, it was Rilla who pushed aside her plate almost untouched. After the first reluctant mouthful I

53

found I was starving and while I ate, I thought out a plan which I intended to carry out alone, something I had no intention of confiding to my sister.

It was lucky, I thought, later in the day, that I was on such good terms with Katya because from her I was able to find out that Stefan had been ordered to have the carriage ready at seven o'clock to drive his master to the rendezvous at the Petrovsky Park. Upstairs in the drawing room there was a conspiracy of silence. Andrei refused even to discuss it, but in the kitchens the servants knew all about everything.

'May the Lord God protect his honour,' said Katya fervently. 'It's many a long day since such a dreadful thing has happened in the house of Kuragin, though they do say that once upon a time Count Andrei was a holy terror; but that was when he was a young officer,' she added hastily, 'long before he was married to the Countess. And as for Prince Leon,' she raised her hands in horror, 'in Petersburg last winter it is said he killed a man only for speaking too saucily to his sister, shot him clean through the heart. . . .'

'Oh do be quiet, Katya. I don't want to hear and anyway I don't believe it. It's nothing but gossip. You shouldn't repeat such things.'

They were all gloating over it, I thought angrily. Well, I had made up my mind that without saying a word to anyone, I was going to stop it. I was going to reach the ground before they did, throw myself between them, appeal to their better feelings. They would have to listen to me then. I would show Rilla . . . I would show them all . . . how stupid it was just to sit back and do nothing.

If I had not been so young and so completely inexperienced in such matters, I would have realized the difficulties that had to be overcome before ever reaching such a desirable result.

To start with, when I crept out of the house shortly before seven, it was still quite dark and the slight thaw had brought with it a thick drizzling mist. I had great trouble in finding a droshky and when I did, the cab driver took a very long time to grasp my few limited words of Russian. He stared at me as if I were out of my senses, then gruffly demanded the fare before he would drive off, still grumbling, and whipping up what must have been the slowest and oldest horse in the whole of Moscow. The cab smelled vilely of stale tobacco, musky perfume and sour rotting straw. When we arrived at the Park, he only very reluctantly agreed to wait for me though recklessly I poured all the money I had with me into his eager horny hands.

By now the sky had lightened into a dull grey morning, damp and bleak. The grass underfoot was soggy with patches of melting snow. I squelched through it in my sheepskin boots. I had only the vaguest notion of the meeting place but I battled on. Behind the pavilion, Katya had said, and I could see the red roof and white walls through a little belt of leafless trees. I clutched my cloak round me and plunged into the freezing undergrowth. As I came out of the tangled path, I caught a glimpse of two carriages drawn up beyond the building. I could see the horses and men moving together and almost wept with relief. I began to run towards them and the next moment I was caught very firmly round the waist and a man's voice said, 'I'm sorry but you must not go any further.'

I struggled violently to free myself. My silk shawl fell back from my head and I found myself facing Michael Federov.

'Oh it's you,' I exclaimed in exasperation. 'Let me go. You must let me go.'

'Mademoiselle Sophie! What in the name of God are you doing here?'

I could see Andrei and Leon moving into position; their seconds were drawing to one side. In a moment it would be too late.

'I must stop them,' I said frantically. 'You don't understand. They must not shoot.'

'No, Mademoiselle.' He still held me, gently enough but very firmly. 'It is you who do not understand. You cannot interfere in an affair of honour, indeed you cannot. It is quite impossible.'

'Why?' I was furious with him. 'What right have you to stop me?'

'Captain Astrov is my commanding officer. I am under his orders.'

'What has that got to do with it?'

'Believe me, it is better that you stay here, really it is. It will be over soon.'

Helplessly I stood and watched with a dreadful feeling of unreality. It was like a scene in a play. It could not really be happening, and yet it was.

'It's the best of three,' whispered the Lieutenant close to my ear. I did not understand him, but I saw the two dark figures bow politely to one another, move apart and raise their right arms. I heard the count. 'One, two, three. . . !' And then what sounded like a single shot.

'By Heaven, he's fired into the air!'

'Who?'

'Count Kuragin.'

'And Prince Leon?'

'He must have missed. One minute, Mademoiselle, and they will fire again.'

It might have been a shooting match in a public gallery instead of men's lives at stake, I thought angrily.

A few seconds seemed like an hour, then another shot rang out and the young man exclaimed excitedly, 'He has winged him this time.'

'Who? Where?'

'Count Andrei. Don't you see? My Captain has wounded him in the arm. Now for the last one.'

But there was no third shot. Instead I heard Leon's furious exclamation. 'God damn it, what's the matter with you? Why don't you shoot? Are you laughing at me? Do you want me to kill you?'

What Andrei said I couldn't hear, but I saw Leon hurl his pistol violently away from him. Then the two men were moving together. They had flung their arms round one another. It was all over and with it there came a sickening sense of anti-climax. Men! I would never understand them. All that agony of mind over nothing, and all I had done was to make a fool of myself!

The young Lieutenant said gently, 'Have you a carriage waiting? Let me take you to it. It's better, Mademoiselle, believe me. I'll not say a word. You can rely on me.'

I was grateful for his consideration and let him lead me back to the waiting droshky. 'You're very kind,' I said, shivering with cold and reaction.

'It is a pleasure,' he put me into the dingy cab, bowing over my hand and closing the door on me.

I don't know quite how I managed it, but Katya opened the door and I slipped into the house and up the stairs to my own room without being seen. My dress was sodden to the knees. I changed quickly into warm dry clothes and then came down quietly to the dining room. Rilla was already there, pale and tense, making a pretence of eating and starting at every sound.

I longed to tell her that it was all right, that I had seen them and Andrei was safe, but I could not do so without relating the story of my escapade and by now I was heartily ashamed of it. I was sipping my first cup of coffee when we heard the carriage and the next moment Andrei had come into the room. His cloak was hanging loosely round his shoulders and he carried his left arm in a sling, but he was smiling cheerfully.

'Well, thank Heaven that's over and no harm done.'

Rilla had stood up, white and trembling. She put out a hand to touch his arm. 'You're hurt.'

'It's nothing, just a scratch. The surgeon dressed it. Leon's a damned bad shot, my dear. I'll really have to take him in hand.'

'So that he can kill you next time, I suppose, or someone else or start a revolution and shoot the Tsar so that you will all be hanged! Why must you do it, Andrei? Why, why?' and Rilla choked into tears and ran out of the room.

It was so unexpected, so unlike my sister, that it was a moment before I could find words. Then I said gently, 'It's only because she is upset. She was so terribly concerned for you.'

'Was she? Sometimes lately I have wondered.'

'But she worships you. . . .'

'No, there is something you do not know.' He glanced at me with a faint bitter smile. 'You see, Sophie, your sister has never forgiven me for the baby's death.'

There was so much pain in his voice that I stared at him, not daring to ask why. For the first time since he had come into our lives, I felt my prejudice and resentment vanish for ever. I wanted to comfort him but did not know how. He stood for a moment as if uncertain, then went quietly out of the room. I heard him go up the stairs and knock at my sister's door. I found myself praying that Rilla would open it.

Chapter 6

'Sophie, my dear child, what are all these tales I have been hearing about you? Only two months in Russia and the most talked of young man in Moscow is shooting at his best friend on your account. Oh how I envy you!'

Madame Lubova, exuberant as ever, pulled me to her, kissed me on both cheeks and then held me at arm's length, critically examining my new spring costume in lime green with its bands of black braid.

'And you look so elegant, so chic!' She wagged a fat finger in front of my nose. 'What has the Countess done to you? She has turned the little duckling into a swan, far too grand to visit old friends.'

'Oh no,' I said quickly, 'you must not think that, dear Madame. I am sorry I have been so long before coming to see you, but there has been so much to do and the days have simply flown by.'

'Of course they have and why should you waste five minutes of your time calling on an old woman like me with all the young men knocking at your door, but you see I am not quite forgotten,' and Madame waved her hand complacently round her crowded drawing room.

The old actress's house was lavishly furnished with overstuffed chairs and sofas, cabinets bursting with priceless objects and plush curtains fringed with gold, yet it still looked as if a gale had blown through it, as untidy and disorderly as she was herself. She wore a rich purple satin morning gown, but her bare feet were thrust into fur slippers, diamonds sparkled in her ears under uncombed grey hair piled up like a crow's nest and there was a grubby mark on the old brown neck above the delicate lace. But to my surprise half fashionable Moscow was gathered there. Madame seemed to keep a salon for artists, actors, poets and young army officers, all standing around talking and laughing.

'Here she is,' announced Madame with a sweeping gesture, 'here is my little Mademoiselle Sophie, heroine of our very latest affaire du coeur,' and I blushed as I saw all eyes turn on me curiously.

Overcome with shyness I went down on my knees to hug the two little dogs who had come racing to greet me. A shrill screech in my ear nearly startled me out of my wits, but it was only Madame's scarlet and blue macaw on his gilded perch.

Michael Federov came to speak to me, bringing with him a young man with bushy black hair and wild brown eyes. Anatol Ryelev was a poet and quite obviously in a state of considerable excitement.

He gripped my hand, thrusting his face close to mine. 'You are from England, Mademoiselle Weston. What do you think of our slave state, eh?'

I was rather taken aback by his vehemence and he went on with a theatrical gesture.

'Michael says you were there in the Red Square yesterday. You saw what happened. Did it not make you sick to your very soul?'

I did not know how to answer though I knew perfectly well to what he referred. Irina had taken me to watch the parade of troops because Leon was there with his regiment. I had been horrified at the brutal way the police beat back the ordinary people crowding the pavements, but worse was to follow. The Grand Duke Nicholas had drawn his sword with a splendid gesture and rode alone across the square to salute his mother, the Dowager Empress, and one of the peasants, stupidly enough, had wandered on to the parade ground almost under his horse's hooves. With a sudden brutal arrogance he had slashed down at him, thrusting him out of his path. The man had been quickly hustled away but not before we had seen the blood and heard the murmur of anger. Involuntarily I had glanced at Leon motionless on his horse at the head of his troop. His face had been without expression, but I could not help wondering what he thought.

'Vile, wasn't it?' Ryelev was saying. 'A taste of the tiger that lives in all tyrants, in all Romanovs. Alexander once promised us freedom, but we still live in chains. . . .'

Michael was trying to hush him and I saw one or two people glance at us uneasily and then deliberately turn their backs. It struck me suddenly that they were afraid. They did not want even to be found listening. Nervously I began to feel I had already had enough of the stuffy overheated room. I was looking for Madame Lubova to say goodbye when the door opened and yet another visitor was shown in. There was no mistaking the tall thin figure in black. Madame gave a scream of pleasure and sailed across the room holding out plump beringed hands.

'Mon cher Jean, at last you are come. I hear you are in Moscow but not a word, not one word can you spare for your old friend. Shame on you!'

'Forgive me, dear lady,' said my old acquaintance from the inn. 'But you know I must not be idle. I have to work to live.' He bent to kiss his hostess's hand and she rapped his cheek indulgently.

'Ah, you rogue, as if I didn't know all about you! How have you lived these last years, gadding about Europe, eh? And now you must meet my little friend. Sophie, my child, let me present Monsieur Jean Reynard.'

He was as out of place among this gay throng as a bird of prey in a cage of bright-coloured humming birds, I thought, as he bowed over my hand. He did not say a word about our previous meetings, but when he raised his head, the tiny expressive shrug behind Madame Lubova's back made me smile in spite of myself.

'In another month I shall be a neighbour of yours at Arachino,' he said quietly.

'You mean you are coming to live nearby?'

'Prince Astrov has engaged me to put some order into his estate at Valdaya. It is his grandson's inheritance but he neglects it shamefully. Prince Leon is too occupied with other matters.' His glance ran over me so that I felt the colour flame into my cheeks. 'It is beggars like myself who have to do the hard work. Maybe I shall have the pleasure of seeing you during the summer.'

For no reason at all I felt a faint chill even in that hot and crowded room. As soon as I could I took my leave. It was a relief to escape into the clean fresh air of the street. It was an enchanting morning. Spring had come with dramatic suddenness. Only a fortnight before on the morning of the duel, it had seemed as if the whole of Moscow was still wrapped in ice, but now the packed snow on the roofs had cascaded into showering avalanches, the great icicles dripping from the gutters had all melted, the streets ran with water and the peasants came crowding into the city with armfuls of silver grey willow in time for Palm Sunday.

The sun was unexpectedly warm and I had no wish to return home immediately. I dismissed Stefan with the carriage and walked briskly along the street, my thoughts busy with the man I had left behind me. It was absurd but I had a feeling that a net was closing in, a threat to Rilla and Andrei, but how or why I did not know, and anyway what could he do? By now I had reached the square. The brilliant sunlight flashed on the scintillating multi-coloured pinnacles of St Basil's Cathedral. Rilla had told me that it was built by Ivan the Terrible and afterwards the architect's eyes had been plucked out to make sure that his masterpiece should remain unique. But that was two hundred years ago. Such savage cruelty belonged to the past, but all the same I found it hard to banish yesterday's incident from my mind.

I looked around me. I had been fascinated by the Ryady Bazaars, huge three-storied buildings which housed a labyrinth of shops. Bearded and booted merchants standing in doorways grabbed at passers-by urging them to enter. Inside it was a strange mingling of magnificence and squalor. Sometimes you could see ragged peasants hunting through cheap remnants beside richly dressed women examining priceless lace through gold lorgnettes. Anything less like the quiet restrained dignity of Bond Street, it would be hard to imagine.

But today I was tempted to explore further. Rilla had told me that I ought not to venture into the poorer parts of the city unless Stefan or one of the servants was with me, but that was ridiculous. I was quite accustomed to looking after myself and I had always wanted to see the open-air markets. I took one of the roads off the square and in five minutes I was back in medieval Russia.

Food stalls stretched in every direction. Peasant housewives, squat sturdy figures with shawls over their heads and huge felt boots, bargained, argued and screamed over plump chickens, shining silvery fish on straw mats, squirming eels in buckets and great joints hanging from iron hooks. Hens cackled, piglets squealed, dogs barked and leather-clad hunters hung with hares, ducks and pheasants strolled among the crowd thrusting their game under customers' noses. A travelling surgeon, the knives of his trade hanging gruesomely from his belt, stood ready offering to lance a boil, pull a tooth, cut off a dog's tail or destroy a troublesome cat. I shuddered at the bloodstained sack at his feet.

But there were other stalls too with leather goods and lacquer ware, undressed sheepskins beside heaps of soiled rags, silk carpets, rush mats and cheap jewellery. There were a great many curious glances directed at me as I wandered from one to the other, but I took no notice. I stopped to look at the silver spread outside a tall dingy brown house whose battered door stood open. The bracelets, necklaces and earrings were exquisitely wrought. The stallkeeper with his tall fur hat, yellow skin and slanting black eyes must be Tartar or Persian, I thought. As I picked up one of the necklets, he let fly a flood in some dialect I could not understand and while I stood there, examining the fragile silver flowers set with tiny stones, my attention was drawn to something else.

A young cavalry officer, elegant in his dark blue uniform, came through the doorway of the house, looked from left to right, then ran quickly down the steps and disappeared into the throng. A moment later he was followed by another, and then another. I counted six in all, each one leaving separately. What could those ugly brown walls and filthy windows be hiding? . . . a Club . . . surely not . . . or could it be something more sordid? I knew there were such places as brothels and houses of assignation but surely not in so vile a spot as this. Then I stiffened because the last to emerge were Leon and Andrei. They shut the door behind them but lingered, talking quietly on the step almost beside me though I was hidden by the rough sack-cloth awning of the stall.

Leon said, 'What is it you have against Jean Reynard that you are so determined to resign now he has returned to join us?'

'My reasons are personal,' replied Andrei curtly. 'I do not care to meet him.'

'Surely you will not let an old grudge persuade you to wreck what you yourself started. We need you, Andrei, we need you and your influence badly. I don't particularly care for him but he has worked loyally for our cause abroad.'

'For his own ends, Leon, and for nothing else, believe me. But he is only part of it. There are other, more important reasons. The leaders of the group would go too far. I want a better Russia, freedom for the serfs, freedom for us all to live our own lives, but not revolution, not bloodshed and not the murder of the Tsar. That would bring only anarchy.'

I shivered. Surely they could not mean what they were saying, or was this what Rilla had been so afraid of? Half guiltily I went on listening.

Leon had lifted his head. I saw the smouldering grey eyes, heard the fervour in his voice. 'History has taught us that the tree of freedom must be watered by blood.'

'Fine phrases, fine phrases, Leon, but have you ever stopped to think what they mean? I know what I am talking about. The Russian peasant is a child, a violent dangerous child. Give him freedom, put weapons in his hands, and he will destroy his world and then weep over the ruins.'

They were speaking so softly that I took a step nearer, the silver necklace still clasped in my hand.

'You did not talk like this five years ago,' said Leon bitterly. Marriage has changed you.'

'That is not true. I have only learned, painfully sometimes, that there is no quick way to an ideal world. . . .'

But I heard no more. The stallkeeper had suddenly leaned across his piled goods; his dirty hand clutched at my arm and he was shouting so loudly that people stopped to stare. The two men swung round.

'Good God, it's Sophie. What on earth are you doing here?'

Andrei took the steps in one stride. The peasant cowered back at the sharp authoritative voice. Andrei threw down some money and he grabbed at it counting the coins and still jabbering excitedly.

'He thought you were stealing his trumpery rubbish. Put it in your pocket. You can give it to one of the serving girls.' Andrei frowned down at me. 'You shouldn't be here at all, you know. Didn't Rilla tell you?'

'She doesn't keep me on a chain,' I answered tartly. 'Besides I wanted to come. Everyone says these markets are the real Russia.'

Andrei smiled. 'The real Russia, I wonder! Do you hear that, Leon? I wish I had time to show you the real Russia, but I'm late already. I should have been somewhere else half an hour ago. Leon, my dear fellow, will you do me a favour? Will you escort Sophie home for me?'

Leon had followed him down the steps. He gave me a polite nod. 'Of course. I should be delighted.'

'I don't need anyone,' I protested.

'Yes, you do. You're far too independent.' Andrei tapped my cheek with one long brown finger. 'Why did I ever marry into such an obstinate pig-headed race? Now you be a good child and do what you're told. Don't forget, Leon,' he went on as he turned away. 'Rilla is expecting you and Irina to join us for the Easter Mass.'

'We will be there.'

'Good.'

Leon watched him go and then turned to me. He did not look any too pleased and I was furious with Andrei for treating me like a schoolgirl and foisting me on to someone who obviously did not want me.

I said icily, 'If it is not too much to ask, Prince Astrov, I would like to see more of the markets before I return home.'

'Certainly. If it is the real Russia you want to see, I can take you to the Khitrov.' Leon's cool sarcastic tone matched mine. 'That's where the tramps live, the homeless, the thieves, the murderers, a dozen families in one stinking hovel with so many brats they are glad to hire them out to the beggars. Dragged barefoot and starving through the mud and slush of the streets, they can earn as much as ten kopecks a day from rich young women like you wanting to see the "real" Russia. I'm afraid you will not be too popular dressed like that and you will have to be careful where you bestow your charity. In the Khitrov they knife one another in the back for a crust of bread or a heel of sausage.'

I was appalled at what he said, but I was indignant too. 'If you have quite finished lecturing me, I would like to remind you that it is not my fault that Andrei forced me on you. I would much prefer to go alone. In fact that is exactly what I intend to do,' and I began to walk quickly down the street. He came after me like a flash.

'No, you don't.'

'Let go my arm.'

We were glaring at one another, then quite suddenly and

64

unexpectedly Leon smiled. It was such a lightning change I was bewildered.

He released my arm. 'Forgive me. That was quite unpardonable. I don't know what came over me to say such things to you. The fact is. . . .'

'You're angry with yourself and so you're punishing me.'

'Perhaps.' He caught my eye and had the grace to look ashamed. 'I'm beginning to think you know me better than I know myself. Come, shall we go?'

I hesitated and then took his proffered arm. We walked on together and he was quite different, friendly and companionable, pausing here and there to explain or point out something of interest. It was still too early in the year for many flowers but one old woman had a basket of violets, only half opened in clumps of green moss. He bought a cluster of them and put them in my hands. The sweet fresh scent reminded me of English woods, but to my surprise I felt no regret, no yearning for home, though not so long ago I had been sure that I would never grow to like Russia or its people.

I wanted to ask him about the conversation I had overheard, what it meant and why they had been meeting in that broken-down house, but I could not do so without betraying that I had been an eavesdropper, something I despised. We had paused to watch the antics of a peasant boy, thin and lithe as a snake, twisting himself into hoops and performing somersaults in the filthy gutter and I plucked up courage to ask one question.

'Are you well acquainted with Jean Reynard?'

Leon gave me a quick glance. 'Hardly at all. Why do you ask?'

'I called on Madame Lubova this morning and he was there. He told me he is to be employed by your grandfather.'

'Yes, he is . . . at Valdaya.'

'Why don't you look after your estate yourself?'

Leon frowned, looking away from me. He paused before he said abruptly, 'Why should I? If the rents come in regularly, that is all I want from them.'

The careless arrogant reply was not what I had expected. I wished I understood him.

'When I saw you first . . . at the inn, do you remember. . . ? You were with Monsieur Reynard then.' I laughed a little. 'I heard you speaking of *"la liberté"* and I wondered what kind of country I had come to with conspirators hatching some fearful plot.'

'My dear Mademoiselle Sophie, you must have been dreaming or reading too many romances.' The face he turned to me was limpid with innocence, the grey eyes dancing with amusement. 'I had met Jean Reynard by chance, a fellow traveller, that was all. At that time I didn't even know his name ... and now, look, here is the bird market I promised you.'

Quite obviously he was not going to tell me anything. Frustrated I turned to where he pointed. There were birds of every description, green linnets, scarlet-throated bullfinches, small brown nightingales, jays and jackdaws, sturdy pigeons and snowy doves, all beating their wings helplessly against their small cages while the bird catcher argued and bargained over the price.

'There you have a picture of the Russian people,' said Leon sombrely. 'Every one of us and all in prison.'

A customer had at last put down his money. He carried the cage away, opened the door and let the bird fly free.

'How wonderful!' I exclaimed. 'To buy them into freedom.'

'Wonderful indeed, only in most cases it is a trick,' replied Leon cynically. 'They are well trained. They will flutter up into the sky, fly a short distance, then return and wait quietly with folded wings for the boy to pick them up, bring them back to their master and resell them.'

'But that is hateful!'

'It's like all of us. We long for freedom, we talk about it night and day, but when it comes to action, we all run back to our cages and sit there too frightened to move.' He turned to me, the grey eyes glowing. 'I'll tell you what we will do, you and I. We will buy as many as we can carry, drive up into the hills and release them there.'

'How marvellous! Could we?'

'Why not?'

He was laughing now and he did not bargain. He tossed down gold and we seized the cages of linnets, nightingales, larks and doves while bystanders stared at us as if we were crazy. Away from the market Leon found a droshky to drive us to the verge of the Sparrow Hills.

High up with the city's spires and domes glittering in the distance, we opened the cages. His hands as he lifted each

66

bird from its prison were so gentle, I felt I was seeing a part of him shown only to very few. When we came to the doves, he said, 'You take these.'

He put the birds one by one into my hands. I felt the tiny heart beating in the fragile body, the tremor of its wings before I threw it up in the air and saw it soar and glide in the soft breeze.

We stood quite still watching them until they had disappeared. Then he turned to me and it seemed the most natural thing in the world to feel his arms round me and his mouth on mine. He pushed back my bonnet, his lips wandered lightly over my hair and my eyes and came back to my mouth, this time with a sudden fierce strength that made me tremble. The last shred of pain attached to Edward's memory was chased away by that kiss. This was something more powerful, more disturbing, though at the moment I could not see beyond it.

How long we stood there, I do not know. It was a time one does not count. Then Leon released me. He did not say anything, only cupped my face in his two hands and looked at me as though he wanted to remember every tiny detail.

Then he dropped his hands and turned away, pushing aside the empty cages. 'I must take you home,' he said, and I followed after him through the wet grass towards the waiting droshky.

In my bedroom I put the violets carefully in water and placed them on my dressing table. Then I leaned forward to look at myself in the mirror. Madame Lubova was right. I had changed and it was not just the fashionable clothes. I had become quite different from the shy stiff prickly young person who had come so unwillingly, nursing imaginary grievances, all the hundreds of miles from England to Russia. In two short months I had become so involved in this new life, I felt as if I had always been part of it, yet there was so much that I still did not understand.

It had been a disturbing morning. The mysterious stranger whom I had dismissed as of no importance had suddenly stepped into our intimate circle. He had acquired a name and a personality. He might have to be reckoned with. At the very first opportunity I must ask Rilla what she knew about him. I had felt differently towards Andrei ever since the duel but I was still a little shy of him. He was charming and easy-going, but I suspected that if his anger was aroused, he could be formidable. I had already noticed that though his servants liked and respected him, they took no liberties.

I began to unbutton my jacket while I thought of the snatch of conversation I had overheard. Revolution belonged to history. It meant France and the guillotine and Napoleon, but that was all long past. It was ten years since Waterloo and Europe was at peace. Maybe these Russians, like young men everywhere, liked to talk of their dreams but never turned them into reality.

While I changed my dress, I could not stop myself thinking of Leon. After the wretchedness of Edward's betrayal, I had believed myself armoured against all charming wayward young men. Never again I had vowed to myself, never again would I give my heart to anyone unless I was sure, absolutely sure. I was well aware that even to think of Leon was madness—wild, arrogant, reckless, hopelessly in debt—nothing that he did or said could be trusted. Then there was his grandfather and Olga.

Resolutely I changed my shoes and washed my hands ready for luncheon, but when I combed my hair, the sweet faint scent of the violets stole up and despite myself, a tiny shiver ran through me. I knew with a frightening certainty that something inside me had responded instantly to him, something that might be hard to kill.

Chapter 7

I asked Rilla about Jean Reynard the next afternoon while I helped her with the preparations for our move to Arachino. Immediately after Easter, the house in Moscow would be shut up except for a few servants and the whole household would be making the three-day journey to the country just south of Petersburg.

My sister looked up from the lists she was checking. 'Jean Reynard? Surely he has not dared to come back,' she said and something in the way she spoke disturbed me. 'He told you that he would be at Valdaya during the summer, but that is only twenty miles from Arachino. Are you sure?'

'That's what he said at Madame Lubova's yesterday morning. Who is he, Rilla?'

'He was an orphan on whom Andrei's father, the old Count, took pity. He brought him up and educated him. When he was old enough, he made him his steward. He managed the estates.'

'What happened?'

'He behaved badly, very badly, and Andrei was forced to dismiss him.'

'Why? What had he done?'

'There was no proof but he believed him responsible for the attack that nearly cost Dmitri's life.'

'How shocking. And was he?'

'I was sure of it, but many people, including Prince Astrov, thought Andrei had acted unjustly. They did not know the facts or that he has provided for him ever since.'

'Provided? You mean he is given an allowance? But whatever for if he was guilty?'

Rilla was not looking at me. She was shredding the quill pen in her hands with nervous fingers. 'Andrei felt he owed it to the memory of his father. After all they had grown up as boys together. So you see, Jean Reynard has no cause to feel any bitterness against the Kuragins.'

'No,' but I was not satisfied. I remembered what he had said at the inn. "He destroyed the one thing that made my life worth living." There was something else, something deeper and more important behind it all, but I knew my sister. If Rilla did not choose to speak of it, no urging on my part would move her.

'Will you tell Andrei?' I asked.

Rilla had picked up another pen and began to trim the quill. 'I could wish he were not coming to Valdaya,' she said evenly, 'but after all there is no reason why we should meet. I shan't mention it. Andrei will have to know, I suppose, but time enough when we are there.'

But after all it was Jean Reynard himself who made sure that Andrei knew and afterwards I wondered if it had been deliberately planned.

Easter, I discovered, was by far the greatest feast of the Russian year and mountains of food were being prepared in the kitchens. Katya called me out one day in Holy Week to look at the eggs, dozens and dozens of them, all being dipped into pans filled with red, green, blue and yellow dyes. There was sugared white cheese for *pashkha*, a delicious cake stuffed with preserved fruits, and soft white dough for the *kulich*. Every cake and biscuit was stamped with XB, Russian initials for Christ is Risen.

Leon and Irina were to have joined us for the midnight mass in the Cathedral of the Assumption but though we waited for them, they did not come, and when we reached the Kremlin, the Cathedral was already packed to the door.

It was a cold clear night and the pale golden domes glimmered against the dark sky. When I looked around me, it seemed as if the stars had come down to earth for everyone in that vast silent crowd carried a lighted taper. A breathless excitement held us in its grip as though we waited for a miracle. Faintly we could hear the singing in the Cathedral. Then the great doors swung open, music and light flowed out; embroidered banners, candles and gold copes moved in a scintillating procession seeking for Christ's sepulchre and certain of His resurrection. The choir's powerful singing mounted up into the sky. A star shot up with a long sparkling tail, then another and another— the blaze of fireworks! Golden rain was falling, lighting up the whole Kremlin. Domes, crosses, towers, eagle-headed battlements floated like a magic ship ready to fly from its moorings and soar into the sky. The earth shook beneath my feet as all the bells of the city rang out in a mad rejoicing. The hymn rose up into a great chant of triumph. 'Christ is risen!' Everyone rich and poor was turning one to another, their faces filled with joy.

Andrei embraced his wife and turned to me, kissing me on both cheeks. I had never felt like this in the dark austere church at home. A great happiness flooded through me. The taper in my hand flared up and unbelievably I thought I saw Leon at a little distance. He must have come late after all. He held no candle and looked so lonely, I could not endure it. I tried to push my way through to him, but there were too many people. When I looked again, he had gone, swallowed up in the crowds.

It was when we were making our way slowly towards the waiting carriage that we met Jean Reynard. He stood directly in our path and Andrei halted. He had been laughing and teasing me, now he was suddenly grimly silent.

There was a smile on Jean's good-looking face but it did not reach his eyes. 'It is four years, Andrei. Isn't it time to let the past bury its dead?'

Andrei stared at him for a long moment. One or two people as they pressed past looked at us in surprise. Then he said quietly, 'Never. Never so long as I live,' and would have walked on but Reynard stopped him with a hand on his arm.

'I am still the man I was. I too have a right to live. Don't think you can deny me for ever.'

The light eyes in the pale face blazed with a naked hatred that made me afraid. Andrei made no reply. He pulled himself free and went on, taking us with him.

A great number of guests had been invited to share the Easter feast. 'They will never eat all that,' I had exclaimed that afternoon standing beside Rilla in the kitchens.

My sister laughed. 'You don't know the Russian appetite.'

We started with wafer-thin pancakes filled with cream and the caviare which I loathed. 'Frogs' spawn,' I called it much to Andrei's amusement. There were pickled herrings with cucumber, and then *borsch*, the favourite Russian soup with white cabbage and beetroot, fish with truffles, pheasant roasted in sour cream with cranberry sauce and the traditional sucking pig, curled up in a rich gravy, the crackling brown and crisp, and a coloured egg in its half-open mouth.

Andrei was a wonderful host and if that evening he seemed to be drinking more than usual, no one would have known it, though now and again I saw Rilla's eyes turned to him.

Lieutenant Federov found himself a seat beside me. He was disappointed at not seeing Irina and I listened to him talking and talking of her while my thoughts chased after Leon and that tense moment with Jean Reynard that had come so swiftly after the Easter blessing. It was four o'clock in the morning before the last guest had gone and an exhausted Rilla kissed me goodnight.

The next day a footman came round with a note from the Astrov palace. The old man had suffered a severe heart attack shortly before midnight and was still very sick. So that explained why the brother and sister had not joined us for the Easter mass.

We were leaving for Arachino at the end of the week and there were a thousand things to be done before we left. I was helping Rilla to supervise the packing on the morning when Madame Leskova called. We hurried downstairs, dusty and untidy, and not at all in the mood to receive fashionable visitors. Madame Leskova rose at once as we entered the drawing room.

'Do forgive me, dear Countess,' she said gushingly to Rilla, 'I know how busy you must be but I felt that as your husband is such a close friend of Prince Leon, you must be the very first to hear our wonderful news.' She paused and looked proudly at her daughter. 'He has asked my little Olga to be his wife.'

Rilla was murmuring polite congratulations but I could not find a single word. An immense anger tinged with contempt went surging through me. How could he have let himself be persuaded after all he had said?

Madame Leskova turned to me, her smile sweet as sugar. 'Olga, my love, do show Mademoiselle Sophie your ring. I am sure she would love to see it.'

Olga looked quite different. The black eyes were sparkling. She drew off her lavender kid glove and stretched out her hand with the gesture of a queen. The ring was magnificent, a huge diamond surrounded with rubies and I loathed it.

Through stiff lips, I said, 'It is beautiful. I congratulate you.'

Much to our relief they did not stay long. There were too many other visits to pay.

'Well, who would have thought it!' exclaimed Rilla when

they had been shown out. 'She's been angling for Leon for over a year now but I must admit I never thought she would capture him, and did you ever see anything more vulgarly ostentatious than that engagement ring? Leon must have been out of his mind.'

'If he chose it,' I said shortly. I was angry with myself because the news had come as a shock, because I had hated the look of triumph in Olga's eyes and more than anything because I found it so hard to believe that Leon would have done such a thing.

It was two days before I heard the truth of the matter from Irina when she came to say goodbye.

'Oh Sophie, it was dreadful,' she said unhappily. 'We really thought the end had come. The priests had already begun to chant the prayers for the dying. All the family were there, the old aunts, the cousins, some of them I had never seen. There was Madame Leskova too with Olga, even Fräulein and the servants, and in front of them all, grandfather cursed Leon for destroying the family honour and causing his death by his wilful disobedience. If he would promise to marry Olga, he said, then and then only could he die in peace, and because Leon would not answer, he went on and on in a hoarse choking voice and the aunts never stopped sobbing. I was kneeling beside the bed and I saw Leon's face. I knew how he felt better than anyone and I wanted so much to help him, but there was nothing I could do. Everyone was looking at him reproachfully and at last he could stand it no longer, and he rushed out of the room. . . .'

'I know,' I said, 'I saw him . . . outside the Cathedral. . . .'

'Is that where he went? He never told me. A little later he came back and it all began over again, only this time it was worse. I don't know whether you can understand, Sophie, but the whole family were against him, accusing, making him feel guilty and ashamed, and though he fights grandfather, he loves him too. In the end he gave way. He fell on his knees and let grandfather join his hand to Olga's and give them his blessing.'

'But Prince Astrov didn't die. . . .'

'No . . . and Sophie, I know it is wicked of me, but I wish he had. He was still alive the next morning and now he is recovering.'

'What will your brother do?'

'I don't know. As soon as the doctors said grandfather was

73

out of danger, he went back to Petersburg without seeing him or Olga again. Madame Leskova is boasting to everyone about the engagement but it's not fair,' she burst out. 'At any other time Leon would never have agreed. It's blackmail.'

With a flash if intuition I understood what Leon had meant when he talked of freedom. It was not only Russia he was thinking of, it was his personal struggle with his grandfather and now Prince Astrov had won.

All the way north I tried to put it out of my mind, but even when we reached Arachino and I saw the village and the golden dome of the little church and the peasants, men and women and children, who came swarming round the carriage with the headman carrying bread and salt to welcome the master after his long absence, I still kept seeing Leon standing isolated among the joyous crowd on that Easter night before he went back to his grandfather's bedside and the prison gates shut on him.

Chapter 8

The carriage followed the track through the birch forest, came up the lime avenue and there was Ryvlach, a rambling gabled house built of wood weathered to silver grey with doors, lintels and window frames carved into beautiful and fantastic designs. I noticed that a whole new wing had been added and only very recently completed.

'It is enchanting. How you must love it,' I exclaimed turning to my sister, but Rilla was staring out of the carriage window, her face pale and her lips trembling, so that my questions died before I could utter them.

Ryvlach was only a few miles from the big house of Arachino and before his marriage, Andrei had lived there with Aunt Vera, his father's sister, who was ninety-six but still very much alive to everything that was going on.

She rarely left her room these days but a pair of bright blue eyes in a wrinkled brown face looked me over with keen interest when Andrei took me up to her pleasant sunny room a day or so after our arrival.

'So you are Sophie,' she said. 'Not so striking as your sister and there is not very much of you, is there? Still it will do, it will do very nicely. Now tell me all about yourself.'

'There's nothing to tell,' I said, amused at the old lady's forthright manner.

'Rubbish, every young woman enjoys talking about herself. Come and sit here beside me, my dear,' and Aunt Vera waved imperiously to the footstool close beside her armchair. 'I've heard a great deal about you already, you know, and about that young rake, Leonid Astrov . . . allowing him to present you to the Grand Duke as his *chère amie* as they used to say in my young days, right under his grandfather's nose too, the very idea!' and Aunt Vera chuckled appreciatively. 'That must have shaken him up and Nicholas too, stiff as a poker he always was, not at all like his brother Alexander, our dear Emperor.'

'You've got it all wrong, Auntie,' interrupted Andrei, 'Sophie did nothing of the sort. It was just an unfortunate mistake and anyway Leon is betrothed to Olga Leskova; it was all over Moscow before we left.'

'More fool he,' remarked the old lady crisply. 'And you too, Andrei, don't imagine I don't know about that duel of yours. You should be ashamed of yourself. All the same it's about time the boy stood up to that grandfather of his. I knew Ivan Astrov when he was no more than a snivelling schoolboy and a nasty bad-tempered lad he was too. Even then he flew into a rage if he couldn't get his own way. Many a time I itched to box his ears and I'd do it now if only I had the use of my legs and could get myself as far as Valdaya.'

She stabbed at the embroidery on her lap as if she would have liked to stick the needle into Prince Astrov himself. I caught the amused twinkle in Andrei's eyes and could not stifle a tiny smile. Aunt Vera pounced on it instantly.

'And don't make fun of me either, grinning like a pair of hyenas. I may be old but I'm not dead yet, not by a long way, and let me tell you something else, young lady, if you have only half the spirit of your sister, you could do a great deal more for that poor boy than the silly little chits he wastes his time running after.'

'Really, Aunt, you shouldn't say such things,' said Andrei, 'you will make Sophie blush.'

'Nonsense. She's not an idiot, is she? She knows what men are and if she doesn't, the sooner she learns the better. I like Leon. He is a nice boy under all that foolishness. He took the trouble to call here on his way to Petersburg and entertained me with all the latest gossip. There are not many young men who would bother their heads about a lonely old woman who could be their grandmother. You remember what I say, my child. How long are you to stay with us?'

'I don't know. It depends on how long Andrei can put up with me.'

'You needn't worry about that. He will do what his wife tells him and quite right too, and that reminds me,' she turned to Andrei accusingly. 'Rilla is not looking well. She is still grieving over the loss of the child and you know what the remedy is for that. Give her another and quickly. A second baby in her arms is the only cure.'

76

'Maybe.' Andrei had moved to the window so that I could not see his face. 'You know as well as I do that is as God wills.'

'What has God to do with it?' snapped the old lady tartly. 'And let me tell you, He helps those who help themselves. I want to see a young brood of Kuragins growing up here at Ryvlach before I die. Besides it's not fair on Paul. All the hopes of the future pinned on that one child of Dmitri's. . . .'

There seemed no way of stopping the old lady and I intervened rather desperately. 'I am looking forward to meeting Paul. Rilla has told me so much about him.'

'She has, has she? I remember the first time she came here. Far too pretty for a governess, I thought to myself, and I was right.'

At least I had succeeded in temporarily diverting Aunt Vera's attention from Andrei and he seized the opportunity to excuse himself and leave us together.

'Now I've upset him,' remarked the old lady as the door closed behind him. 'But somebody's got to say it. I know Andrei. He can be driven only so far and he's nearing the end of his patience.'

I was beginning to realize that myself. Ever since we had arrived at Ryvlach, Rilla had been quite unlike herself, touchy and out of temper. The slightest thing upset her and she was sharp with everyone, including Andrei; and though he said nothing, I guessed at the tight control he was keeping over himself. I thought perhaps it was because this was the first time they had returned to the house since the death of the child and I wanted to help but what could I do when neither of them would speak of what lay between them?

Even more than in Moscow I was astonished to see how well Rilla had adjusted herself to a way of life so different from our humble home in Fulham.

'You've no idea what it was like at the beginning,' she said to me one day, 'the serfs brought in vast quantities of game, cheese, eggs, fruit, butter and so on and no one ever dreamed of checking it. It just disappeared or went bad. The stillrooms were crammed with home-made pear cheese, chestnut jam, candied walnuts, all kinds of preserves and then forgotten till they went mouldy. Rats and mice had a feast day and moths were devouring carpets and furs and curtains until I took it in hand.'

It could not have been easy either, I thought, with illiterate peasants who hated change and whose only method of counting was a wooden tally. We lived luxuriously but not wastefully and Rilla seemed to know the name of every servant down to the merest scrap of a stable boy, and a great number of the villagers and the outdoor serfs too.

'There's never been anyone like her,' said Marya admiringly the first time I met her. 'She is Andrei's right hand. She helps him in everything. He could never do as much as he does without her.'

Marya was a wonderful person, kind, placid and warm-hearted. I liked her at once. She lived at Arachino with her husband Simon and their two children. She was half sister to the Kuragins, the old Count's daughter by a peasant mistress, and as seemed to be the custom in Russia, she had been well educated and brought up with the family. She cared for Dmitri and looked after his household, but it was quite obvious that it was Andrei for whom she had most affection.

May came in with an unexpected blaze of heat and one afternoon when we had all driven over to the big house, it was warm enough to sit out on the lawn in front of the high stone terrace that ran all along the south side of the garden.

The air was honeysweet with budding limes. Paul was playing with his bear cub. The little creature was fastened by a long chain to a stake in the grass and at barely six weeks old seemed no more than a delightful bundle of light brown fur.

Paul was ten, a tall slim boy with Andrei's dark hair and his father's luminous brown eyes. 'Simon shot Kali's mother,' he explained to me very seriously. 'You see, Sophie, he had to because she had savaged one of the villagers, but he brought the baby home otherwise it would have died. We had to feed it with a bottle at first, just like Nikki.'

'Isn't it rather a dangerous playmate? What did your father say?'

'I don't think Papa notices what pets I have. Uncle Andrei says I can keep him till the autumn then he will have to be sent away because of Tanya and Nikki. You see he'll be bigger than they are by then, perhaps even bigger than me.'

Tanya, a lively little three-year-old, and Nikki just eight months, peacefully sleeping in his cradle, were Marya's two children. On the other side of the grass Andrei was talking to Simon, who was in charge not only of the Arachino stables but also of the stud of fine pure-bred Arab horses that he was slowly building up at Ryvlach.

Paul was certainly right about his father. The first time I had seen Dmitri, I had found it hard to believe he was Andrei's brother. He could not be much more than fifty but looked years and years older. The shock of the accident had turned his hair white. He moved slowly and his brown eyes had a remote look as if he lived in some other faraway world and only brought himself back to the present with an effort. He greeted me with his gentle smile and probably forgot me the next moment. He still rode and hunted, but though Andrei consulted him on matters concerning the estate, I doubted if he took much interest. One thing was certain, he was not crazy as Jean Reynard had spitefully hinted. I wondered why.

On my first visit to the house Paul had taken me up to the schoolroom to show me his pets, a squirrel in a cage and a spaniel with a litter of puppies. As we went up the stairs my eye had been caught by a painting hanging in an upper corridor. It was a portrait of a young woman of such striking beauty she seemed to leap out of the canvas, and I stopped fascinated by the pale face with the coronet of shining black hair and the slim taut figure in a dark green riding habit.

'That's my Mamma,' said Paul. 'She was killed, you know, when her horse threw her over the edge of the old quarry. It was when Papa was shot.'

'She was very beautiful. Why is the picture hung here where no one can see it?'

'Uncle Andrei did that. You see, Papa was very sick and when he got better and they had to tell him about Mamma, he could not bear to look at it any longer!'

It was little wonder that Dmitri sometimes appeared so stricken even now, four years after the tragedy.

It was wonderfully peaceful on the lawn that warm afternoon. An early bee was buzzing drowsily in the grass beside me and I thought about the letter that had come from Irina.

'We have heard nothing from Leon,' she wrote, 'but soon now we shall be at Valdaya. Grandfather has invited Olga and her mother too . . . you will come and visit us, Sophie, won't you? Stay for a week . . . or longer if your sister can spare you. . . .'

I was not sure if I wanted to go. It was not that I did not like Irina, but Petersburg was not far away, and it was more than likely that Leon would be there too, at least part of the time. It would be so much better not to see him and yet. . . . Deliberately I switched my thoughts away from him. I looked across at Rilla, who was lying back in the chaise-longue, her eyes closed. Aunt Vera was right. She did look exhausted. She did far too much. Lately I had begun to worry about her.

The servants had brought out the samovar and Marya began to pour the tea. She said, 'Paul, run and find Tanya for me, will you, and then you can come and carry round the tea.'

'Tanya was here a moment ago,' I said, and then gave a little gasp. The child had climbed up the steep stone steps and was running joyously along the edge of the terrace, a good six feet up from the lawn. I was afraid to call out in case it should startle her and then it all happened so quickly no one had time to prevent it. Dmitri came out of the drawing room, the big Borzoi that went everywhere with him bounding ahead. Tanya, poised on the edge, turned to wave to the dog, took a false step and went over backwards down the steep rocky side of the terrace.

Andrei was the first to reach her. The child hung limp in his arms as he lifted her. Marya sprang to her feet, but before she could move or speak, Rilla had sat bolt upright, her face white as paper, her eyes wide and dark as if she had woken up out of a nightmare.

'Oh God, what have you done to her?' she cried out so fiercely and accusingly that Andrei halted.

In a flash it was all over. He brought the child to Marya and already the shock had passed. The little girl was sitting up, noisily crying. Her old nurse had come bustling up and she was carried into the house.

Andrei had come to his wife's side. He stood looking down at her. 'What is it, Rilla? Are you ill?'

'No, of course not.' She did not look at him. 'It's just the sun. It has given me a headache. I'll go indoors for a little.'

'I'll come with you,' I said quickly.

'No, no, please. I don't want anyone.' Rilla got up, pushing aside my outstretched hand and walked away from us over the grass.

Andrei said abruptly, 'I am going to the stables with Simon, Sophie. Let me know when you and Rilla are ready to leave.'

Marya was coming back from the house. 'It's not serious, only bruises and scratches. Anfisa is bathing them.' Her eyes followed Andrei as he went across the garden. 'I thought the trouble was over between them, but it's not. Rilla doesn't seem to know what she is doing to him.'

'That is what Aunt Vera said. Marya, what happened? What has gone wrong?'

'Haven't they told you?'

'I have tried and tried to make Rilla tell me. She will not speak of it.'

'Perhaps you should know.' Marya lifted Nikki from his cradle. 'Come up to the nursery with me. I want to make quite sure that Tanya is not really hurt.'

When both children were safely in bed with Anfisa watching beside them, Marya said, 'Come and sit down. Perhaps you may be able to do more than any of us. We are too close to them both. You see, it all happened on the night of the fire.'

'Fire?' Horror touched me. 'You mean the baby was burned.'

'Not quite. But I must go back a little if you are to understand how it happened. When Andrei knew they were to have a child he was overjoyed. You know Ryvlach. It is not large. He decided to rebuild the old wing which had been falling down for years and turn it into nurseries. Rilla was against it. She thought it too far from where they themselves slept, but he was insistent so she gave in and he went ahead with his plans. He wanted so much to please her and the rooms were lovely, large and airy. He went to endless trouble and expense, even importing furniture from Europe and installing fireplaces in the English style instead of our wood stoves. When the baby was born, only a month after my Nikki, I don't think I have seen two people more proud and happy.'

'What happened?'

'It was a night in December. Rilla had not been out anywhere since the baby's coming and Dmitri had decided to hold a party for Nikki's christening. It was very unusual. He prefers to live quietly and Andrei who was to be godfather felt he had to be there. He persuaded Rilla to come with him. It was intensely cold so the baby was left behind. That evening the snow came down as it does sometimes here, so thick and heavy that every road was high with the drifts. Rilla wanted to go home in spite of it, but Andrei was worried about her. He said that the morning was soon enough . . . and that night the fire broke out.'

81

'But why? How?'

'We never knew. I think perhaps the servants were not used to open fires and piled up logs and fuel too high against the bitter cold and then when the blaze spread, they panicked. It was about three o'clock in the morning when Stefan came hammering at our door. Andrei wanted Rilla to stay here but she would not, so Simon and I went with them. It was a nightmare journey, the horses floundering through the snow and when we got there, the whole wing was ablaze. They were trying hard to fight it, but the snow and ice made it difficult. The water froze in the buckets as they fetched it. Rilla would have plunged into the flames if Andrei had not prevented her. He put her in Simon's arms and went in himself though everyone tried to stop him.' Marya paused for a moment. 'Even now I can't think of it without turning sick. Somehow he reached the cradle and brought the baby out. I don't think I shall ever forget seeing him come through the doorway, the fire behind him, his face scorched and blackened. Rilla ran to him but it was a dead child he put in her arms, not burned or hurt in any way, but quite dead. He was so tiny and the smoke had suffocated him.'

'How terrible!' I felt the tears spring into my eyes.

'There's not much more. At first we thought she would go out of her mind. It was shock, the doctor said, and Andrei was part of it, you see. Every time he came to the bedside, she shivered and moaned. She would not look at him or speak to him. When she began to recover, she conquered it. Your sister is brave and good and with her reason she knows she is wrong to blame him, but it is there, Sophie, like a glass wall between them that she can't break through. Dr Arnoud says time will cure it, but nearly six months have gone by and Andrei suffers though he says nothing. Sometimes it frightens me. You see, I know the Kuragins. I've known them all my life. They are passionate men and they feel deeply.' Marya leaned forward, putting her warm hand on mine. 'The doctor said we should not remind her of it, so deliberately we never speak of that night and Andrei has been strict with the servants, but now I wonder if we are wrong. Why don't you try and persuade her to confide in you?'

But it was not so easy. Close though we had always been Rilla was still my elder sister, proud, self-contained and reserved about things that mattered most to her. All the way back to

Ryvlach I thought about it and it was still in my mind when I undressed. I opened the little gilt casket to put away my few trinkets and saw the necklace of Persian silver Andrei had bought me at the market. It glimmered like moonshine in the light of the lamp. I thought how pretty it was and a wave of sympathy for him and for Rilla flooded through me. How sad it was that they should be throwing away something so precious between them while Leon was tied to a girl for whom he cared nothing, tied by a promise to a selfish cantankerous old man who thought he was dying. The sudden opening of the door startled me but it was only Rilla, pale as a moth in her white dressing gown.

I looked at her questioningly. 'Is anything wrong?'

'No. I feel restless tonight. I just wanted to talk a little. Do you mind?'

'No, of course not, silly. Let's have a cosy gossip like we used to have in the old days.'

Rilla smiled. 'How long ago that seems. What did Irina have to say? You didn't tell me.'

'Only that soon they are coming to Valdaya.'

'She did not mention Jean Reynard.'

'No.'

'It worries me. I'm sure he has done this deliberately. He has some plan to injure Andrei. I am certain of it.'

'But, Rilla, what can he do?'

'I don't know, but he is subtle and clever. He knows how to twist things to his own advantage.' My sister was moving round the room as if she could not stay still, picking up garments, refolding them and putting them down again. Suddenly she swung round. 'What did you and Marya talk about so long this afternoon?'

I hesitated for a moment. 'She told me about the fire.'

'So now you know.'

'Why didn't you tell me yourself?'

'I couldn't.' Rilla beat her hands together with a desperate gesture. 'Oh God, what am I to do, Sophie, what am I to do?' She was shaking with hard dry sobs and I put my arms around her, drawing her down to sit beside me on the bed.

She was staring in front of her, the words coming jerkily as if they were forced out of her.

'This afternoon when I saw Andrei with Tanya . . . it all came

83

back . . . the horror . . . the nightmare . . . I see it over and over again.' She was trembling. 'Every time he comes near me, I hear the roar of the fire, I can even smell the smoke. I can't bear him to touch me. If he takes me in his arms, I go cold and sick and now he doesn't come any longer . . . and I love him, Sophie, I love him with all my heart and I am driving him away from me.'

'No, you're not. He will be patient. He will wait.'

'You don't know Andrei. You don't know what happened before . . . if I lose him, I will kill myself.'

'Rilla, you are talking foolishly.'

'Am I?' She looked at me, her eyes distraught. 'He is a man women die for.' For an instant it seemed as if she would have said something more but with a brave effort she pulled herself together. She put out a hand to touch my cheek. 'Poor child, you're so young. It's not fair to burden you with our troubles.' She got up again, moving across to the dressing table, staring at herself in the mirror. 'I'm even losing what little looks I once had. I see Andrei glance at another woman and go cold with terror.'

'You don't need to. He thinks only of you.'

'Does he?' Her eye fell on the silver necklace and she picked it up. 'This is pretty. Where did you get it?'

'Andrei gave it to me.'

'Andrei? You never told me.'

'I never thought about it. It was one morning in the market near the Ryady bazaars. The stallkeeper thought I was stealing it.' I laughed a little. 'I don't know what I should have done if Andrei had not been there. He put down some money . . . trumpery rubbish he called it, but I kept it because I like it.'

Rilla was staring at me. 'And because he gave it to you,' she said slowly. 'How many times did you and Andrei meet without saying a word to me?'

'None. It was sheer chance that we met that day. He was with Leon.'

'In the food market? Don't be ridiculous. Why are you lying?'

'I'm not lying. Whatever is the matter with you?'

'I know how attractive Andrei is, none better.' Swiftly Rilla came to me, seizing my shoulder, the fingers digging through the thin silk of my dressing gown. 'If you and he. . . .'

'Rilla!' I shook myself free. 'How can you say such things? Are you crazy?'

'Oh God!' She buried her face in her hands. 'I'm sorry, Sophie, I'm sorry. I don't know what possessed me . . . sometimes I think I am crazy to feel as I do. . . .'

'Oh, darling, of course you're not. It's just that you are tired and not well. Let me take you to bed. In the morning you will feel quite different.'

She let me take her back to her room and tuck her up in the big four-poster bed. She looked very frail against the piled white pillows and I was anxious about her when I went back to my own room.

Sometimes in the past I had envied my sister, but all the same I loved her dearly and it maddened me to feel so helpless. For almost the first time in my life I longed for Mamma. It would have been good to talk it over with her, but it was no use thinking of that. She was thousands of miles away. Whatever our problems, Rilla's or mine, we had to work them out in our own way.

Chapter 9

I was up early the next morning. The sun came pouring in through my window and the garden looked so inviting that I was dressed and out by seven o'clock. The air was sweet with the fresh scent of cut grass. I saw Andrei going towards the stables, Malika trotting at his heels. He waved to me but did not stop. I remembered what Rilla had said . . . 'He is a man women die for,' and I thought with a pang of Leon holding the birds in his hands before he released them. It struck me then that in him just as in Andrei there existed that fatal charm that is so irresistible and so impossible to define, but to believe that the magical moment when Leon kissed me meant as much to him as it did to me was only foolish.

I had already turned towards the house when Katya came to tell me that breakfast was ready, but that the Countess was not yet out of bed. It was so unusual that I went at once to ask Rilla if she was unwell and found her complaining of a headache and sore throat. By noon when Andrei returned to luncheon, she was in such a fever that he sent for the doctor and towards evening he came, a little brown nut of a man, bustling in and shaking his head over her.

'All you young ladies are the same, leading a gay life in the city, burning the candle at both ends, and then coming down to the country and expecting me to find a cure!' He talked on and on while he made a careful examination. 'There now, it's no more than a spring cold, but you've got to take care. I told you before, you don't eat enough.' A pair of eyes, bright as an inquisitive bird, looked me up and down. 'You feed your sister up, Mademoiselle. She's got nerves like frayed violin strings. She wants some flesh on her bones. I'll give you something to ease the throat, but it's you who can cure yourself, you know that, my dear Countess.'

He might be a good doctor but he was certainly a chatterbox, I thought, as I accompanied him down the stairs. But then something caught my attention and I found myself listening with all my ears.

'I was at Valdaya this morning,' he was saying, 'your message reached me there. That's why I am late. Fine goings-on, I must say!'

'Has Prince Astrov been taken ill again?'

'It's not the old man, but the young one. Driving down from Petersburg like a madman and doing his best to kill himself!'

'Has there been an accident?' I remembered vividly that crazy trip to the Sparrow Hills and despite myself I felt my heart miss a beat.

'Accident!' Dr Arnoud was drawing on his gloves in the hall. 'My dear Mademoiselle, it is only by the mercy of God he's not a murderer as well as a lunatic. What can you expect driving half-broken thoroughbreds over our appalling country tracks? The young lady was thrown out on her head.'

'Young lady?' I felt stifled. 'Was it . . . his fiancée?'

'Ah no.' Dr Arnoud paused and gave me a sly grin. 'There's the rub, as they say. Poor Olga Leskova waiting nice as you please for her betrothed to make an appearance and what happens? In he comes with a ravishing young woman in his arms, more dead than alive, and the fat is in the fire, I can tell you. I thought his grandfather would have an apoplexy.'

'And Prince Leon? Is he hurt?'

'Bruised from head to foot and a fractured arm. I set it myself. It will keep him out of mischief for a few weeks, that's one good thing.'

He climbed into his carriage and took the reins from the stable boy, but I had to know. I said quickly, 'And the young lady, doctor, who was she?'

'Now that's telling. I might perhaps hazard a guess. She was sitting up and abusing him roundly before I left and I've only heard language like that in the theatre. . . . Tell Count Andrei I will look in again tomorrow,' and with a flick of his whip, he was off down the drive.

How could Leon do such a thing? Flaunting one of his mistresses in front of his grandfather, to say nothing of Olga! And I had thought . . . just for an instant I had believed. . . . that something real and true had sprung to life between us! What a fool I had been! Well, that settled it. Whatever happened, I was not going to Valdaya. I had no intention of becoming the next victim of Prince Leon's all-conquering charm.

I went in search of Andrei to tell him what the doctor had said about Rilla and found him at last with the horses. The stables lay at a little distance from the house. Newly built and enlarged, they surrounded an old stone courtyard. When I came through the arched gateway, I saw Andrei standing by the water trough, his whip in his hand, Simon close behind him and one of the peasants sprawled on the ground at his feet.

Andrei rarely raised his voice and he was not shouting now, but he was tight-lipped with anger. I saw him raise the whip and the man on the ground writhed as it bit across his cheek. He snarled out something and I thought Andrei would have struck again, but he did not. He said something in Russian to Simon and abruptly strode away. Frightened faces peering out of half-open doors hurriedly withdrew out of his sight. The peasant slowly dragged himself to his feet and I saw quite clearly the mark of the lash across the dark cheek. He spat viciously after his master, then cringed as Simon's hand came down roughly on his shoulder, forcing him away.

Nobody had noticed me. I did not know whether to go or stay. Then I saw Stefan in the coach house and hurried across to ask him what had happened. He did not look at me, but went on vigorously polishing the brass carriage lamps.

'The master has ordered Musaka to be flogged.'

'Oh no.' Such things did not happen at Ryvlach. Rilla had said so a hundred times. 'Why? What has he done?'

'He has been stealing the fodder. Keeping the horses short and selling it.'

'Is that all?'

'It's more than enough, Mademoiselle. Two of them are sick with the rubbish he has been tipping into the mangers and one of them a mare in foal.' Stefan spat on the cloth in his hand and rubbed harder than ever. 'You know how the master feels about his horses, apart from the money they cost him. He lost his temper and Musaka was insolent.'

So Andrei was taking out his frustrations on his serfs. When I saw him at luncheon, he was so grimly silent I did not dare to question him. It was only afterwards I learned from Katya that he had changed his mind about the flogging. Instead the man was dismissed from the favoured position in the stables and condemned to the hardest field labour.

'No more than he deserves,' said Katya. 'He was always a sullen brute. He's lucky to miss the lash. The master is too soft.'

A few days later she reported with contempt that Musaka had deserted his wife and children and mysteriously disappeared. 'Good riddance too!' she went on. 'It won't have reached your ears, Mademoiselle, but he has been spreading tales about the Count.'

'What tales?'

She looked uncomfortable. 'That he was under his wife's thumb, no longer master in his own house ... no man likes to hear things like that.'

So that was what had provoked Andrei to such unusual violence. Even the servants were talking. It was little wonder that he looked so stormy these days.

Rilla was no better when Dr Arnoud came the next day nor the day after. It was nothing really serious and yet she did not seem able to throw off the infection. Sometimes I wondered if it was a retreat from something she did not want to face.

One morning at breakfast another letter came from Irina urging, almost begging me to go to Valdaya.

Andrei looked up from his coffee. 'Why don't you go? There's quite a party there, I understand. It's lonely for you here. I don't feel inclined to entertain while Rilla is sick.'

I shook my head decisively. 'I don't want to leave her.'

'As you please.' Andrei was almost out of the room when he came back half impatiently, tapping his boot with the crop in his hand.

'Would you like to ride with me this morning? I have to visit one of our farms and I'm taking Paul with me. The boy ought to know something about the estates.'

I was not a brilliant horsewoman like my sister. I only liked the slowest and safest of horses. I said shyly, 'I'd like to very much if you can put up with me.'

'Silly child, we're not going to run races. Get yourself dressed and be quick about it.'

Joyously I did as I was told.

After that I rode out with him nearly every day, sometimes with Paul, but quite often alone, and I found out many things about him. Occasionally he would talk entertainingly and at other times he would ride without saying a single word, but I respected his moods and enjoyed being with him, and it never once occurred to me what Rilla might be thinking, sick and unhappy, in the great lonely bed upstairs.

I would go into her room in the early morning to ask how she was and to tell her what we were going to do that day. Then I would kiss her and hurry off, never dreaming that I was leaving her a prey to all sorts of foolish fantasies.

It was about a fortnight later that one day as we turned our horses for home, Andrei suggested that we should visit the monastery at Kustevo.

'Do you remember saying you wanted to see the real Russia? Well, Kustevo goes back to the first Prince of Muscovy, long before Petersburg was even dreamed of. It's a place of pilgrimage. They come—great processions of them—on certain feast days. The monks possess an icon, a sacred painting of Mother and Child which is said to work miracles.'

'Do you believe that?'

Andrei shrugged his shoulders. 'What I believe hardly matters. Thousands of others do.'

The monastery was built on the bank of a river. We saw the gold-spangled blue domes of the church rising out of the green forest. As we came up to the white walls, there was no sound but birdsong and the murmur of running water. The old man who opened the gate to us wore a long white robe. He bowed low to Andrei and then, with folded hands and lowered eyes, led us to the door of the church.

Out of the brilliant sunshine, it was cool and dark, but a forest of candles burned around the miraculous icon. The colours were faded and brown with age and the bottom of the painting worn and dimmed by the kisses of multitudes of worshippers, but the face of the Child, pale and calm, was still beautiful. Andrei stood beside me, his expression unreadable, but I wondered if he thought of his own dead son and whether, sophisticated and cynical though he was, he too hoped for a miracle like the humble pilgrims who came to pray.

Afterwards, though I was not allowed to enter the monastery buildings, we were permitted to walk in the gardens. We wandered along by the little stream, clear as crystal over brown stones, crossed a tiny bridge and followed the slope up to the high stone wall. Great trees of lilac overshadowed it, already bursting into flower. Andrei plucked one of the sprays of heavy white blossom.

'It's too early,' he said. 'We shall be lucky if there are no more night frosts to blast it.' He put the flowers into my hands and I smelled the sweet fresh fragrance. He was looking down at me half smiling. 'Tell me, Sophie, do you still resent me? Am I still the ogre who carried off your sister?'

'Oh no. Don't remind me of how foolish I was. I think Rilla is very fortunate.'

'Do you? I'm afraid it's a long time since she has thought so.'

'It will be all right,' I said impulsively. 'It must be. I'm sure of it.'

'You're a sweet child.' He put a finger under my chin and tilted my face to look up at him. 'And a great comfort. I don't quite know what I might have done these past weeks if you had not been here.' He bent his head and kissed me lightly on the lips. 'That's by way of saying thank you, and now come along. The horses have been kept waiting long enough.'

Hand in hand we went back to the gate. The strange impelling chant of the monks followed us as we rode past the monastery walls towards Ryvlach.

After that I lost my shyness. I found it easier to talk to him and one evening when we had supped companionably together, I asked him about the conversation I had overheard between him and Leon on the day we had met in the market.

Andrei was lying back in one of the deep armchairs and I pulled up a footstool to sit beside him. He did not answer immediately and when he did, I had a notion that he was feeling his way, careful not to say too much.

'There are quite a number of us,' he said, 'who would like to make changes in our Russian constitution. Freedom for the serfs for one thing. Better conditions for factory workers. You are a stranger, Sophie, from a country that is not a slave state like ours. You criticize your Kings, your statesmen, your government in speech and in print, even in your Houses of Parliament, and in most cases suffer no harm from it. If we were to do one quarter of what is everyday practice in London, we would end our days in a filthy cell in the Peter and Paul prison or find ourselves exiled to the salt mines of Siberia, parted forever from wife and children. And so those of us who feel strongly about such things meet sometimes to talk of reform and in our own way try to carry out our ideals.'

'As you do here.'

'As I try to do . . . yes.'

'Is that all?'

'What more could there be? Even that we have to keep secret.'

'And that's why you were meeting in that old house?'

'That's why. What did you think we were doing, plotting to overset the state? That's what Rilla believes. She worries about me too much.' Andrei smiled a little bitterly. 'By now she should have learned that Russians talk but very seldom act.'

'That's what Leon said.'

'Ah well, Leon . . . he is still young enough to be quite certain he can put the whole world to rights in five minutes.'

'And yet he often behaves so badly.'

'You mean this ridiculous engagement. God knows what will come of it. I wish I had some influence with Prince Astrov, but he and I have been at loggerheads ever since he was my commanding officer in my own early days in the Guards.' Andrei sat up suddenly. 'What's the meaning of all these questions? You are not falling in love with Leon, I hope. That would be a folly I would not wish for anyone.'

'No, of course not. I like Irina and I just feel . . . sorry for him, that's all.'

'That's a dangerous feeling, the most dangerous of all.'

'But you like him too. Otherwise you'd never have fired into the air at that stupid duel.'

'How do you know what I did?'

'I saw you.' I suddenly realized what I had said and stopped short.

'You were there . . . Good God! Whatever made you do such a thing?'

'Nobody else would . . . I thought I could prevent it.'

'By throwing yourself between us like the heroine of a melodrama.' Andrei began to laugh. 'Oh, Sophie, Sophie, what a child you are.'

'I'm not a child. And you won't tell Leon?'

'I promise—on my word of honour. But whatever you do, don't let him capture your heart.' Andrei was still smiling and he put an arm round me. 'I like you, Sophie. I don't want you to be hurt.'

'I won't be,' and impulsively I put my arms round his neck and kissed him as I might have kissed my brother, and at that moment Rilla came into the room.

Andrei did not remove his arm from round my shoulders. He merely looked up and said coolly, 'You shouldn't be walking about the house like a ghost, my dear. You will catch cold.'

Startled, I saw my sister was in her dressing gown and barefoot. I wondered how long she had been there listening. I got up quickly.

'What is the matter? Are you feeling worse? Shall I fetch you something?'

In the soft glow of the lamp, Rilla's face looked white and tense. She said quietly, 'You had better go to bed, Sophie.'

'Not before you tell me what is the matter.'

'Do you need to ask?' Her voice rose sharply. 'Go to bed.'

Andrei said, 'Go, Sophie. It would be best.'

It had all meant nothing. Surely Rilla must realize that and yet she was looking at us as if she hated us both. I went slowly from the room. In the hall I paused. I could not leave them like that. I would go back, explain ... my hand on the door handle I heard my sister say, 'How could you? All these weeks ... you should be ashamed ... Sophie of all people ... a mere child. . . .'

And Andrei's reply, proud and resentful. 'What am I supposed to have done? What are you accusing me of this time?'

The words were flying between them, stinging and bitter. I ran up the stairs to my own room because I could not bear to hear any more. Perhaps it would be better if I went away, but where? To go home to England would take weeks of preparation. The night was warm. I felt stifled and flung open the windows, distressed because there seemed so little I could do. Distractedly I began to undress and then I stopped. I could hear someone coming up the stairs and then a door shut. Perhaps I could talk to Rilla quietly in her own room, make her see how absurd it was. I opened the door. Andrei was coming along the corridor. I had never seen him look like that before. He went past me as if I didn't exist, paused outside his wife's door, then kicked it open and slammed it shut behind him. Aunt Vera was right. This time she had driven him too far.

If I tried to interfere now, it would only make the situation worse. In that instant I made up my mind. I would go to Valdaya. I pulled the small travelling bag from the wardrobe. I would pack now and Stefan could drive me over early in the morning. While I folded underclothes and tried to select dresses, I wondered about the two who loved one another and whom only a tragic accident had parted and amid, my anxiety for them, there was something else, something I tried hard to stifle, an excitement, an anticipation. I had made a firm resolution to avoid Leon. It was going to be broken by circumstances outside my control and I knew very well that I was glad of it.

In the morning, however, my determination wavered, but Andrei took matters into his own hands. He came into the morning room where I was trying hard to swallow a cup of coffee and said abruptly, 'I have sent a note to Prince Astrov. Put your things together and I'll drive you over to Valdaya.'

'I've packed already, but I don't want to leave Rilla.'

'I can look after my wife,' and I knew by the look on his face that last night had settled nothing between them. Then he smiled faintly. 'Believe me, my child, it will be better for all of us. Now go and put on your bonnet.'

But after all it was Stefan who brought the carriage round and not Andrei. The mare whom Musaka had done his best to destroy had chosen this inconvenient moment to drop her foal, and it was a tricky business with a delicate animal and no horse doctor within miles.

Andrei came to the carriage to say goodbye, his coat off, the sleeves of his white shirt rolled up and sweat on his face.

'You'll let me know . . . about everything,' I said anxiously.

'I will. Don't worry.'

'Oh Andrei . . . Rilla wouldn't see me. . . .' despite all my brave resolution, I was ready to burst into tears.

'It's not your quarrel, little one. We must settle our own differences.' Andrei put his hand on mine. 'And mind what I told you about Leon,' then he stood back.

Stefan whipped up the horses and as the carriage swayed and bumped over the rough country roads, my spirits began to rise. Irina had told me much of Valdaya where she and her brother had spent their childhood. And if Leon were there, well I had learned a great deal during the weeks at Ryvlach. It was a challenge I could meet. I hated to leave Rilla but after all I was only twenty and when Stefan looked over his shoulder and then pointed ahead, waving his whip towards the great iron gates guarded by two stone lions, I found myself trembling with excitement and anticipation.

Chapter 10

Valdaya was a long low white house that had once been magnificent, surrounded by gardens, beautiful still but now overgrown and neglected. The drive was thick with moss and overshadowed by tall ragged firs. The moment I entered the house, I felt chilled. The huge rooms with their painted ceilings and stately portraits of long dead Astrovs were faded, their brilliance dimmed by years of dust and decay. But I soon found that though the estates might be mortgaged as Leon had said, his grandfather still lived in the lavish prodigal style of a bygone age, not at all like the informality of Ryvlach or even Arachino. The house always seemed to be crowded. Guests came and went almost unheeded. Two elderly aunts, so alike that I could never tell them apart, lived there permanently. Then there were others, shabby elderly figures, who appeared for meals, and then vanished again to their rooms in some distant wing. Poverty-stricken relatives, I discovered, who came with begging tales of hard luck and remained to live at Prince Astrov's expense.

In the first few days I was there, I felt bewildered. Of the master of the house I saw scarcely anything. He only appeared once a day at the head of the long table, so stern and forbidding that hardly anyone dared to utter a word. He acknowledged my existence with a frosty nod on my first evening and never spoke to me again. I would have felt utterly lost if it had not been for Irina. Despite all the resolutions I had made, I looked eagerly for Leon and he was not there.

'He is away for a day or two,' Irina explained when we were sitting together in the drawing room after dinner.

'Has he quite recovered from his accident?'

'Oh yes,' she gave a hasty glance round the room and then drew me into a corner. 'It really was the funniest thing in the world. You see, Leon hardly knew Carlotta Franconi. He was just giving her a lift because she wanted to visit friends who live near here. She is a dancer and never has any money. She was furious with him and so was grandfather, and Olga went all stiff and prickly, and it was all for the wrong reasons.'

'Didn't Leon explain?'

'Oh no, that's not his way. He let it all rage above his head and next day calmly took her on to her destination.'

It was ridiculous to feel so relieved and happy.

'He will be back for grandfather's name day of course,' went on Irina.

'Name day?'

'Didn't Rilla tell you about that? We celebrate it just like your birthday. Grandfather's name is Ivan, that is John in English, so on St John's day, everyone calls with good wishes and gifts. It has always been a great occasion. The gardens are lit up and the serfs come and dance for us. It can be good fun. You'll see.'

'It is a wonderful opportunity to present Olga to the neighbourhood as the future Princess Astrov,' said Madame Leskova smoothly, looking up from the tapestry frame on which she had been working, 'particularly as the young couple will be making their home here, isn't that so, my pet?' and she smiled archly at her daughter sitting beside her.

Olga was the most silent girl I had ever met and I could not make up my mind whether she was shy or merely sullen. Although both she and her mother had greeted me with expressions of pleasure, I was very aware of their dislike. I had an idea that the night of the ball still rankled and they held it against me. I tried to be friendly with Olga but it met with no response and Irina merely shrugged her shoulders impatiently.

'She dislikes riding, she doesn't care for dogs and Madame Leskova says she is delicate and mustn't walk too far or she will get overtired. What can you do in the country with a girl like that?' she remarked scornfully.

And what was more important, what on earth would Leon find in her was the thought that flashed through my mind.

One thing I could not help noticing from the very start and that was the influence Jean Reynard already seemed to possess over the household. It was strange when he was so quiet and unobtrusive. He never raised his voice and yet the servants all deferred to him, even Prince Astrov treated him with respect. He had greeted me with impeccable courtesy and a subtle insidious charm that in spite of myself I found difficult to

97

resist. In his presence even Olga bloomed and I found it hard to believe what Rilla had said about him except on one occasion.

It was a few days after my arrival at Valdaya. One day when were all at luncheon, Irina happened to mention Ryvlach.

'I always thought it such a lovely house,' she said, turning to me, 'and I was so sorry about the fire. Leon was telling me that wonderful progress has been made with the rebuilding.'

'Yes, it has,' I said. 'It is quite finished.'

Jean Reynard had raised his head. 'Fire?' he asked.

'Yes, it was last winter,' explained Irina. 'It was such a terrible tragedy that I could never bring myself to talk about it to anyone. Andrei's baby son died in the blaze.'

'Is that so? I had no idea.'

I happened to be looking directly at him and I could have sworn he smiled. In an instant it had vanished, he was saying something grave and sympathetic, but I could not escape the impression that somehow he had found the information pleasing and had stored it for further use.

Leon returned on the eve of his grandfather's feast day. He came late, after dinner was over, striding into the drawing room still in his riding dress, and he had brought Michael Federov with him. It was curious, I thought, how the whole room seemed to spring to life at his entrance though apart from greeting the old aunts who fluttered up to him with little welcoming nods and kisses, he ignored the rest of the company and came immediately to where Irina was sitting behind the samovar.

'Just what I need to wash the dust of the road out of my throat,' he said and dropped a kiss on his sister's cheek. 'See who I've brought with me. Aren't you pleased?' he whispered and waved a hand towards his young Lieutenant.

I saw Irina's quick blush as I brought my glass of tea to the table. That Leon had not expected me to be there was obvious. For the first time I saw him disconcerted. For an instant our eyes met and neither said a word, then Madame Leskova's voice, sugar sweet and insistent, cut across the room.

'Aren't you forgetting someone, my dear Leon? Olga has been counting the minutes while you have been away. Isn't that so, my love?'

I saw a flicker of anger cross his face before he shrugged his shoulders and went to kiss his fiancee's hand. Michael Federov had joined us, speaking to Irina and including me in his greeting. I scarcely heard him. My heart was beating so fast I felt confused and angry with myself. I had known he was coming. I had schooled myself to act with calm indifference and here I was as disturbed as any schoolgirl. If the very sight of him was to arouse such a tumult of feeling, it boded ill for the days I must spend at Valdaya.

The next morning it was easy to avoid Leon. There was a constant stream of visitors to greet old Prince Astrov seated in state in a red velvet chair in the drawing room and I was kept busy helping Irina serve tea and coffee, smiling and chatting with strangers until my face ached. Olga had become a different person. Elaborately dressed, she stood by the old Prince's chair and again and again throughout the morning she called Leon imperiously to her side, commanding him, so that one or two of the guests smiled at it, and once when I was busying myself putting some roses in water, I heard one of them say under his breath, 'Merciful Heaven, what a change is here! The young cub has been brought to heel at last!'

Olga's a fool, I thought to myself scornfully. That's no way to treat him. Surely she can see he is being driven against his will.

I had half expected that Andrei would ride over during the day as so many other neighbours had done, but he sent Stefan instead with two of the hunting Borzois as a gift. They were lovely gentle creatures and Irina who adored dogs was enchanted with them.

'Grandfather would send them to the stables, but I shan't let him,' she said defiantly. 'I shall keep Ruslan and Melka in the house.'

Already the musicians had arrived. There was to be dancing in the drawing room. The carpets were rolled up, servants were polishing the floor and the windows were open on to the lawn. The June day had been glorious with burning sunshine. But in the evening when I went upstairs to dress, the heat had lessened though it was still very warm. I looked through my wardrobe. Rilla had been generous and I had several to choose from. With a conscious reaction against Olga's finery, I took out the simplest of them all, a white muslin over ivory satin, lightly embroidered with silver thread.

I looked in the mirror and, as so often happened, was unsatisfied with what I saw. I was too thin and small and pale. I had no jewels, no diamonds like Rilla or rubies like Olga. I fastened the silver necklet Andrei had bought for me round my neck. The fragile flowers were set with tiny green stones. I hunted through my drawer and threaded a green velvet ribbon into my hair.

I never afterwards remembered the first part of the evening. What happened later drove it out of my mind. There was no lack of partners and I suppose I must have danced and eaten ices and smiled while all the time my eyes sought for Leon and saw him dancing with Olga, remaining constantly at her side, laughing, drinking champagne, and never once glancing in my direction.

There had been a sharp exchange between him and his grand-father early in the evening when he had first come down the grand staircase into the hall. The old man looked him up and down, the elegant black evening coat, the fine lace cravat, the tight trousers strapped under his shoes. He said cuttingly, 'Are you ashamed of the regiment that you dress yourself like a damned civil servant?'

'The uniform was never my choice,' was the curt reply and I wondered how much lay behind that simple act of defiance.

The serf dancers arrived at eleven o'clock, but it was still light. I was only just growing accustomed to these long Northern nights when darkness only falls for a few hours and the evenings are filled with a silvery radiance unlike anything in England. The dancers were to perform on the lawns and chairs had been set out for the guests in a half circle. The candle-lit globes hanging in the trees shone like golden fruit. The air was fragrant with the scent of flowers. Near where I was standing by an old stone bench I could smell the sweet heavy perfume of the syringa. The vibrant rhythm of the music was disturbing and my eyes were dazzled by the dancers whirling in a maze of brilliant coloured skirts and stamping feet. The hand slipped into mine startled me. Leon's voice, warm and husky, was in my ear.

'Come with me, Sophie. I want to show you something.'

Did he think he could neglect me and then expect me to run at his bidding? I shook my head. 'No. I am watching the dancers.'

'Is that the real reason?'

His hand came out and turned my face towards him. I was

100

forced to meet the grey eyes, challenging, filled with laughter. 'Are you afraid of me?'

'No.'

'What is it then?'

And the reckless little devil that lived inside me prompted me to be bold, to dare anything. 'Where are we going?'

Leon smiled. 'You'll see.'

He slid round the back of the bench and into the shrubbery and I followed after him. Hand in hand we took a path across the rose garden, round the stone wall of the cherry orchard and into a neglected wilderness of trees and bushes which I had not yet explored.

I hesitated for an instant and he glanced down at me.

'Scared?'

'No.'

'Come on then.'

And through the trees we went, the path overgrown and mossy so that I slipped in my silver sandals and when I stumbled, he put an arm round my waist. A long way beyond the copse in a grassy clearing there was a wooden hut, long and low, with straw thatching and windows all along one side. I stared at it in astonishment.

'Where are we?'

Leon was hunting for a key in his pocket. He unlocked the door and flung it wide.

'Ira and I used to call this our kingdom. My father had it built for us when we were children. We used to spend hours and hours here. It was our secret place. Here we felt we were safe from everybody, even from our nurse.'

'And now?'

Leon did not answer. He was busy with the lamp on the table while I looked round me. There was a spicy smell of cedarwood mingled with paint and oil and turpentine. As the light bloomed, I saw that the hut was roughly furnished with a big wooden table, one or two fine old chairs and a red velvet sofa that had seen better days. There were faded Persian rugs on the wooden floor, but what struck me immediately was the easel set up at one end, the palette, paint and brushes heaped on the table and the canvases stacked face to the wall.

'It is a studio!' I exclaimed in surprise.

'Yes.'

'Yours?'

Leon had been holding the lamp high so that its radiance illuminated the whole room. He put it down slowly, his eyes devouring me as if he were seeing me for the first time.

'By God, I never dreamed . . . the silver, the emerald . . . it's like moonlight on water . . . how lovely you are.'

'No . . . no, I'm not. I wish you would not say such things. . . .'

'Sophie, Sophie, do you know what you do to me?'

He was moving towards me and I backed away nervously.

'No . . . please. . . .'

But he had taken me into his arms and it was sweet to listen to him, to respond to his kisses with an abandon that matched his own, but only for an instant. I was not to be swept off my feet for a second time. I had suffered once and one does not forget so easily. I fought to free myself.

'You should not do this. You belong to Olga.'

'Damn Olga! Do you think I care a rush for her?'

'You are engaged to her. . . .'

'Engagements can be broken. . . .'

'Not by me. I will not listen to you,' I said breathlessly, but he shut my mouth with his kisses, drawing me down with him on to the sofa. It was madness. I must stop him, I must, before I was overwhelmed, before I was lost in this new dreadful sweetness that made my whole body tremble.

I snatched a hand free and hit him hard across the face. The shock of it loosened his grip, I tore myself away, fiercely angry, the words tumbling over one another.

'Is this where you bring all your women? Well, I'm not one of them . . . I should never have listened to you . . . I ought to have known . . . Andrei warned me against you. . . .'

'What did he say?'

'It doesn't matter.'

He held my wrist in a grip of iron. 'Tell me . . . what did he say?'

It was absurd but I was fighting an overwhelming desire to burst into tears. 'Nothing, I tell you . . . only that any woman would be a fool to lose her heart to you.'

'And is that what has happened to you, Sophie? Is it?'

'If it were, do you imagine I would tell you so that you could boast of your conquest to all your friends?'

'I would not boast, Sophie, believe me . . . I would feel too

102

honoured.' He dropped my wrist and leaned back against the sofa. 'Go if you wish, but I did not bring you here for this, truly I did not.' He gave me that boyish grin that had something so young and appealing in it. 'That was an ... accident for which you must blame yourself. You should not look so enchanting.'

I would not listen to him. I got up, uncertain, confused by his changes of mood and desperately afraid of my own feelings.

'I ought to go....'

'In a moment we'll go together, but first ... if you will be patient with me ... let me show you what I brought you to see.'

He had risen and picked up one of the canvases from the wall. He set it up on the easel and turned it to face me. I was looking at myself, the bonnet pushed back, my hair touched by wintry sunshine, and in my outstretched hand one of the doves poised for flight. It was unfinished, a sketch merely, but it had captured the spirit of that moment on the Sparrow Hills and I caught my breath.

'It's beautiful ... far more beautiful than I could ever be....'

'No, it's not half so lovely. I did it too long afterwards.'

'You? You mean you painted it?' I looked all round the room. 'Are all these yours too?'

He nodded. 'Most of them are not worth the canvas they're painted on. I'll show them to you some other time perhaps.'

'But if you are an artist, why do you keep it secret? Why don't you show them to everyone?'

'Why?' He smiled wryly. 'Do you really want to know?'

'Yes ... yes, of course.' I had forgotten that I ought to go, that it must be very late and we would both be missed.

'It's simple enough. You've seen the house, you've seen the portraits. Great grandfather who fought with Peter the Great at the battle of Poltava, grandfather who commanded a regiment under Catherine, Uncle Sergei who lost a leg in Turkey, father who died at Borodino ... what other course was ever open to me? I was fourteen when father was killed. I implored my grandfather to let me study at the Academy of Arts or even at Petersburg University; he did not listen. I doubt if he even heard me. An Astrov study painting with a lot of serfs and the sons of village priests ... it was unthinkable! I was sent to the Imperial Corps of Pages where my name had been entered when I was born. Do you know what that is, Sophie? The crack

103

military school. I must be a soldier like the rest of us . . . with no wars to fight. . . .'

'But you went on painting?'

'Oh yes, sometimes, when I'm in the mood, in between guard duty at the Winter Palace, military reviews, exercises at the Cavalry school, manoeuvres in some God-forsaken provincial town. . . .'

'But Michael Federov says your men worship you. . . .'

'The men?' Leon smiled dryly. 'Only because I treat the poor devils like human beings instead of animals, and because, now and then, I've stood between them and a few floggings. I owe that to Andrei. He was my first Captain. He made me see that we treated our horses and dogs better than the men who served under us. It was a good lesson, something I've never forgotten.'

Breathlessly I exclaimed, 'But you're not fourteen now. Why don't you break free, do what you've always wanted to do?'

'A good question to which there's no good answer.' Leon took a restless stride up and down the room and then swung round to face me. 'Because it's too late. I told you once. I'm like the rest of the family. I've got into the habit of it. It's a pleasant enough life so long as you don't think. I drink too much, I gamble, I hunt and race my horses. . . .'

'And marry a girl you despise for the sake of her money and torment her for the rest of your life and hers,' I broke in fiercely.

It brought Leon up short. 'That's not true. You know that. I'd never have let myself be persuaded if grandfather had not been so desperately sick. . . .'

'I know Irina says he blackmailed you into it when you thought he was dying, but why didn't you stand up to him?'

'It is not so easy. . . .'

'Do you know what I think, Prince Leonid Astrov, for all your boasts and your duels and your fine doings . . . you're a coward. You hide behind excuses because you haven't the courage to stand on your own two feet and face up to what you ought to do.'

For an instant the grey eyes darkened into anger and sitting bolt upright on the sofa, my hands clasped in my lap, I faced him resolutely while inwardly I quaked with terror.

Then unexpectedly Leon flung back his head and laughed. 'Well, that's straight from the shoulder at any rate. No one has ever said that to me before and gone unpunished.' He sat down beside me on the sofa. 'You're an astonishing young woman, Sophie, did you know that? So small, so quiet and the spirit of a lion. Maybe you're right. I don't know. If I promise to think of it seriously, will you do something for me?'

'What is it?'

'Will you come here sometimes and sit for me? I've wanted to paint you properly ever since that day when we drove up to the hills, remember?'

'But I could not come here alone . . . it would not be right. . . .'

'And what would people say?' he mocked me smiling. 'Bring Ira with you if you like. I promise to behave myself and no one knows of this place or cares about it except my sister and myself so we shall be quite safe. Will you, Sophie, please?'

'I don't know. . . .' It was difficult to resist when everything inside me was urging me to do what he asked. 'Maybe . . . if Ira will come. . . .'

'Good,' he said instantly. 'Then that's settled and now we must go back.'

It was shadowy and cool in the gardens and I shivered in my thin dress. He drew me close against him with an arm round my shoulders. In the drawing room they were dancing still. As we came across the lawn, I could see the couples swirling round in the mazurka and I drew back, feeling I could not face them, not now, dishevelled and untidy, and with him.

'I'm tired,' I whispered. 'I shall go to bed.'

'Coward!' He was smiling down at me in the faint light. I felt the feather-light touch of his lips on mine, heard him whisper, 'Don't forget, you've promised,' and then he had gone in through one of the long windows, leaving me to walk wearily into the hall and up the great staircase.

In the quiet of my own room I sat by the open window and thought what a fool I was. I would never admit it, not to Ira, not to anyone, but within myself I faced up to the truth. I was in grave danger of falling in love with Leon in spite of all my brave determination and instead of resolutely turning my back on him, I was going forward into something that would invariably only make it far worse when the day of reckoning came. Because it was all quite hopeless, I was sure of that. There was Olga . . . every instinct of decency told me I ought to leave

105

Valdaya tomorrow and every fibre of my being rebelled and was determined to stay.

Lying restlessly on the bed with only the thin sheet for covering, I tried to banish the memory of his arms round me and the guilty delight of his kisses by wondering how he would paint me and what excuses I could find to cover my escape to the studio, and I would not admit even for a moment how foolish it was or the sad truth that those who play with fire invariably get scorched.

Chapter 11

At the beginning of July the weather turned breathlessly hot, but riding through the birch forest at seven in the morning, it was still cool and fresh. Leon had gone ahead with the two dogs, his gun slung over his shoulder. Michael and Irina ambled along close together and I deliberately hung back a little. I knew that Irina was deeply in love with Lieutenant Federov though I doubted whether her grandfather would ever agree to their marriage. He was the younger son of an old aristocratic family, but they were not rich and he had several brothers and sisters.

I let my pony pick his own way while I thought of the week that had gone by since the day of the party. I had been to the studio only once with Ira, and Leon had drawn sketch after sketch turning my face this way and that until I had burst out laughing and offered to stand on my head.

'What the devil is it all for?' he said, throwing down his pencil in disgust. 'What in God's name am I trying to do?'

'Creating something, finding out about yourself,' I dared to say.

'Don't lecture,' was the swift reply, but he smiled at me while Irina lit the battered samovar and brewed tea. We sipped it from tall glasses with slices of lemon and talked and talked.

'It's like the old days,' said Irina happily, 'when you came home from the Academy and we used to hide ourselves down here . . . do you remember, Leon?'

'Indeed I do, and a hateful little brat you were too, for ever tagging at my heels,' teased Leon, but I was conscious of the strong affection between brother and sister and I felt shut out until they both turned to me asking questions, drawing me into their shared intimacy.

To my surprise I found myself telling them things I rarely confided to anyone, foolish things like what it felt like to be always poor and how hard it was to endure when the money you had saved week by week for a new dress had to go on boots for your little brothers if they were not to go barefoot.

'You see there was Rilla and my brother Jamie. They were so much cleverer than I was. I was always the odd one out,' I confessed and blushed because I had never talked about that secret resentment to anyone else and had always been a little ashamed of it. Now I saw the grey eyes fixed on me and felt a melting sweetness though he had not so much as touched my hand.

Leon could be so many different people, brusque, arrogant, without mercy sometimes towards anyone he disliked, yet he was never unkind to the old aunts who tried everybody's patience; and when Ruslan developed a festering boil on his paw, he patiently bathed and bandaged it day after day until it was cured.

A squirrel went racing across the path and ran chittering up into the trees. I looked up to find myself on the edge of the forest and no sign of the others. I wondered if I had taken the wrong path. The track followed a little rise alongside a deep valley. Honeysuckle, convolvulus, wild briar knotted together with brambles down a steep slope and I reined in to break off a branch of late flowering hawthorn, its bittersweet scent strong in the hot sun.

My eyes dazzled and it was a moment before I saw another rider a little ahead of me, absolutely motionless, staring down into the mass of flowers and foliage. I recognized Jean Reynard and while I watched, a man in rough working clothes came running from the opposite direction and joined him. They spoke together, then the peasant broke away and came hurrying down the track and I saw the thin seam of the scar left by the whip across his cheek and was sure it was Musaka whom I had last seen in the stableyard at Ryvlach. I could not imagine what he could be doing here and urged my horse forward at the same time as Reynard came trotting down the slope towards me.

'The others have gone ahead,' he called as he came up. 'They passed some minutes ago.'

'That man just now,' I said quickly. 'I'm certain I recognized him. Isn't he the serf who ran away from Ryvlach because he was punished for stealing?'

'You must be mistaken, Mademoiselle. He lives in the village here. He came to ask me about the forestry work. They are thinning out the young trees.'

It could be true but although I still felt doubtful, I was not sure enough to press the point. Reynard had ridden up alongside me. He nodded towards the steep slope of flowers and trees.

'Do you know what this place is?'

'No. I've never ridden up here before. How beautiful it is.'

'It's an old quarry which has not been used for many years. A place for lovers wouldn't you say?' He gave me a quick side-long glance. 'This is the spot where Paul's mother rode her horse over the edge.'

'Surely it was an accident.'

'That is what was said, but it was not so. Natalya deliberately plunged to her death and do you know why? Because her lover had deserted her.'

'Her lover?'

Something in his tone repelled me. I didn't want to listen, but he had leaned over, his hand on my wrist, those strange eyes fixed on mine so that I could not stir.

'She killed herself because she was carrying Andrei Kuragin's child. They didn't tell you that, did they?' he said. 'He had eyes only for someone else—your sister, Mademoiselle Sophie.'

'It's not true. I don't believe you. Why are you saying this to me?'

'Why indeed?' He released my wrist. 'Except that it may serve as a warning.'

'You must be mad to speak like that. What has all this to do with me?'

'You should know that better than I.'

There was a threat in the quiet voice and I had a sudden frightening feeling that he was thinking of Leon and that his hatred embraced us all. For some reason he wanted to destroy the whole world because it had denied him what he had desired.

I could not get away from him quickly enough. The beauty of the valley had become horrible to me. I threw away the flowering branch and trotted my horse forward. In a few minutes to my relief I saw the others coming back to look for me. Leon came cantering down the track.

'You look upset. What has happened?'

'Nothing. I have been talking to Jean Reynard.'

'Jean? What has he been saying?'

But I could not tell him. I could only say, 'I wish he were not here.'

'But why, Sophie? What has he done? He doesn't interfere with us, and he is extremely efficient.'

'Too efficient,' I exclaimed, and my uneasiness made me angry. 'It is absurd. You ought to manage your estate yourself.'

He smiled at me. 'It's not mine yet, you know, not until I marry. I have a shrewd notion my father thought I might lose it all at the card table or on the race track.' He had turned his horse to ride beside me. 'As a matter of fact I did try my hand at it a year or so ago.'

'What happened?'

He looked at me ruefully. 'You remember the birds we released from their cages. Well, I wanted to do that with my serfs. I gave them their freedom, but far from being content, they wanted more and more. There were riots and bloodshed, endless arguments and no work was done at all. The harvest rotted while they quarrelled over their share, to say nothing of mine. There was nothing to be done but to bring them all back on to the old treadmill once again.'

'Andrei says freedom must be earned. You have to learn how to use it.'

'I'm beginning to think he is right. Yet it seems to me that simply to be free is worth almost any sacrifice. Our nurse was fond of telling us an old fairy tale that I used to think stupid when I was a child. It took time for me to understand its true meaning.'

'What is it?'

We had entered the wood and the sunlight glinting through the silvery trunks of the birches dappled the path before us with moving shadows.

'There was once a Tsar,' he went on, 'who suspecting his wife of unfaithfulness ordered her to be placed with her son in a barrel. Then he had it tightly sealed and cast into the sea.'

'How savage!'

'It's only a fairy tale,' he said with a smile. 'At any rate the barrel floated on the waters for a great many years and the boy grew and grew till his head pressed against the top of the barrel and his feet against the bottom. Every day he felt more cramped and one morning he said, "Mother, I cannot go on

110

like this. Allow me to stretch to my full height and know freedom."

' "My dear son," answered his mother, "beware of doing such a dangerous thing for the barrel will burst and you will drown us both in the salt sea."

'The Tsarevitch thought for a moment then he said, "Better to stretch oneself just once and know freedom even if it only brings destruction." '

'And did he?'

'That's what I used to ask my nurse, but she didn't know the answer any more than I do, even now.'

And I guessed that he was thinking of his own problem and how in honour and without bringing ruin on his grandfather, he was to escape from a hateful situation that imprisoned him as closely as the barrel had enclosed the unhappy Prince.

We had come to the edge of the woods where the track divided. Leon said, 'Would you prefer to ride on with Irina and Michael? I have to go to the village.'

'May I come with you?'

'If you wish.' He smiled. 'Yakov will be in the seventh heaven if I bring you to visit him.'

I knew about Yakov. He was an old serf who had been born and bred at Valdaya and as was the Russian custom had been put in charge of the young Leon from childhood. He had taught him to ride and shoot and track wolf and bear, and had served him faithfully from the day he went to the military academy until a carriage accident had turned him into a helpless cripple.

Irina told me once that hardly a day passed without Leon spending a few minutes in the old man's scrupulously clean little hut, amusing him with army gossip and leaving a piece of gold or a handful of fine cigars among the few treasured possessions on the carved chest beside his chair.

'It's a week since I've seen him,' went on Leon, half laughing, 'and the old man will want to know the reason why. By God, he was a tyrant. Every time I got in a scrape he used to give me a long lecture and once when I lost a whole quarter's allowance in one night at the card table, he brought me his pitiful life savings to keep me out of the clutches of the money-lending sharks.'

'Did you take them?'

'No, it would have felt like robbery. I found the money somewhere.'

We had come in sight of a straggling line of huts nothing at all like the neat tidy village of Arachino. I was shocked at the neglect, the ragged thatch, the unglazed holes that served as windows. Through the doors already open against the heat, I caught a glimpse of the animals that shared the bare rooms with their owners, a thin goat, a mangy dog, a few scrawny hens pecking in the dirt. But despite the wretched look of poverty, there were smiles for Leon from the women as we rode through. He waved his hand to them cheerfully. At the far end, a little apart from the rest, was a cottage built partly of brick, neat and cleanly kept with green lettuces, beans and even a few flowers growing in the little garden.

Leon dismounted, threw the reins to one of the village children, said, 'Wait here for a moment,' and plunged into the hut. In a couple of minutes he was back, his face dark with anger. 'This is Jean's doing.'

'Why? What has happened?'

'God damn it, who is master here, he or I? The old man can no longer do a day's work so he has had him turned out, sent him to the infirmary to die.'

'Perhaps he is sick.'

'That has nothing to do with it. I gave him my promise.' He jerked himself back into the saddle. 'I'll see Yakov first and then, by Heaven, I'll make Jean sweat for it.'

'I'll come with you.'

'Better not. You don't know what the infirmary is like.'

'All the same I'd like to come.'

The grey eyes scanned my face. Then he said briefly, 'Very well, but don't say I didn't warn you.'

The infirmary was a long narrow building with few windows. A suffocating stench of dirt and sickness met me at the door and nearly drove me back. Leon went striding ahead and it took all my courage to follow after him. It was dark inside and very hot. Flies buzzed everywhere and hollow eyes in dark bearded faces stared at me apathetically from the mattresses ranged on either side. At the far end Leon had gone down on his knees, his voice deliberately warm and reassuring.

'I'll get you out of this place, you old rascal, never fear.'

The wrinkled brown face on the hard pillow with the thatch

of grey hair and grizzled beard broke into a smile. A gnarled hand clutched at the long slim fingers on the rough black blanket.

'Don't you trouble yourself about me, Leonid Karlovitch, I'm like an old horse. When you've no more use for it, you send it to the knacker's yard.'

'No! Not you, Yakov, never. If needs be, I'll have you carried to the house.'

'And what would his excellency have to say about that, eh? Old Yakov treated like some great prince ... that would never do.'

I was surprised by the concern on Leon's face and the gentleness with which he was stroking the old peasant's work-worn hand.

The brown eyes bright as a squirrel were turned to me. 'And is this young lady to be your bride? It is good of you, Barina, to come and show old Yakov your pretty face.'

I caught Leon's imploring look and came close to the bed. There was a sour smell from the soiled blankets, but I put my hand on his.

'Leon has told me so much about you.'

A look of mischievous pleasure shone for a second on the old man's face. 'A rare time I had with him. He was a wild one and no mistake, but he always had a good heart, Barina. I tell you that, I who have known him since he was no higher than a sparrow. You remember that, whatever dance he leads you.'

We stayed a little longer, then went out of the infirmary together. Thankfully I took a deep breath of the clean air. Leon lifted me on to my horse, saying nothing, then he looked up at me.

'It was kind of you. Olga would never have come.'

'She might if you had asked her.'

'No.' He paused and then went on savagely. 'An old dog would be given more care and Yakov means more to me than my own father. ...' He broke off and threw a coin to the boy who had been holding our horses. He was moodily silent as we rode back to Valdaya.

So much had happened, it seemed strange to find that it was not yet ten and breakfast was still on the table. Michael and Irina were drinking coffee and Olga glanced up as Leon came

113

into the room, the black eyes going swiftly from him to me.

He said abruptly, 'Where is Jean Reynard?'

She shrugged her shoulders. 'In his office, I suppose. Has something happened?'

Leon did not answer her. He went out leaving the door flung wide and must have met Jean in the hall for their raised voices could be heard all too clearly.

'What the devil do you mean by turning Yakov out of his cottage?'

'My dear Leon,' came Jean's smooth reply, 'the old man is sick and incapable. He is better off where he is.'

'He was proud of his independence,' said Leon angrily. 'His father and his grandfather had lived in that miserable hut. Surely he could be allowed to die there.'

'Not when it is needed for someone else—good workers, who are worth their hire.'

'I don't care who they are. I had given my promise to Yakov. Build your workers something else if needs be.'

'With what may I ask? I am here to run the estate and not indulge your fits of sentimental generosity.'

'By God, have you no heart? Andrei warned me about you and I didn't believe him.'

'If it were not for me, Leonid Karlovitch, you and your grandfather could be sweating in a debtor's prison by now.'

'I think you forget yourself,' said Leon haughtily. 'You are not master here.'

'Neither are you, and I am not to be treated like one of your serfs. Don't think you can insult me without paying the price.'

It was there in the cold fury of his voice, the jealousy, the envy that corroded him and influenced everything he did. Leon's contemptuous laugh reached us at the table so that Irina looked up startled.

'You must be out of your mind. Put Yakov back in his cottage or else it will be the worse for you.'

He did not come back to the dining room and no one said anything. Michael and Irina went on eating and Olga rang the bell for fresh coffee.

Ironically enough, all Leon's efforts were wasted. A few days later, before he could be moved back to his cottage, old Yakov died in his sleep and Jean made no comment, only wore an infuriating look of triumph on his handsome face.

114

The days passed and I sometimes felt I was leading a double life. I took part in all the pleasurable activities of summer in the country : riding in the early morning, trips to beauty spots in the neighbourhood, music in the evenings. There was even English croquet on the lawn, but at the same time there were those stolen hours when I found excuses to escape through the gardens to the studio hut so that the portrait began to take shape and the intimacy between us grew and blossomed.

Occasionally Prince Astrov would appear from his study, address a gruff word to me and pay marked attention to Olga as if to make up for his grandson's neglect. Leon was courteous to her, but little more. When strangers were present, he would stay at her side for a time, then find some excuse to disappear. Sometimes I watched the sullen black eyes fixed on him and wondered how anyone could swallow so much simply for the sake of becoming the Princess Astrov.

If I had not been so blinded by my own feelings, I would have realized that it could not go on; that sooner or later there would come discovery. There were too many curious eyes to observe my going and coming. I did not allow myself to think of what I was doing, I dare not, and it did not strike me that to any keen observer, I must have given myself away every time my eyes rested on Leon.

One afternoon there was an unpleasant little scene with Olga. The intense heat had broken in a thunderstorm the night before and all day it had rained heavily. During luncheon I caught a look from Leon that meant he would be waiting for me in the studio despite the rain and despite the fact that when we were all confined to the house, my absence was bound to be remarked on.

The portrait was almost finished, but he had not yet allowed me to see it. When he put down his brushes, he would throw an old paint-stained rag over the easel. 'Time enough when it is done,' he would say and I had an idea that it meant more to him than anything he had done up to now and that he was half afraid to put it to the test.

Sometimes he would work absorbedly in total silence. Then afterwards I would make tea and we would talk endlessly forgetting time. It seemed to me then that I was seeing another and different Leon and I realized that beneath his air of careless indifference, he loved Valdaya passionately and dreamed

115

of the changes he would make there when it became his own.

On this particular afternoon with the rain battering against the windows and the two dogs who provided such a useful excuse for a walk lying curled up on the rugs, Leon threw down his brush, stretched himself contentedly and said, 'One more day and it will be finished.'

'Are you pleased with it?'

He shrugged his shoulders. 'Is anyone ever satisfied with anything?'

He pulled off the peasant smock he used when he was painting. The fine white shirt was open at the throat. The tawny hair was ruffled and untidy. There was a smear of paint on one cheek and on the strong fingers he was wiping on the towel. Soon, too soon, it would be all over, I thought, and what would happen then? Did he feel anything at all for me or was he just using me because I was there and so willing to be used? I still didn't know.

He picked up his coat, then dropped it again and turned to look at me. 'Sophie,' he said and took a step towards me.

'Yes.' I didn't know why I trembled. In all the time we had spent together, he had never made love to me or kissed me or even taken my hand. I got up quickly and began unnecessarily to rearrange the wild flowers I had picked on my way through the woods and thrust into an old stone jar.

'Sophie, I have not thanked you.'

'There is no need.'

'But there is. I don't know anyone else who would have done what you have done and been so patient with me.'

'I have done nothing.'

'You have done everything.'

He took my hand and gently, with none of the violence he had shown before, he kissed me on the lips. For an instant he held me very close, my head against his breast, and I wondered if these hours we had shared had given him the tranquillity and sense of fulfilment that they had brought to me. I felt inexpressibly happy and yet desolate that they must end so soon.

We locked up in silence and went our separate ways back to the house as usual.

When I came into the hall, my cloak soaked by the rain, tendrils of damp hair escaping from the silk scarf I had tied over my head, Ruslan and Melka following at my heels, I met Olga coming out of the drawing room.

'How devoted you must be to the dogs to spend such a terrible afternoon exercising them,' she said, black eyes taking in the sodden shoes, the mud on the hem of my cloak.

'I like walking,' I said briefly.

'What an extraordinary English trait that is. Do you also like solitude or do you find company in the woods?'

'I don't know what you mean.'

'Nothing of course, only it seems strange ... did you by chance meet Leon during your wanderings?'

'No, why should I?'

'Valdaya is not so large. It seems odd that two lovers of lonely walks should not meet somewhere.'

'I have seen no one.' I made a move to pass her, but she stopped me, her hand on my arm.

'Leon is mine, you know. I don't intend giving him up to anyone.'

'Why should you?'

'I just wanted you to know, that's all.'

I shook her off. 'If that is all you have to say, I would like to change my wet shoes and stockings.'

Escaping up the stairs, I knew Olga had guessed at something though it must be far from the truth. Irina was the only one who knew about Leon's painting, not even Michael had been let into the secret, but then never before had Leon spent so much time working in the studio. It crossed my mind that I ought to warn him, but I was aware that soon he had to return to Petersburg and I could not bear to lose what might be our last opportunity to be alone together.

Chapter 12

It was a day or so later and the sun was sparkling on a rain-washed world when I sat down one morning, pen in hand, to write to Ryvlach. I had already spent a month at Valdaya and felt guiltily conscious of how little I had thought of my sister during that time. Simon had ridden over one morning bringing a long letter from Marya which amidst details of Paul and the children told me very little of what I wanted to know and there was only a brief note from Andrei.

'Rilla is up and about again,' he wrote, 'but gets tired very quickly. The mare has made a wonderful recovery and her filly is a beauty. We have called her Sonya which is Russian for Sophie, you know, so when are you coming back to see your namesake?'

I wondered how things were between him and Rilla. Once I would have been only too ready to believe every word of the story Jean Reynard had told me, but not now when I knew Andrei so much better. Yet I could not help remembering what Rilla had said about him and I wondered if somewhere in the past lay the root of her distress at the baby's death.

I was just sealing my letter when someone tapped at the door and before I could say anything, Irina had come swiftly into the room, slamming the door behind her and leaning back against it, her face flushed.

'I told him not to do it,' she said in a breathless rush, 'I begged him not to. I knew what would happen, but he insisted. He said it wasn't honourable, feeling as he did, to go on as we were and now grandfather has ordered him out of the house. Oh Sophie, what am I to do?' and she choked into angry tears.

She looked so distressed that I dropped my letter and went to her. 'Ira darling, what is it? What has happened? Who has done what?'

'It's Michael,' she whispered. 'You know how we feel about one another. This morning he wouldn't listen to me any more.

He went to grandfather and asked him formally for his permission and he refused absolutely.'

'But why? What reason did he give?'

'None. He never does. He doesn't want me to be happy,' she exclaimed passionately.

'Oh no, Ira, I'm sure that is not true. . . .'

'It is, it is, Sophie. Just because Michael will only inherit a small estate and hasn't a great name like the Astrovs, he is to be sent packing and I am to go on living in that hateful gloomy house in Moscow until I die, but I won't, I won't . . . I'll run away . . . I'll do something terrible and disgrace him, then grandfather will have something to be angry about. . . .'

Poor Irina, it was not easy to comfort her when there was so little I could say. 'Does Leon know?' I asked after a while.

'Not yet. He will be furious but what can he do.'

Little enough, but all the same it deepened the bitterness between him and Prince Astrov. He did not appear at luncheon that day and we were all together in the drawing room, the old aunts, the cousins, Olga, Irina and myself, when he came in, his face bleak as the east wind. He ignored the company and went straight to his grandfather.

'I am told, sir, that you have ordered my friend out of the house.'

'I have done no such thing. Lieutenant Federov had the good sense to realize he had outstayed his welcome.'

'That is a lie.' Leon did not raise his voice but we could hear every word he said. 'I know that Michael wants to marry Irina and why shouldn't he?'

'I am your sister's guardian and I decide what is best for her,' replied the old man stiffly.

'Isn't it enough that you command my life? Do you want to destroy Irina's happiness too?'

'I refuse to discuss it with you. This is not the time or place.'

'It never is, is it grandfather? But I'll tell you one thing. I am fond of my sister and if I can help her to get what she wants, then I will do so and be damned to you!' and Leon went out of the room, the door closing quietly behind him, leaving a shattered silence.

For two days he was absent, no one knowing where he had gone, and my heart sank. I was sorry for Irina and, without Michael or Leon, the house seemed very quiet and the days long. Then as suddenly as he had left, he came back. I saw him leading his horse into the courtyard, both of them thick with dust as if they had been riding hard. There were others there and he did not say anything directly to me, only looked, and I knew why he had returned. Like a song in my heart was the certainty that in the afternoon I would be going to the studio and nothing else mattered.

Olga had a headache and was lying down, but it was not until three o'clock that I could escape, Ruslan and Melka bounding ahead as usual. When I reached the hut, the door was open and he was waiting for me impatiently. I asked him where he had been.

'Nowhere,' he said briefly. 'Just riding and thinking. If I'd stayed here, God knows what I might have done. Let's get to work.'

He painted concentratedly for an hour, then he stood back. 'If I touch it once more I shall ruin it. Come and see.' He held out his hand and I came to join him, curious and yet half afraid.

I knew nothing of painting except for the few dull family portraits in the houses I had visited and to me the picture was something startlingly new and wonderful. There was no formal background, but out of sky and cloud there emerged a head and shoulders of a young girl in a pink muslin dress without formal beauty but with grace and fineness of bone, slight and delicate, with laughter in the violet eyes, tenderness in the mouth and character in the chin.

'That is not me,' I exclaimed. 'It cannot be. It is not possible.'

'It's how I see you,' said Leon, and a ripple of pure happiness ran through me that he of all men should find me beautiful.

'What will you do with it?'

'God knows. I've done it. That's enough for the present.'

He sounded happy and relaxed. He hummed a little tune as he cleaned his brushes and, dragging myself away from the portrait, I went on turning over the canvases, many of which I had already seen. Most of them were unfinished, quick impressions of a horse, a dog, a bird. There was one of Irina and another of a wrinkled brown face that I recognized as Yakov. Last of all, pushed away in a corner, looking dusty and untouched as if it had lain there for years, there was a picture so unexpected and so horrible that I stared at it for a moment in silence. It was

120

crudely done by an amateurish hand, but violence leaped out of the canvas. A man was being flogged, the whip curling round the naked back, the blood starting from the lashes, and in the background, grotesquely contorted, a figure swung from a gallows.

I said, 'Leon, what was it that made you paint this?'

He came to stand beside me. 'Oh that! I did that a long time ago. It was like . . . like an exorcism if you like, something I had to do to rid myself of nightmares.'

'I don't understand.'

'I was about sixteen, I suppose, when it happened. There was a revolt among the peasants and some of our serfs were involved. After it was put down, punishment was savage. My grandfather forced me to watch. It was a useful lesson, he said; if we were to survive as a class, then we must learn how to deal with those who threatened us.' He smiled a little. 'It did not have the effect he hoped. I remember I disgraced myself by being sick. Then for weeks I used to dream of it. Long afterwards I painted it, badly as you see, but somehow it helped. Let's turn it to the wall and forget it.'

But though he dismissed it so lightly, I did not find it so easy to forget and it brought back to my mind the house in the market.

I said, 'Is that one of the things that makes you feel as you do about the serfs, about wanting to change everything?'

'What do you know about that?'

'Andrei told me something. But what can you do? Surely no one would want revolution.'

'No, of course not,' he said smiling. 'But we have certain ideas of what could be done. Russia needs reform.'

'Are you sure that is all?'

'Of course it is.' Like Andrei, he was speaking as though I were a child, too simple and young to be treated seriously, and I felt sure that there was more behind it than either of them was willing to admit.

I said slowly, 'You said once that freedom was a tree that must be watered with blood.'

'Did I? One says all manner of foolish things,' he replied easily. He was shrugging himself into his coat. He stood for a moment, frowning, his eyes on the ground before he turned to me, speaking seriously, the casual manner vanished.

121

'Sophie, I don't know how to say this . . . you will laugh at me for a fool and you have every right to do so, and yet. . . .' He raised his eyes and looked me full in the face. 'Sophie, if I were to ask you, would you marry me?'

'Marry you?' I could not believe my ears. I felt confused, bewildered and filled with joy all at once. 'But you cannot . . . it is impossible. . . .'

'I know all that,' he said impatiently. 'There is Olga and I am going to be condemned as every kind of vile wretch if I break our engagement and yet that is what I intend to do and very soon though God knows, it is not going to be easy.'

'But there's your grandfather. . . .'

'You told me once it was high time I stood up to him. Are you going to blame me for doing just that?'

'No . . . oh no, only. . . .'

'Only nothing.' Abruptly he came to me, taking both my hands. 'Only tell me this . . . do you care what I do? Will it matter so much to you whether you marry Prince Leonid Astrov or plain Leon Karlovitch who may have a hard struggle to keep his head above water?'

'What kind of an answer do you want?'

'Just a plain one because I've been nerving myself to say this for the last couple of days and I can't endure to wait a moment longer.'

A little bubble of laughter escaped me. 'Oh Leon, how foolish you are. . . .'

'Does that mean. . . ?'

'It means,' I took a deep breath. 'It means I would marry you tomorrow if you wanted me and I'm not afraid of what people will say or of being poor. I've never been anything else. I know far more than you about it.'

'Oh Sophie, why didn't I ask you to marry me the day I took you driving in the Sparrow Hills?'

'If you had, I most certainly would have refused. Have you forgotten you were on the point of fighting a duel with Andrei? It would have been most improper.'

He laughed and hugged me. 'Why can I never do anything right? All my life I seem to have played the fool in one way or another, but now it will be different. I wish I had something to give you, but what can I find here at Valdaya? Wait a minute though,' he opened a drawer, rummaged through it

122

for a moment and came back to me. 'Don't laugh at it. It's very old, belonged to my grandmother, I believe, though I never knew her.'

It was a gold ring, heavy and old-fashioned, with a square green stone engraved with the head of a lion. He put it on my finger. 'A pledge from me to you. We shall have to wait, my darling, do you mind?'

I shook my head and he kissed me, lightly at first, then more and more passionately until momentarily everything was blotted out in joy.

'So this is where you spend your time,' the harsh voice rasped across us and dazedly we broke apart.

Prince Astrov stood in the open doorway leaning on his ebony stick, the hooded eyes bright in the old brown face. 'A pretty picture I must say!' he went on cuttingly. He came further into the room waving his cane contemptuously at the canvas on the easel. 'I thought I had cured you of this nonsense. It seems I was mistaken.'

'This place belongs to me,' said Leon coolly. He had not moved from my side and I felt his fingers close on mine. 'What I do here is my affair.'

'Is it indeed? One part of it concerns me very deeply.' His eyes flickered over me. 'Is this young woman your mistress that you meet here day after day in secret?'

'No, she is not. She has just done me the honour of promising to be my wife.'

'Have you forgotten that you are living in the same house as your affianced bride? Is this more of your play-acting or have you taken leave of your senses?'

'It seems to me that I have only just come to them. I am not fourteen now, grandfather, and I will not be forced into a marriage I loathe.'

'You should have thought of that when you gave your promise.'

'A promise that was forced out of me against my will. I shall tell Olga so when I return to the house.'

'You are a fool, Leonid. What do you think will be said of you? An Astrov marry this ... this little English nobody....' he spat out the words with an angry disdain.

'And what is Olga?' retorted Leon. 'Her father peddled silks and muslins all through Russia to Turkey and if it wasn't for the money shovelled over his counters, his daughter would never have been allowed to step across your threshold.'

'Don't dare to speak to me like that!'

'Deny it if you please, it is the truth. An Astrov selling his honour like a shopkeeper selling cheeses!'

A dull red flush had suffused the old man's face. He raised his silver-headed cane. I thought he would strike Leon, but instead he brought it down on the portrait slashing at it again and again until the canvas was ripped and ruined.

With a cry of rage Leon sprang at his grandfather. There was murder in his face as he wrenched the stick out of his hand. In another moment he would have brought it down on the old man's head if I had not seized his arm.

'No, Leon, no . . . you must not. . . .'

I felt him straining against me, then slowly he let his arm fall. The fury died out of his eyes. He threw the stick away from him.

'You can thank Sophie that I didn't kill you,' he muttered thickly.

For a long moment they stood staring at one another, the small erect figure of the old Prince still formidable, but it was he who stirred first. He bent and picked up the stick and moved stiffly to the door. When he turned and spoke, his words seemed to fall heavy as lead.

'You've forgotten one thing, Leon. Part of that money you despise has already been used. It has paid your debts as well as mine. You had better remember that before you jilt Olga Leskova. The St Petersburg courts will find it very amusing when she sues you for the return of her dowry and Mademoiselle Sophie may find the prospect of a honeymoon in a debtor's prison a little discouraging.'

Leon watched him go heavily down the step and disappear along the path. Then he passed his hand over his face. 'I never knew about the money, Sophie. Believe me, I did not.'

It was a shock, but just then I hardly realized its importance. I could only ask, 'How did he find out about this place?'

'God knows. Someone must have followed us here.'

Jean Reynard, I thought, and was certain I was right. He had found a way to punish Leon for that public humiliation.

Leon was staring at the ruined picture and the sick look on his face made me want to weep. I touched his hand.

124

'You can paint it again.'

'No, you never recapture anything. But that doesn't matter any more.' He moved restlessly. 'That damned money! It's like a millstone round my neck, but I'll not let it drown me. Somehow or other I'll get free.'

There was such a look of desperation on his face that I said quickly, 'What will you do?'

'How do I know? There must be some way. Do you hate me for dragging you into this wretched tangle? I could have killed my grandfather for what he said to you.'

'And what good would that have done?'

'Nothing at all except to get me hanged.' The old gay grin that was so much part of him appeared for a second and then vanished. 'I'm not much good, Sophie, but whatever happens, I meant what I said, every word of it. Will you remember that?'

I nodded, afraid to speak lest I should burst into tears. The whole afternoon had been too much. Walking back to the house, the early evening sun sent our shadows dancing before us. The gardens slumbered peacefully in the heat, bees buzzing in the velvet petals of the roses, fat blackbirds pecking lazily at the crumbs one of the maids had scattered on the grass, the soft moan of doves in the lime trees. The turmoil was only in our own hearts, I thought wearily. The long windows were open in the drawing room. We went in together and Olga looked up from the sofa where she had been lying. She stretched out a hand to Leon.

'My head is better now. Come and talk to me, dearest.'

In a pale gown of mousseline de soie with her dark hair loosened, she looked seductively helpless. With a pang I saw Leon hesitate and then go to her. All that had happened that afternoon seemed suddenly like a wild dream that could never be realized. How was he ever to break free? This was the real world and I might as well face up to it.

I did not go down to supper that evening and when Irina came knocking at the door and asking if there was anything wrong, I said that I was tired and going to bed early. But when I was undressed, it was too hot and I was too restless. In my white wrapper I sat by the open window watching the moon flood the garden with its unearthly light. What had I expected Leon to do? Stand up in front of them all and tell Olga brutally that he did not intend to go through with their marriage, shame her in front of everyone? No honourable man could behave in such a way, and yet a little worm of disappointment curled inside me because he had not done so, because everything was going on the same as before.

There was a gentle knock at the door and I called 'Come in', thinking it was Irina coming to say goodnight. It would be wonderfully comforting to confide in her, but she had her own problem and it did not seem fair to burden her with what was only between Leon and I.

But it was not Irina but Olga who came quietly into the room closing the door behind her.

'Do you mind?' she said. 'There is something I feel I must say to you.'

'No, of course not.'

I looked at her with a tiny stir of apprehension. There had never been any hint of friendship between us so why should she choose this moment to come to me? The mellow candlelight softened the rather angular lines of her face into something approaching beauty. The long dark hair was unbraided and fell almost to her waist over the dressing gown of blue corded silk.

I moved from the window to the dressing table. 'I was just going to bed. What is it you wanted to tell me?'

'Just this.' Olga came to stand beside me. Unwillingly I saw the reflection in the mirror. Beside me she looked tall and graceful, with a poise and confidence I had always envied.

'You are a stranger in Russia,' Olga was saying. 'I don't think you quite understand our ways nor the type of man Leon is. He is like so many others, so wilful and impetuous. It's like all the fuss he has made about Irina. There are better matches than Michael Federov and he knows it, but it amuses him to behave outrageously. He thinks it proves his independence, but I assure you that it means nothing.'

'Why are you saying all this to me?'

'Oh come, Sophie, I am not blind. I have seen the attentions he has been paying you these last few weeks. He is charming and attractive, is he not? No one appreciates that better than I. It is all too easy to lose one's head over him. It is just that I want to make sure you don't misunderstand.'

'I don't know what you are talking about.'

126

'I think you do.' Olga's gentle tone had hardened. 'It all means so little, you know. Any young girl is a challenge and he can never resist showing off. I've seen it and said nothing. After all it is his last fling before we are married, but now I feel it has gone too far. It is so thoughtless of him and I don't want to see you hurt. It is only right that you should know.'

'Know what?'

'That the date of our marriage is fixed. It is to be in the autumn, little more than two months away.'

'I don't believe you.'

'Why should I lie? You can ask my mother or Prince Astrov if you wish. The marriage settlements are all signed.' The black eyes watched me. 'Oh my dear, I am so sorry. What has he been saying to you?'

I longed to tell her, to fling it defiantly in her face, to say, 'You may have bought him, but it is I whom he loves.' But a sudden paralysing doubt kept me silent. After all it was true that I knew him so little. All I had heard of him, all the words of warning went scurrying through my mind. I turned my back on Olga so that she should not read the dismay in my face.

'He has said nothing to me,' I answered in a stifled voice.

Passionately I wished she would go away, but she went on insistently. 'I did not mean to tell you this . . . I have not told anyone . . . but you see, my dear, in Russia a betrothal is as binding as a marriage and. . . .'

A numbness had seized me. I could hardly get the words out. 'What are you trying to tell me?'

'I don't know how to say it . . . but maybe it will help you to realize . . . Leon and I . . . well, I should not have permitted it, but he was so urgent . . . and after all it is only a few months to our marriage. . . .'

It could not be true, it could not. It was impossible that he and Olga should have been lovers . . . and yet would any woman confess to such a thing if it were not true? I felt sick. I gripped a corner of the dressing table to keep myself steady. Then I turned to face Olga.

'Thank you for giving me your confidence. It must have been very painful for you, but really there was no need. I am not a child, you know, and I've grown up in a harsh world, far harsher than yours. I know how to look after myself.'

For an instant there was a measuring look between us, then Olga dropped her eyes. 'You'll say nothing about this?'

'Why should I? What you do is your own affair,' but inside me I thought she does not care if I do. She will hold it over him like a threat.

When Olga had slipped soft-footed through the door, I could not stay still. I paced up and down the room, at one moment refusing to believe a word she had said and at the next, raging with a furious anger against Leon.

I lay on the bed, my eyes burning, staring into the hot darkness, my throat aching with the tears I would not shed. It was like the misery of Edward's rejection all over again. What was wrong with me that men found me so easy to deceive? About one thing I was quite certain. I could not stay at Valdaya. A sharp longing for home and my sister overwhelmed me. Surely by now Rilla would hold nothing against me. But before I went, I must see Leon. I must speak to him. Just one reassuring word would be enough to still my torturing doubts. But when I came down to breakfast, heavy-eyed from my sleepless night, it was only to hear that he had left the house. Long before anyone was up, he had ordered the horses to be saddled and had returned to Petersburg.

'There is so much to be done,' said Olga smoothly. 'He asked me to excuse him for not making his farewells to you, Sophie. He felt sure you would understand. You don't look well, my dear. Shall I pour you some tea?'

It seemed to me that everyone round the table was staring at me, Olga's black eyes full of secret meaning and Jean Reynard smiling with pleasure at another's pain. It took every ounce of my courage to smile back, to take the cup and say quietly:

'Would you be kind enough, Monsieur Reynard, to ask Prince Astrov if he can spare the carriage? I would like to return to Ryvlach. My sister is not well and needs me.'

Chapter 13

Coming back to Ryvlach was like coming home. How strange it was, I thought, that it had taken the month away to make me realize it. When I ran through the house, I saw them all there in the garden, Marya with the children, Rilla with an old ,straw hat tied over her bright hair, snipping off dead roses in the border, and Andrei stretched lazily on the grass, a pile of books beside him.

It was Paul who saw me first. He came racing across the lawn shouting 'It's Sophie!' and flung his arms round my waist. Then they were all exclaiming in surprise. Andrei sat up, Marya was smiling, even Malika came to push his cold nose into my hand, waving his great plume of a tail. It was absurd to be so pleased, to feel that here was where I belonged, but it was my sister who really mattered.

Rilla had put down her basket. She was coming towards me with outstretched hands, 'Sophie darling, what a surprise and how lovely to see you.' The look on her face told me all I wanted to know. I hugged her with a feeling of joy that the anger and jealousy had only been part of her sickness and now could be forgotten.

'What made you leave so suddenly?' Andrei was asking. 'If you had let us know, I would have sent Stefan to fetch you.'

'Oh I don't know. I just felt I had been away long enough.'

'Nothing has happened, has it? Old Prince Astrov hasn't been taken sick ... or anything?' Rilla was looking at me anxiously.

'No, of course he hasn't. I've had a marvellous time but all the same it's good to be back.'

'Paul dear, run and tell Katya to bring fresh tea,' said Rilla, and when it came, we all sat around talking and exchanging news and I told them about the name day party and all I had seen and done except I did not mention Leon and said nothing of what had mattered most.

Then there were Nikki's two teeth to be examined and admired, Tanya had a new doll with a pink wax face and clothes that came off right down to silk shift and lace-trimmed knickers, and Paul kept interrupting to say, 'We've something to show you, Sophie, haven't we, Uncle Andrei?'

I don't quite know how Yakov's name cropped up. It was when I happened to mention the village and Rilla looked at me curiously.

'You didn't say Leon was there. Were you riding alone with him every day?'

'No, of course not,' I said hurriedly. 'Michael and Ira were always with us. Olga does not care for horses.'

'I remember old Yakov,' remarked Andrei. 'He was the joke of the Mess when I was still with the Guards. He was like a mother hen fussing over one chick. The cadets used to rag poor Leon about it unmercifully. He took it pretty well, I must say. I think he was fond of the old devil in his own way.'

'He was very distressed when he died,' and I told them how the old man had been turned out of his cottage and something of the quarrel with Jean.

I saw Rilla glance quickly at Andrei, but he only said quietly, 'Jean never permitted pity to stand between him and what he wanted. All the same it might have been wiser if Leon had kept his mouth shut.'

'How could he?' I retorted indignantly. 'It was mean and cruel.'

Andrei shrugged his shoulders and I was on the point of telling him about Musaka when Nikki, feeling he had been neglected long enough, set up such a wail of rage that it set Tanya off and Marya laughed as she picked up the baby.

'He's hungry,' she said. 'It's high time I took them both home.'

In the bustle of seeing them off in the little carriage Marya liked to drive herself, the subject of Jean Reynard was forgotten and afterwards there seemed no point in mentioning my vague suspicions.

Paul had not gone with Marya. He and his brown bear cub were staying at Ryvlach for a few weeks. He was dancing up and down with impatience and tugging at my hand.

'Do come to the stables now, please,' he urged. 'I've been

130

teaching Kali to beg for sugar and Rilla won't let me keep him in the house.'

'I should think not indeed,' Andrei ruffled the boy's dark hair. 'She spoils you quite enough as it is. The truth is, Sophie, he can't wait to show you Sonya.'

'And I can't wait to see her,' I replied gaily. 'Will you come too, Rilla?'

'No, I must go in and make sure your room is ready for you. You've taken us by surprise. Don't be late for supper all of you.'

It was a lovely evening, the sky clear and serene with tiny high-flying clouds and a slight breeze filled with the scent of tobacco plants and the purple plumbago bordering the path. After a month of tension, of happiness and doubt and stretched nerves, it was wonderful to feel the peace of Ryvlach. Whatever might still lie between Rilla and Andrei, there was no strife or bitterness, no uneasy atmosphere or warring temperaments, rasping against one another. A feeling of contentment flowed over me as I walked beside Andrei with Paul and Malika racing ahead.

The most valuable horses of the stud Andrei was slowly building up were brought in from the paddocks each evening. Their names were written above their stalls, Bajazet, Cazimir, Roxana, all chosen to fit their Eastern breeding, all except the new filly born at Ryvlach. Sonya was beautiful, her coat had the rich gloss of a ripe chestnut with mane and tail of a darker brown. She tossed her head with a shy wild grace when I stretched out a hand to touch the soft nose.

Paul could contain himself no longer. He was bursting with pride. 'Uncle Andrei has given her to me. When she is old enough and has been broken to the saddle, I'm going to have her to ride for my very own.'

Watching the man and boy together, I wondered if Andrei was thinking of the son he might have had and whether he and Rilla had yet found a way to cross the barrier that the baby's death had raised between them. I remembered the last night I had spent at Ryvlach and the glimpse I had of him then, grim-faced, stern, nothing like his usual casual easy charm. What Jean had said about him still lingered at the back of my mind though I rejected it. Perhaps there was more in common between him and Leon than I had thought; something fierce and untamed, so that one was never quite sure of them. Had Rilla found that as I was finding it? One part of me would have liked to tell him everything and ask his advice. I sometimes thought he knew Leon better than anyone, but how could I when it was all so uncertain? Only a day away from Valdaya and the whole month I had spent there seemed like a fantastic dream.

I duly admired Kali sitting up beautifully for sugar and then tumbling over backwards to shrieks of laughter from Paul. A comfortable place had been made for him in an empty stable where he was fastened with a long chain.

Walking back to the house and talking about the horses, I said without thinking, 'You ought to ask Leon to paint Sonya for you, just as she is now,' and would have bitten back the words, but it was too late.

Andrei looked at me sharply. 'How did you know about that?'

'He . . . he showed me some of his sketches one day.'

'Did he? You are highly honoured. Leon keeps that part of his life hidden from everyone, except perhaps his sister.'

'But you know about it.'

'By the merest chance. His comrades in the regiment would make fine sport of it if they found out. The dashing brilliant Prince Leonid daubing paint on canvas like a beggarly serf!' Andrei smiled a little. 'Leon leads a double life. He has a little flat in Petersburg . . . on one of the islands of the Neva . . . I don't know exactly where.' I was conscious of Andrei's blue eyes on me, shrewd but kind. 'Has his grandfather had a change of heart or was he perhaps sharing his secret with Olga?'

'Oh no,' I said quickly. 'I mean . . . they were not there, no one was. He just showed them to me.'

'I see.' We walked on a few steps in silence, then Andrei said quietly, 'You know, Sophie, Leon has not yet discovered what he asks from life. He is restless and unhappy and he turns from one thing to the other, always seeking and not finding what he wants. He paints, he has grand ideas about reforming Russia and freeing all the serfs, once or twice he has fallen desperately in love. But whatever he is looking for, he will have to discover for himself, even if he hurts others in the process. Do you understand what I mean?'

'I think so.'

I knew that he had guessed a little of what I felt and was trying to warn me that anything Leon might promise could not be trusted even though at the time he might mean what he said. I felt disheartened and yet elated because in spite of everything, Leon had shared with me something that was precious to him. We did not speak of him again and I said nothing to my sister. Rilla still thought of me as the little girl she had loved and protected, but that was four years ago, four years in which I had learned a great deal.

I had been back at Ryvlach about a fortnight when I heard about the fair. It was August and the heat had become intense. During the day the sun blazed down baking the earth to brown crumbling dust. The flowers wilted and the lawns grew parched because even the wells that supplied Ryvlach and Arachino with water had begun to run short and very little could be spared to the gardens.

The morning of the fair was hotter than ever. It was a holiday for the whole village and Andrei had given permission to any of the house serfs, who wished, to go and enjoy themselves. Katya came to show herself off to me, whirling round in her new scarlet skirts, black eyes sparkling, tossing her head and giggling when one of the footmen caught her round the trim waist and gave her a smacking kiss. She boxed his ears, but looked pleased all the same, and I was envious, wishing I too was running off with Leon, light-hearted and gay, without a trouble in the world.

In the late afternoon Andrei drove us over to see some of the fun. We strolled among the stalls, the crowds of merrymakers parting respectfully before us wherever we went. There were all kinds of pretty knick-knacks carried in the pedlars' packs from far distant places. One old man in a long brown pilgrim's gown was selling icons. His straggling white hair and long silky beard made him look like an Old Testament prophet and I wondered what he could be doing peddling icons at a fair.

'He is a *starets*,' explained Andrei, 'what you would call in English a hermit. Someone who by meditation and prayers has acquired the power to help and guide others.'

'Do you mean he is a monk?' I asked curiously.

'Some of them are and some not. This old man is called Kozima. He has a cell at the monastery we visited, but his great gift is for painting and he brings his icons to sell cheaply to those who are too poor to buy in the cities.'

The gnarled hands of the peasants beside me touched the paintings with reverence, their voices hushed, as if for the moment the noise and gaiety of the fair did not exist for them. The icons were small and I turned them over curiously, the Virgin, the Holy Child, and strange saints whose names I had never heard, each face with a still calm beauty of its own.

'The artist does not look for realism,' went on Andrei. 'An icon is a mystery and the painting of it is a holy undertaking. The artist believes that the spirit of the saint enters into him and guides his brush and his colours are mixed with water that has been blessed. Would you like one?'

I lingered over the choosing, at last picking out St George whose red-gold hair and proud uplifted head reminded me of Leon. On a blue horse with lifted spear he struck at the scarlet dragon writhing at his feet.

Andrei put down the money and the old man leaned forward, gripping my wrist and speaking in Russian.

'What does he say?'

'He says that your eyes are the eyes of innocence and with those you can conquer all evil and that if you pray before the icon with faith and simplicity, the saint will grant you your heart's desire.'

I smiled my thanks and the old man smiled back. For some inexplicable reason I felt a great wave of happiness wash over me as if the icon was already touching me with its miraculous power.

We did not stay much longer. 'This heat,' exclaimed Rilla. 'And the dust! I can scarcely breathe.'

I laughed and was not sorry to climb back into the carriage. At Ryvlach it was strangely quiet with hardly a servant left in the house and we ate a cold supper on the terrace under the stars with only the mellow glow of the candles beneath their glass globes.

By late evening it had grown cooler though there was still not a breath of wind. Paul had been sent to bed. Rilla had gone up to her room, but Andrei was still reading on the terrace with the light at his elbow. Feeling restless, I called Malika and thought I would walk a little in the garden before going to bed.

Fireflies glimmered here and there among the bushes like tiny stars. Gnats hummed in pockets of warm air as I wandered down the path. I had tried to school myself to patience, but although every morning when Stefan came in with the postbag, I could hardly wait for Andrei to open it, no word had come from Leon. At one moment I would make up my mind to forget the whole episode, pretend that it had never happened, and in the very next breath I would see again Olga's sly look of triumph and long to wipe it off her face. Above all there was the dull ache of memory, Leon's face with its swift changes from gravity to laughter, the compelling grey eyes meeting mine with the joy of a shared secret, his voice whispering huskily, 'Why did I never meet you before?'

I was so deep in thought that l did not realize I had taken the path to the stables till I heard a frightened whinny followed by another, then the stamping of feet, and quite suddenly I knew why. I smelled it first, the unmistakable smell of burning wood. Someone must have lighted a bonfire and carelessly left it smouldering. Then I saw the coils of blue smoke. I stared at them for an instant, unwilling to believe what I saw, then I went racing back to the house, stumbling in my haste and calling out breathlessly as I came up to the terrace.

'The stables ... they're on fire ... I could see the smoke. . . .'

'On fire? Are you sure?' Andrei threw down his book and got to his feet. 'By God, and there's hardly a soul left on the place. Call Rilla, will you? Ask her to send someone over to Arachino. Simon will bring help. I'll get down there at once.'

The next few moments were frantic. Rilla came running down the stairs, half-dressed, a shawl round her shoulders. Kostya, the half-witted son of the cook who had been left behind, was roused from his bed and sent racing off to Arachino with a scribbled note.

'It will be some time before Simon gets here,' said Rilla. 'We'll have to help, Sophie. We're going to need buckets, as many as we can carry. There's the well for the stables, we can get water from there.'

Paul had been roused by the noise. He was half way down the stairs in his nightshirt before we saw him.

'Go back to bed,' exclaimed Rilla. 'There's nothing you can do. It will be all right.'

'There's Kali. He's chained up in the stables.'

'Don't worry. We'll get him out. Now go back to your room, there's a good boy. Anichka, see that he stays there,' she said to the fat old cook who had appeared from the kitchens looking scared.

By the time we reached the stables, the fire had spread and

135

already had taken firm hold on the timbers, baked dry by the sun. Flames were shooting up, red and gold, against the darkening sky. Stefan with some of the men had already returned from the fair. They had formed a chain, filling buckets and passing them from one to the other, but they were pitifully inadequate to quell the fury of the fire.

Andrei, his coat off, his white shirt already filthy, was directing operations. Some of the horses had been brought out. They reared and plunged, whinnying with fright in the smoke and heat. They were having trouble with Sonya. Terrified, she had backed away into the farthest corner of the stall. Through the smoke I saw Andrei go in with the men. I heard his voice, calling to her, coaxing her. Slowly they dragged her out, kicking, biting and struggling.

Rilla and I took our place in the line of water carriers. How long we stood there, I had no idea. My hands were blistered, the front of my dress soaked from the spilling water, my eyes smarting and painful from the smoke. Once I looked up and was horrified to see Paul, barefooted and with a coat pulled on over his nightshirt, standing by the shivering trembling Sonya, his eyes fixed on the stable.

I was just going to mention it to Rilla when the man working the ropes of the well, shouted, 'The level has dropped. We'll get no more from here,' and sweating and panting, we stopped for a second to take breath.

Through the shifting clouds of smoke I could see that Simon had arrived and was standing with Andrei. All the horses had been got out, but without water there was little more we could do. We would have to watch the flames consume the buildings that Andrei had mortgaged half his estate to build and on which he had placed such high hopes.

One of the men shouted, 'There's the pond. We could get water from the pond.'

It was true, but it was some distance away, thick and slimy with weed. Still it might save something. While the men organized another line of carriers to pass the buckets, I remembered Paul. I looked frantically from one to the other, but he was nowhere to be seen. I seized my sister by the arm.

'Where's Paul?'

'Paul?' Rilla turned a white face smudged with smoke. 'We left Paul at the house.'

136

'No, he was here. I saw him just a minute ago. He must have followed us. He said something about his bear cub.'

'The bear! Oh God, no one has remembered it. Andrei!' Rilla's cry brought him swinging round. 'Where's Kali? We can't find Paul anywhere.'

'What on earth were you doing to bring the boy down here?'

'He followed us,' I said quickly. 'It's not Rilla's fault. She told him to stay at Ryvlach, but I think he was worried about his bear.'

'Oh Andrei, he can't have gone in there to fetch him . . . can he?'

I saw my sister's pale face, tense and strained, and realized suddenly that she must be reliving all the horror of that terrible night last winter.

'I had forgotten the bear,' exclaimed Andrei.

For an instant we were all stunned into silence. The fire had reached the end of the stable buildings but had not yet burst into flames. Thick smoke billowed out from the doorway.

I said frantically, 'He must be somewhere.'

The men looked at one another helplessly. One or two of them scattered, shouting his name.

Andrei said, 'I am going in.'

'You can't.' Simon gripped him by the arm. 'At any minute the roof will collapse.'

'Don't you understand? The boy's gone in after his bear.' Andrei shook him off. 'Get out of my way.'

I dipped my flimsy scarf into the last pail of slimy water and gave it to Andrei. He wrapped it round his mouth and plunged through the doorway. Rilla, pale as death, was still as if carved out of stone. No one spoke, no one moved.

A long scarlet tongue shot up from the peaked roof and someone screamed. I heard the crackle and roar of the fire creeping nearer and nearer. To wait was unbearable and yet there was nothing anyone could do. Then Andrei appeared in the opening. He was carrying Paul in his arms. He seemed to stagger, then he threw the child forward out of danger as part of the roof crashed behind him with a shower of golden sparks and a wave of heat. Through the clouds of black smoke Andrei hurled himself forward and fell on his face, a dozen willing hands seizing him and dragging him away from the falling timbers.

137

Paul had scrambled to his feet. He was sobbing wildly. 'I couldn't undo the chain . . . It was too hot . . . I tried and tried, but Uncle Andrei would not let me stay. . . .' His tears choked him and I put my arms round the shaking child trying to soothe him while my eyes sought anxiously after Andrei.

Rilla had thrust her way through the men and was on her knees beside him. She said, 'Stand back all of you. We don't know how much he may be hurt. Simon, help me and send Stefan for Dr Arnoud.'

But Andrei was already struggling to sit up. Paul broke free and ran to him, tears still streaking his face.

'I couldn't save Kali. He was so frightened and I couldn't get him free,' he sobbed.

'I know. I am sorry, Paul.'

'Oh Uncle. . . .' the boy flung his arms round Andrei's neck begging for comfort and I saw his face contract with pain.

Simon bent down, gently lifted the child and set him on his feet. 'There now,' he said quietly, 'your uncle saved your life though he couldn't save poor Kali. Try and remember that.'

One of the men was helping Andrei up. He stood swaying a little, holding on to Rilla. I saw how she looked at him and thought how strange it was that the disaster of the fire had done what no doctor, no reasoning, no will power had been able to do. By what was almost a miracle he had been given back to her and she saw him not as the murderer of her baby but as the man who had risked his life to save a child, the man she loved with all her heart.

We left Simon doing what he could to salvage the blackened ruins of the stables. Andrei would have stayed longer, but Rilla urged him to come away and he yielded at last because the first numbness was being succeeded by pain that was obviously almost more than he could endure.

We went back to the house slowly and at a glance from Rilla I took Paul upstairs to put him to bed. The boy was silent now as I washed his face and hands, found a clean nightshirt that did not smell sickeningly of the smoke and tucked him into bed. When I bent to kiss him, he suddenly sat up again.

'Sophie, do you think Kali knows that I tried to rescue him?'

'Yes, of course he does, darling,' I said soothingly. 'Try not to think about it.'

He clutched at my hand, large eyes imploring me. 'Uncle Andrei won't die, will he? Not like Kali.'

'No. The doctor will be here soon. He will make him better. Now lie down and Anichka shall bring you some hot milk and sit with you till you go to sleep.'

When I came down the stairs to the drawing room, Andrei was lying back in the chair with his eyes closed. Rilla had done what she could till the doctor came. She had cut away the burned rags of his shirt. He was lucky to have escaped more serious hurt. The falling timbers had bruised and lacerated his shoulder and scored a furrow down his right arm which was raw and ugly. She had wrung out clean linen in cool water, smeared it with goose grease and laid it over the burned flesh.

Andrei stirred when I came into the room. He sat up wincing with the pain of the sudden movement. 'How did it start?' he said. 'Was it deliberate or was it just carelessness on someone's part? I have to know.'

'Don't worry about it now, Andrei. It won't do any good. You can go into all that afterwards.'

'But I must. If Sophie had not taken that walk, everything could have been destroyed. Why should it happen tonight of all nights when no one was there? Doesn't that look as though it were planned? Who hates me so much that they would do such a thing?'

'There is Musaka,' I said slowly.

'Musaka? But it's weeks since he ran off and nothing has been heard of him anywhere.'

'I saw him at Valdaya . . . he was talking with Jean Reynard,' and I remembered the look on Jean's face when Irina had spoken of the fire and was certain I was right.

Rilla stiffened and Andrei stared at her. 'Musaka and Jean. . . .' he repeated, but got no further. The doctor came hurrying in with Simon. Dmitri, greatly agitated, had come with them. He crossed at once to Andrei.

'I was away from the house. They've only just told me. I came immediately. My dear brother, what can I say? If it had not been for you, Paul would. . . .'

He could not go on and Andrei smiled. 'It's all right, Mitya. The boy is safe, that's all that matters. Go up and see him if you like.'

'Now, now, gentlemen,' interrupted Dr Arnoud. 'No more of

this now. Plenty of time for talking later. Let me attend to my patient if you please.'

Simon urged Dmitri away while Rilla stayed beside Andrei and I waited in case there was anything I could do. The doctor said little which was unlike him, but I thought his face looked grave as he treated the burns and laid a light bandage of gauze over them. Then he straightened himself.

'I am sorry to have to say this, but the pain and shock will be far worse tomorrow than now. So take it easy, my dear sir, I beg of you. I will leave something with the Countess that will help you to sleep and I'll be back tomorrow.'

When the doctor had gone, Rilla said, 'You'd be much better in bed, Andrei. I'll get Simon to help you upstairs.'

'Be damned to that,' he said impatiently. 'I want to speak with him first. Fetch him, will you, Sophie?'

The pain of the dressing had told on him. He looked white and sick, but he spoke with grim determination and when I came back with Simon and Dmitri, he pulled himself upright with an effort.

'Has Musaka been seen anywhere in this neighbourhood in the last few weeks?'

'Musaka?' repeated Simon in surprise. 'Not that I know of. Why? Do you think he is responsible for the fire?'

'I don't know, but I just don't believe that it was an accident. Make enquiries after him, start a hunt and when you can get anywhere near the burned-out ashes that have been left to us,' he went on savagely, 'take some of the men and search. There may be some evidence.'

'It won't be easy to find, too much has gone, but I'll do what I can.'

'Good . . . and the horses . . . are they all right?'

'Don't fret yourself about them. They can be housed at Arachino,' put in Dmitri quickly. 'And if there's any difficulty about rebuilding . . . well, I know you are an independent devil . . . but come to me.'

'I hope it won't be necessary, but thank you all the same.'

'Andrei needs rest,' interrupted Rilla firmly. 'You can come back and talk about all this tomorrow,' and she urged them away.

140

When she returned and helped Andrei from the chair, he stood for a moment, leaning on her.

'Could it be Jean?' he said, 'Could it, Rilla? Does he want to destroy us all? By the mercy of God nothing has been lost except that wretched little bear cub, but it could have been much worse ... Paul, the horses, even Ryvlach if the wind had been in this direction.'

'Perhaps we are mistaken ... perhaps it was just an accident and with everything so dried up by this heat....' said Rilla.

But Andrei was not listening to her. He went on broodingly, 'I thought it was all over, finished with, forgotten, but it seems that some things we do pursue us and will not let us live in peace.'

'Leave it, Andrei. There's nothing we can do tonight and tomorrow it may look different.'

But in the morning, we forgot Musaka and Jean Reynard and who had been responsible for the fire. Andrei was sick and feverish and Dr Arnoud looked very grave indeed. For the next few days he scarcely seemed to leave the house and that dread thought—blood poisoning—was in all our minds though no one dared to speak it aloud.

One evening towards the end of that nerve-wracking week, I was with my sister in the bedroom. It was still very hot and the windows were open to let in as much cool air as possible. Andrei had been very restless all day, but now at last he had fallen into an uneasy sleep. Rilla wiped the sweat from his face with a linen towel and came to stand beside me. She leaned her head against the window frame, looking out on the garden awash with a pale milky twilight.

'It's all gone, Sophie, all that terrible barrier I had built up inside myself. When Andrei went in to fetch Paul, I thought I would die ... then he was there and it was like a miracle, but now ... oh Sophie....'

The tears were running silently down her face and I put my arm round her. 'He will not die, he cannot, not now, I am sure of it,' I whispered.

We were very close at that moment and partly to distract her thoughts, I said quietly, 'There's something I've been wanting to tell you, something Jean Reynard said to me at Valdaya. I didn't believe it, but I think you ought to know.'

'What did he say?'

'It was the day I saw him with Musaka, when we were riding up by the old quarry. He told me that Paul's mother had killed herself because she was carrying Andrei's child.'

Rilla's eyes flashed angry green fire. 'That damnable lie! Jean is like a snake, everything he says is smeared with poison.' She looked at me for an instant, then sat down on the window seat. 'It's something we don't speak of, something we kept from Dmitri and everyone, but perhaps you should know, especially now when Jean has come back into our lives.'

'Did Natalya really ride her horse over the quarry as he said?'

'Yes, she did, but it was not Andrei's child, but Jean's who died with her.'

It was so unexpected that I stared at her and Rilla sighed. 'I know it is hard to believe, but it is true all the same,' and she went on with her story of love and hate while the shadows lengthened in the room, the little lamp glowed red in front of the icon and there was no other sound but the heavy breathing of the man lying in the bed.

'You've seen her portrait. You know how young and beautiful Natalya was, less than half Dmitri's age, and she and Andrei. . . .'

'You mean they were lovers?'

'Yes. Oh it had happened before ever I came to Arachino. He had wanted her to go away with him, but she would not.'

'Did you know about it?'

'I guessed at it and very painful it was too,' Rilla smiled wryly at the memory of old torments, 'but what I didn't know for a long time was that it was ended between them. Only when he came back that hot summer after a long absence, Natalya would not accept it. She still loved him, you see, she wanted him and when he rejected her, she grew desperate and Jean had always desired her. I suppose she believed it would drive Andrei into jealousy, bring him back to her, but it didn't work out like that.'

'Because he had fallen in love with you?'

'Partly and partly because he had changed.' Rilla paused for a moment and then went on quickly. 'Natalya said to me once that when Jean touched her, it was like being possessed by a devil. I think he both fascinated and terrified her. I told you how he planned the attack on Dmitri that nearly cost his life,

142

but I've not told you the most important thing of all, what it was that drove him to such a terrible action. You see, Sophie, Jean is Andrei's half brother. The old Count was a man who loved many women and Jean's mother was a distant cousin married to a Frenchman. When she died, her son was brought up with Andrei and Dmitri, but always the bastard, always made to feel he was eating the bread of charity, and he resented it. He wanted money, he wanted power and position, he envied the two brothers who had so much more than he and he thought, with Dmitri dead and Paul heir to the Kuragin estates, he could achieve all he desired through Natalya, but she cheated him. That night we were all sure that Dmitri could not live and in the morning she rode out and drove her horse over the quarry to her death.'

I could see it all so clearly, the hushed house, the beautiful desperate young wife and the bitter envious man who had staked everything on her and lost.

'What happened?' I asked at last.

'You know the rest. Andrei's anger was beyond all reason, not only because of Dmitri but for Natalya too. He threw him from the house that very night. Afterwards he arranged for money to be put at his disposal, but Jean has never touched it. He has the pride of the devil and a hatred beyond words. He must have fed on it for years so that now I wonder if he is quite sane.'

I wondered too, remembering the glitter in those strange eyes. It was like a festering wound, an obsession which possessed him and coloured everything he did, and I shivered a little because it seemed to stretch out, striking not only at Andrei but at all those who came within his circle.

'All the Kuragins have it,' Rilla said slowly, 'a streak of wildness, a temper and a pride that does not appear on the surface and Jean has it too, maybe in even greater measure because it has had to be suppressed.'

We sat close together for a moment or two and I thought that my sister and I were still strangers, still feeling our way in a world that sometimes we found hard to understand. I said, 'I know what you mean. I think Leon is the same.'

'Leon?' Rilla looked at me sharply. 'How much did you see of him at Valdaya, Sophie? I've often wondered.'

But I was not yet ready to tell my sister everything. I put her question aside hurriedly.

'You needn't worry about me, but I can't help seeing what he is like, and Irina tells me things about her brother.'

'Well, he will be married soon and a good thing too,' said Rilla, getting up and going back to the bed.

My heart missed a beat. 'How do you know? Have you heard from someone?'

'It is all over Petersburg apparently. Madame Leskova has lost no time in proclaiming it as the wedding of the season with the Grand Duke himself present, maybe even the Tsar if she is lucky.'

So Leon had done nothing, nothing at all. All his promises, all his fine words, were lies, mere empty air. It took me a minute before I could take in what Rilla was saying.

'I think Andrei is better, Sophie. Come and look. He feels cooler and he is sleeping more easily.'

I pulled myself together. This was what was important, this was reality, not my foolish dreams. I hurried to my sister's side, sharing her relief and trying to quieten the agitation in my own heart.

Chapter 14

After that night Andrei recovered very quickly. He was soon out of bed and though he had to keep his arm in a sling and the burns were slower to heal than Dr Arnoud would have wished, he insisted on going about the estate as usual.

'A Guards officer learns to ride without hands,' he said teasingly to Rilla when she protested. 'How else do you think we managed in a cavalry charge? At one time I used to be able to ride with pistol in one hand, sabre in the other and the reins in my teeth.'

I could not but be aware how things had changed between them. They seemed to glow with a renewed happiness. It was not that they caressed one another or indeed behaved any differently in public, but now and again I would see the look in Andrei's eyes when they rested on his wife and though I was happy for my sister, I sometimes envied her. They included me in everything they did and yet I felt shut out. I had no part in their shared joy.

The cause of the fire had not yet been discovered. Simon's searches among the ruins of the stables had brought to light some rather doubtful evidence. A heap of kindling—hay, straw and wood shavings piled together with some oily rags—was suspicious but provided no proof. Not a word had come in about Musaka. His wife had sworn with tears and curses that he had abandoned her and his children and she had seen nothing of him. The doubt and feeling of threat continued to haunt us.

Paul was still at Ryvlach. His tutor had returned from leave of absence during the summer and rode over every morning, but holidays were not yet quite over and lessons were confined to a couple of hours each day. Peter Ilyitch was a quiet pleasant young man who simply worshipped Rilla, a fact which Andrei found highly amusing. Paul still mourned a little for his bear cub, but with the resilience of children the horror died quicker with him than it did with us. I still shivered when I passed the charred blackened stable yard and thought of what might so very easily have brought tragedy.

Rebuilding had already been taken in hand. Winter comes early in Russia and Andrei was determined to get as much done as possible before the frost and snow stopped all outside work. Dmitri used to ride over to consult with him. I think the shock of the fire and the danger to Paul had shaken him out of his withdrawal.

At the end of August there were already touches of autumn in the gardens and woods, a golden leaf here and there, the pink of spindleberry and the fiery red of rowan. The fruit was ripening in the orchards, rosy apples and brown-skinned pears, and the wasps swarmed over the fallen plums juicy under their split scarlet skins.

Dmitri came in one morning with news of the horse fair which was held at a village about thirty miles south of Arachino.

'There should be some interesting stock for sale this year,' he said to Andrei. 'I hear some of the Tartars will be bringing the pick of their herds from the Steppes. They're a set of thieving rogues but they know how to choose the mares. Do you feel strong enough to make the trip with me?'

Andrei was interested at once. It was Rilla who interrupted firmly. 'You shall not go unless I go with you.'

'You see, Mitya, how she treats me. I'm not allowed out of my wife's sight. It's not at all suitable for you, my dear. The company's rough and the accommodation at the inn is appalling. I shan't be able to look after you. I shall need all my wits about me if I'm not to be cheated. Those nomadic horse traders drive a hard bargain.'

But Rilla was insistent. I think she could not bear to have him away from her for more than a few hours. 'Stefan can take care of us and Sophie will be with me. What could be more proper?'

So it was settled and I was all eagerness to go anywhere that would stop me brooding. It was more than a month since I had left Valdaya and a growing resentment was festering in my heart that Leon who had promised so much had left me without a single word.

Paul of course wanted to come with us, but that Andrei would not permit. Much to his disappointment he was left in the care of his tutor for the two days we would be away.

146

We set out very early in the morning when the dew still spangled the grass. Stefan drove Rilla and me in the carriage with Andrei and Dmitri sometimes cantering ahead, sometimes riding on either side. By the time we arrived at the village, it was already crammed. The auction was held in the fields just outside and as we drove up, I thought I had never seen a more colourful spectacle. The Tartar horsemen had pitched their tents of dark felt on the rim of the huge open space. They were small bow-legged men, with tall fur hats, slanting black eyes and brown leathery skins. Wild and barbaric, they swaggered amongst the peasants showing off their fine boots, their many-coloured kaftans and the silver-hilted knives stuck in their broad leather belts.

Andrei had been right. As far as I could see there were no other women of our class there, though there were plenty of gypsies with shawls over their greasy black hair, baskets on their arms and sloe-eyed babies slung at their backs. The buyers were all gathered together at one side of the field; landowners who, like Andrei, preferred to choose for themselves, agents from some of the princely estates and a fair sprinkling of cavalry officers from the crack regiments on the look-out for good mounts for their men.

Dmitri and Andrei were greeted at once by a dozen acquaintances and after making sure that we were well placed, they disappeared among the other men. Stefan had drawn up the carriage alongside the field and let down the hood so that we could see everything comfortably from where we were sitting. I was glad I had listened to Rilla and had brought a parasol for the sun was hot and the dust terrific.

They had already begun to bring out the horses and the customers surged forward watching their owners leading them around the field and putting them through their paces before bidding started. I was not like my sister. I knew nothing about the points for which one must carefully look before making a purchase.

'They keep the best till last,' explained Rilla. 'That's the man to watch . . . Khan Jehangir.'

I looked where she pointed and saw a tall man, thin as a reed, with a hooked nose and narrow black moustachios curling round his mouth. He leaned against the pole of his tent smiling contemptuously.

'He will bring out his horses this afternoon,' she went on, 'and then the bargaining will really begin.'

The morning passed very quickly and there was a break when Stefan lifted out the picnic lunch we had brought in the carriage. Andrei and Dmitri came to join us bringing a couple of acquaintances with them. The visitors bowed to Rilla and me, politely concealing their astonishment, and very happy to share the lavish meal spread out on the grass. There was cold chicken, grouse stuffed with truffles, a salad of sliced tomato, cucumber and pimento, and bottles of Tokay, cool and golden, for us, with vodka for the gentlemen. Their talk of course was all of horses and largely incomprehensible to me though Rilla listened and occasionally made a remark that obviously surprised the guests with its shrewdness.

My attention wandered as I sipped my wine. Men of every type thronged the ground from cavalry officers in brilliant uniforms down to ragged beggars and to my surprise I saw that another carriage had drawn up at a little distance with two handsomely dressed women sitting in it. Curious to see who else had braved the male gathering, I leaned forward to get a better view. They turned to speak to someone and there was no mistaking them. It was Olga and her mother and the man with them was Leon.

It had never occurred to me that he might be there and yet nothing was more probable. No doubt like the other officers he was buying on behalf of the regiment. But that he should have brought Olga to such a meeting, that he should be there so intimately by her side, almost as if they were already married ... it was more than I could endure. Rilla had noticed nothing. I put up my parasol quickly, anxious to avoid recognition. Anger and resentment so choked me that I could not swallow another mouthful.

There must have been some change in my looks because Rilla said, 'You are pale, Sophie. Are you all right?' and Andrei leaning across, bottle in hand to refill my glass, remarked, 'Is the heat too much for you? Would you like to go inside and rest?'

But that was the last thing I wanted. I shook my head gulping the wine gratefully. It ran through me, warming and strengthening.

'No, I'm far too fascinated. When does the auction start again?'

'Very soon now. Khan Jehangir has a marvel up his sleeve so they say. Nobody has seen her yet, a mare in a million.'

The men left us to go back to the ring and when bidding began again, I concentrated my attention on it, feverishly asking Rilla questions, determined not to spare one glance at Olga or Leon. Presently the Khan moved from the opening of his tent to the centre of the ground and two of his tribesmen brought before him a horse that even to my inexperienced eyes seemed to be something quite outstanding. She was the colour of pale gold, her mane and tail brushed to a shining floss silk. She had a narrow beautiful head and wild eyes like dark brown velvet. Rilla drew a sharp breath.

'Andrei is going to beggar himself for that one,' she murmured.

At first the bidding was brisk and general, but as it rose higher they began to drop out and it narrowed at last to only three, one of whom was Andrei. We stood up in the carriage to see better and Rilla gripped my arm.

'Do you see over there?' she said. 'It's Jean Reynard. He must be buying for Prince Astrov and Leon is here too. Whatever is he thinking of? He is bidding against his grandfather.'

The price had already risen to what seemed to me an impossible sum. Then Leon stopped and I could see quite plainly on his face the look of baffled despair that I had seen once or twice before at Valdaya. I wondered why he wanted the horse so passionately. When I looked at Andrei and Jean, they were standing each side of the ring and they never uttered a word, just raised a finger as the auctioneer glanced from one to the other while the rest of the customers clustered in a watching group whispering to one another.

'They will never stop,' murmured Rilla to me. 'They will neither of them give way.'

It was the Khan himself who put an end to it. He strode suddenly into the centre of the ring and raised his hand. He was speaking, his voice harsh, strident with authority.

'What does he say?'

Rilla was frowning. 'He has such a queer accent, it's difficult to understand. I think he says he has changed his mind. He will not sell the mare to the highest bidder, but only to the man strong enough to master her, and that like all women, she is capricious and will obey only where she loves.'

'How fantastic.'

149

'These people are strange, half pagan still and deeply super-stitious, and they value their horses more than life itself.'

'Will they do as he asks?'

'They have no choice if they want her. These tribal chieftains are like kings in their own country. They do what they please. The Khan once refused to sell his horses even to the Tsar.' Rilla looked worried. 'Andrei will risk it and he should not. These horses from the Steppes are only half broken to the saddle. Any-thing could happen. I'm going down to him, Sophie. You don't mind if I leave you?'

I knew what she meant. Andrei rode magnificently, but his right arm was still almost useless. In a match of this kind Jean Reynard would have all the advantage. I stood up to watch them. Dmitri was arguing with Andrei. Then I saw Rilla reach his side and put her hand pleadingly on his arm. There was a buzz of excitement at the unusual sequel to the day's bargain-ing. Anxiety for Andrei had for the moment blotted out every-thing else so that Leon's voice startled me. He had come to the side of the carriage.

He said urgently, 'Sophie, I've been waiting and waiting for an opportunity to find you alone.'

He was bare-headed. The breeze ruffled the tawny hair and there was a pleading look in the grey eyes raised to mine. It nearly undid me, but I had been deceived once and I had made up my mind that it was not going to happen again. Pride came to my aid . . . pride and the memory of Edward. I drew away from him. I said coolly, 'I don't understand what you can have to say to me.'

'I've been wanting to write to you . . . I've wanted to explain . . .'

'What is there to explain? I understand perfectly. Olga told me everything.'

'Olga? What did she tell you?'

The quick look he gave me angered me. I thought of what Olga had said when she came to me at Valdaya that night, the look of triumph in her eyes in the morning when she told me he had left the house. I said, 'Do I need to repeat it? I would prefer not to discuss it.'

Down on the field they were already getting ready for the contest. I saw Andrei gently free himself from Rilla and walk towards the Khan.

Leon was saying, 'What has happened to you, Sophie? Why have you changed?' There was a note of anger in his voice.

Jean Reynard detached himself from the men around him and moved towards the centre. They were saddling the mare. They must have been tossing a coin as to who was to ride first because I saw the gleam of gold. Quite suddenly my anxiety for Andrei and my anger against Leon fused and became too much for me. I said, 'It is not I who have changed but you. Why did you lie to me? Why did you tell me that Olga meant nothing to you?'

'Nor does she?'

I turned to face him. 'How can I believe that when you and she . . . you and she. . . .' But I could not say it aloud, and Leon leaped up into the carriage beside me. He gripped my shoulders. 'Damn you, Sophie, will you listen to me?'

I wrenched myself away. 'No, I will not. Go back to your bride. Go back to where you belong.'

If I had my pride, so had he. I kept my eyes fixed on the field where the Khan's tribesmen were pushing back the spectators so that the space was left free and if I expected Leon to go on pleading, I was wrong. When I summoned courage to look round, he had gone, but not back to Olga. I could not see him anywhere though my eyes swept hungrily all round the eager chattering crowd.

I swallowed the bitter angry tears and forced myself to concentrate on the strange contest that was about to take place down there in front of unheeding people who saw it only as an amusing battle over a horse at the whim of an unpredictable barbarian from the Steppes. I wondered if anyone else but us knew that the two men who did not so much as glance at one another were half brothers who had loved the same woman, had brought her to her death and were at deadly enmity.

I called Stefan to ask what had been decided.

'Three times round the ring, Barina, and may God preserve his honour,' he replied fervently.

Jean Reynard was to ride first. He stood waiting, immaculate in his black coat and high stock. Then he vaulted into the saddle and it had begun.

I was no judge and perhaps it was as much due to my imagination as anything else, but though he rode well, it seemed to me that there was a cruelty in the tight rein and that the delicate creature sensed and resented it. He was conquering her, but it was with savagery, with an iron hand that crushed all that grace and beauty and fire. Three times they went round the field and then she broke. When he would have brought her to a standstill before the tall silent figure of the Tartar Chief, she suddenly threw up her head and bolted. Taken unawares he could not immediately hold her. The spectators scattered in terror. I saw Andrei step quickly back taking Rilla with him. Faced with one of the dark tents, the mare shied violently, nearly unseating Jean, but by a miracle of horsemanship he brought her round forcing her back to the ring, sweating, trembling, ears flung back, teeth bared. There was a round of applause when he dismounted and threw the reins to one of the Tartar tribesmen.

With Andrei it was quite different. He had a hard struggle from the very start. The mare was nervous and distressed. She jerked and pulled away, shying at everything. A blowing leaf, someone coughing, was enough to set her dancing and rearing. Andrei had whipped off the silk sling, but he kept his right hand in his pocket and held the reins in his left. He rode gently, almost casually, and when she trembled and threw up her head, he leaned forward, speaking to her coaxingly. It was not a master conquering a slave, but a partnership between horse and man. All would have been well if some foolish person in the crowd unable to restrain his enthusiasm had not waved his hat and cheered as they came round for the third time. The startled mare reared up and then bucked, kicking out with her hind legs. Andrei taken by surprise was thrown to one side losing a stirrup and, hampered by his useless arm, could not regain his balance. He slipped sideways and I caught my breath. Tangled in the reins he was being dragged across the dusty field. There was a gasp from the crowd. I saw Rilla make a move and Dmitri put out a hand to hold her back. Then something quite astounding happened. Before anyone could reach her, the mare stood still, head drooping, waiting while Andrei freed himself and scrambled to his feet. She was quivering, rubbing her head against him when he fondled her before he led her back to the Khan who stood quite motionless, no expression on his face.

It was his decision and I had no idea of how such a man would react, a man whose life was probably filled with deeds of savagery and violence. He was speaking. I heard a cheer. Then Andrei was smiling and threw his arm round the neck of the horse. Rilla had run to him and the Khan was shaking him by the hand.

Stefan, his round peasant face wreathed in smiles, was speaking excitedly. 'Do you know what he said, Barina? The mare has recognized her master. Three men she has savaged, but not he who has won her love, so Count Andrei has her, but at what a price? God forgive me, but where is it to come from?'

I could not stay in the carriage. I climbed down and pushed my way through to Andrei and Dmitri. The peasants stared at me in my lilac muslin, still holding my cream lace parasol. As I came up I saw that Jean Reynard was there before me. The three of them were together and though physically they were so different—Dmitri, bulky, grey-haired, a little stooped, Andrei with his casual grace and Jean, always so fastidiously elegant—there was about them one of those curious family resemblances so unmistakable that I wondered why everyone did not see it as I did.

I heard Jean say, 'Fortune smiles on you, Andrei. You had better take care. She is a fickle goddess.'

I think Andrei must have fallen on his damaged arm. He held it stiffly as if it pained him. His coat was thick with the dust of the ring and he limped a little, but he faced Jean with a cool pride.

'Is that intended as a threat?'

'Not a threat, my dear Andrei, a warning.'

'Of what? I have no more runaway serfs for you to bribe.'

It was a shot in the dark, but it registered. A muscle in Jean's pale cheek tightened, but he replied calmly enough.

'Do you listen to the lying tales your serfs invent for you? You are too indulgent. Next time you may not escape so lightly.'

There was insolence in the quiet voice and Andrei made an angry movement.

Dmitri said, 'What is all this?'

Jean turned to look at him. 'Life has many surprises, hasn't it? For four years I believed you dead, Dmitri, and now I find I was wrong. It was Natalya who killed herself while the rest of us live on.'

I saw the shock on Dmitri's face. He said dully, 'It was an accident.'

'Didn't they tell you? The child who died with Natalya was not yours, but mine.'

It was unbelievably brutal and Dmitri turned to his brother, bewildered, pathetically seeking reassurance.

153

'It is not true, tell him it is not true.'

'Of course it is not true. Take no notice.'

'Do you call me a liar?'

There was a gasp from those who listened so greedily and I thought, Jean is doing this deliberately hoping to provoke an open quarrel. I saw anger flame into Andrei's eyes but he controlled it. It was Dmitri who erupted into violence. That quiet gentleman who never raised his hand against anyone hurled himself at the man who mocked him and they went down together into the dust of the field. He was a big man and powerful. He had his hands on Jean's throat.

'Damn you!' he was saying over and over again. 'Damn you! Damn you!'

It took the combined strength of Andrei and one of the men who stood by to drag him to his feet. He stood shaking, breathing heavily, while his victim picked himself up, his fine black coat torn and filthy, his neckcloth ripped from his throat, his face a white expressionless mask.

I don't know what everyone expected, an explosion of rage perhaps or a demand for an instant apology. Neither was forthcoming. With one thin hand he flicked disdainfully at the dirt on his coat.

'Madmen can be dangerous. You should watch your brother, Andrei,' he said quietly and walked away into the crowd who parted silently to let him pass.

Andrei took Dmitri's arm and together we moved to the inn. It was past five by now and too late to make the long journey back to Ryvlach. The inn could provide little comfort in the way of lodgings, but there was a bed for Rilla and me and, since there was no private parlour, Andrei ordered food to be served in the room he would share with Dmitri.

Rilla had taken our small bag upstairs. It was still stiflingly hot and Andrei flung open the windows and came back to the table.

'I don't know about you but I need a drink,' he said calmly and began to pour the wine Stefan had brought in from the carriage.

Dmitri took the glass handed to him, but he did not drink. His eyes on Andrei's face he said slowly, 'You knew all the time. Why didn't you tell me? Why?'

'You forget, Dmitri. You were sick . . . very sick . . . and afterwards ... well, she was dead and it didn't seem to matter any longer.'

'You let me go on living in a fool's paradise, believing she had come back to me and it was all a lie.' With a despairing gesture he brought his fist down on the table. 'She never loved me, never. First it was you, then that damned murdering bastard Jean Reynard....'

I could not bear it. I wanted to comfort him and I thought I knew exactly how Natalya must have felt on that terrible morning when she went over the cliff. I ran to kneel beside him, putting my hand on his big brown one.

'But she did love you, don't you see? She proved it. She thought you were dying and she hated Jean. She could not endure that he should triumph over you. That was why she killed herself....'

'She's right,' said Andrei gently. 'The child is right. She sees more clearly than we do.'

Dmitri smiled and touched my cheek. 'Maybe,' he said, 'maybe,' but the pain was going from the brown eyes.

When Rilla came back and we sat down to supper, it was as if a storm had come and gone and we could talk of other things, of Andrei's success, of the horse and plans for her future.

Just as the candles had been lighted and the samovar brought in we had an unexpected visitor. The door was flung open and Leon appeared, dusty and hot from hard riding.

'I hoped I might find you still here,' he said. 'Olga is staying with the Kirstovs. I saw her and her mother safely there and came back at once. Can I speak to you, Andrei, alone?'

'What about?' Andrei glanced round at us. 'I have no secrets from anyone here.'

I watched Leon from my seat by the window and did not know whether I was glad or sorry to see him again. Against my will hope sprang up in me, but it was not I for whom he had returned, nor was it anything to do with Jean.

He leaned back against the door, head flung back as if he were braving the whole world. 'I want to know if you will sell me the horse.'

'What!' Andrei sounded amused. 'Oh come, Leon, this is preposterous. You can't mean it. Forgive me saying it, but where are you going to find her price even if I were willing to sell which I am not.'

'I'd find it somewhere.'

'From the Jews, I suppose, at some outrageous interest.'

'That's my affair.'

'Maybe, but it could be mine too. Oh sit down, man. Sophie, give him some tea. Let's be sensible about this, for Heaven's sake. Why do you want her so badly?'

Leon let himself drop into one of the chairs at the table. He did not even look at me when I put the glass of tea at his elbow. He leaned forward, intent, his eyes fixed on Andrei's face.

'I want to ride her in the races at Peterhof.'

'But you have horses already.'

'None like her.'

'The races are barely six weeks away,' objected Rilla.

'I know, but I was watching her this afternoon. I spoke to some of the Khan's men ... she's magnificent, better than anything that has come out of the Steppes for years. With her, I could win. I'm certain of it.'

'Never, my dear boy,' rumbled Dmitri. 'You're mad even to think of such a crazy notion. In time perhaps, but not now. She's nervous as a kitten. It's a devilishly hard course. You'd never keep her to it.'

'Why is it so important to you?' said Andrei slowly. 'You've never cared about winning before. It's not for the honour of the regiment, I'm damned sure of that.'

Leon flushed. 'I have my reasons.'

'I won't sell her to you, that's certain, but I might let you ride her for me.'

'Oh no, Andrei, why should you? He is asking too much,' protested Rilla.

'It's all right, my dear.' I saw Andrei's hand close over hers. He was a man to make his own decisions. He smiled. 'If he wins, it could even double her value.'

'Why should he ride your horse to death simply to win enough to pay his debts,' went on Rilla indignantly.

'I won't. She'll be safe with me,' said Leon quickly. 'You can trust me, Andrei, you know you can.'

'Yes, I know. Give me a day to think it over, Leon, then I'll send word to you. Where will you be? In Petersburg?'

'Yes, I'm returning there tomorrow. It's generous of you. You'll never know how much it means to me.'

'Maybe I do, more than you think.'

Andrei had always liked Leon and it struck me suddenly that perhaps in him he saw his own youth and had a protective feeling towards a young man without father or brother to guide him and eternally in rebellion against a stern and unrelenting grandfather. How much else he guessed, I did not understand till afterwards. I was already regretting my rejection of the afternoon, but I still had my pride. Nothing would induce me to speak first and Leon gave me neither opportunity nor encouragement.

He stood up at once. 'I mustn't stay. I have to go back to the Kirstovs and then to Petersburg early in the morning. You have been far kinder than I dared to hope.'

He had turned to Rilla, taking her hand and kissing it with the charm I knew so well. 'Don't be angry with me, Countess. I swear that Andrei will not regret it.'

While he made his farewells, I slipped through the door ahead of him. I scarcely knew why except that he was going back to Olga and the very thought gave me pain.

When he came through the door I was on the dark landing and he passed me with no more than a courteous goodnight, but one step down he stopped and turned back. I could see his face, pale in the half light, looking up at me.

'You don't trust me, do you, Sophie? You think me liar and cheat. Well, when I've proved you wrong, I will come back.'

He ran quickly down the stairs, spurs jangling, shouting for his horse as he went out into the inn yard, leaving me standing there, one part of me longing to run after him, the other holding back, telling me not to be a fool, not to make myself cheap, and then it was too late. He had gone.

Chapter 15

A fortnight later, incredible as it seemed, I too was on my way to Petersburg, Katya beside me in the carriage bubbling over with excitement, Stefan on the box and my luggage in the boot.

A few days after we came back from the horse fair, a letter arrived from Madame Lubova, lamenting that she had seen nothing of me during the summer and inviting me to spend a few weeks with her now she had moved to Petersburg for the winter season.

At first I was not sure whether I wanted to go or not and Rilla was very much against it.

'Madame Lubova entertains all kinds of unsuitable people. She adores gambling too, and she encourages the young officers ... there was quite a scandal last year. You're too young, Sophie.'

It was my elder sister speaking and I rebelled instantly. 'Oh Rilla, I've not been brought up in grand society any more than you were till you married Andrei and I'm not a child, you know, I'm nearly twenty-one. I can look after myself.'

'I don't know so much. Besides, isn't it rather foolish to go now when Andrei and I will be in Petersburg at the end of September. We must be there for the races now that Andrei is going to let Leon ride Varenka.'

I knew there had been arguments over the mare, but Andrei had made up his mind and she had been sent to Leon in the charge of two of his most experienced stablemen.

Surprisingly when Rilla tackled him on the question of my visit to Madame Lubova, Andrei was on my side.

'Why shouldn't she go if she can stand the old witch?' he said. 'I warn you, Sophie, she will have you running all over the place, fetching and carrying not only for her but for her horrible little dogs.'

'I don't mind,' I said stoutly, 'I'm used to it, besides I like Togo and Mitzi.'

In the end it was Aunt Vera who made up my mind for me. She was a remarkable old lady. She still kept up a vast correspondence and I sometimes thought she knew more about what went on than anyone. She used to invite me to take tea with her and once started would go on and on about her lively youth under the Empress Catherine in a Russia that seemed to me far more barbaric and dramatic than the times we lived in. One afternoon she began talking about the races.

'I was seventeen,' she said, 'when my father permitted me to accompany him and my Mamma for the first time and I was madly in love with a young man in the Hussars. The last race is a steeple-chase, you know, and the very devil of a course. It carries the highest stakes and only the most daring riders, or the most desperate, ever have the courage to attempt it. Of course my eyes were glued to it, my Igor was so handsome and his horse the most beautiful creature in the world. He was going magnificently and then at the last hazard, a cruel one with a great stretch of water and a five-foot fence, over he went and crashed. They came down so heavily, the horse's back was broken and my hero went rolling over and over in the mud with a broken neck. I screamed so loudly, my Mamma thought I would have a fit and I cried for a week afterwards, quite sure my heart was broken for ever, but of course it wasn't, it never is. Let us hope nothing like that happens to Leonid Karlovitch.'

'Oh no,' I exclaimed, aghast at her tragic tale. 'It couldn't . . . it mustn't . . . not now.'

Aunt Vera went on stabbing away with her needle for a few moments, then she gave me a quick look. 'Tell me, my child, have you lost your heart to that young scamp?'

The unexpected question took me by surprise. I hardly knew how to answer. I turned away lest my face should give too much away. 'How can you think such a thing? He is engaged to Olga.'

'What has that got to do with it? Engagements have been broken before now. Has he been making love to you?'

'No, of course not,' I said indignantly, but I knew the colour had come up into my cheeks.

'Oh Sophie, don't be such a little ninny. Do you think I don't know how a girl looks when she is in love with a man? It may be more than half a century ago, but I've been kissed too, you know, more than once and very enjoyable it was too.' She leaned over and put her old veined hand on mine. 'It's not a crime,

159

child. Leon is an engaging rascal and from all I hear, his fool of a grandfather is tying him up with a girl he detests.'

'Oh he is,' I burst out, 'and Leon is desperately unhappy about it, but what can he do?'

'So he has confided that much to you, has he? Don't you think you had better tell me exactly what did happen at Valdaya?'

It was strange, but the sympathy in her voice, her very detachment from ordinary everyday life, seemed to unlock the floodgates. I could not stop myself. I poured out the whole story, or nearly all of it.

'So that's why he wants Andrei's horse,' she said quietly when I had stammered to an end. 'If he's lucky, he will win enough to throw back the money his grandfather has borrowed and tell Olga Leskova she can whistle for a husband.'

Why hadn't I realized it before! I was horrified at his recklessness. 'But it's crazy. Nobody can be sure of winning. Anything could happen.'

'Exactly, my dear, but I'm afraid that is the man you've chosen to set your heart on. The risk, the spice of danger, is what he lives for. Does your sister know about this, or Andrei?'

'No, I've not told anyone, not even Irina. It was something between Leon and myself . . . and now I've let him think I don't care, and I do, I do . . . Aunt Vera, what ought I to do?'

'It's a pretty tangle, isn't it, and God forbid that I should judge between you. But I'll tell you one thing, Sophie, and I mean it. If you want him, go to Petersburg. Show Olga Leskova, show Leon, that you are someone to be reckoned with, prove that you're worth fighting for.'

I stared at her. 'But how can I? It would not be right . . . it would look as if I were running after him. . . .'

'What does that matter? Do you believe in him, or don't you? Make up your mind. My dear child, Leon will need all you can give him. I know. My father was a tyrant too. Why do you think I never married? Because when it came to the point, I had not the courage to stand up to him, so don't you make the same mistake.'

I didn't believe her. She had never lacked spirit. She was just saying it to encourage me.'

'There is something else too, my dear. Leon fights his grand-

160

father, but he loves him too. Remember that. It may help you to understand him.'

So here I was in the carriage within a few miles of Petersburg still without a single notion in my head as to what I was going to do when I got there.

Madame Lubova's house was not large, but her way of living was as luxurious and untidy as it had been in Moscow. She welcomed me with shrieks of pleasure. Even Colette smiled frostily and Phillips permitted himself a warm, 'Delighted to see you looking so well, Miss.'

It all turned out very much as Andrei had foretold. I was running here, there and everywhere. It was, 'Sophie, fetch me my shawl.' 'Sophie, I've lost my earrings.' 'Sophie darling, do take Togo and Mitzi walking,' or feed them, or brush and comb them or give them their bath! But I didn't mind. In a way I rather enjoyed it even if she did fly into rages one minute and kiss me the next. She was generous too. She took me everywhere with her and in her crowded drawing room I was flung into the very heart of fashionable society.

It seemed that every gossip in Petersburg called on Madame Lubova at some time or other and Leon's engagement was the topic of every scandalmonger. I loathed the venomous tongues that blackened him without knowing any of the true facts.

There was something else too, something I had forgotten in the stress of the fire and Andrei's illness, but which now reminded me of the day in the market, the old brown house and Andrei saying there were those who met in secret to plan a new Russia. It was not that anyone spoke to me of such matters or even talked of them openly, but as I served the tea and listened to the talk going on around me, I heard much that disturbed me. One evening that wild young poet, Ryelev, more than a little drunk, began reciting verses that caused some of the guests to look uneasily at one another.

He had climbed unsteadily on to a chair,

'Beneath the shade of servitude
No golden fruit will grow,
When all things cramp the human mind
No mighty deeds we know. . . .'

he was declaiming at the top of his voice until someone said, 'Shut up, for God's sake. You'll get us all arrested!' and pulled him down.

I spoke of it to Madame Lubova and she waved her hand airily. 'Hot air, my dear child. I know Ryelev. He has a wife and a couple of babies. Do you think he would risk anything happening to them? These poets! They have to write their verses about something, I suppose.'

I had been in Petersburg just over a week when one evening Madame Lubova asked me to accompany her to the opera. I wore my pink velvet gown and when I looked in the mirror, I could not help remembering the last time I had worn it when I danced with Leon and it had all begun. Only seven months ago and it seemed a lifetime away. Some imp of mischief urged me to take out the ring Leon had given me and put it on my finger. It gave me a secret pleasure to feel its weight under my long white glove.

Madame Lubova always went everywhere in great style and we had a box where we could both see and be seen. We were early and we had just seated ourselves when I looked up from studying the programme to see Olga entering the box opposite. She looked magnificent in amber satin with pearls in her black hair and on her white neck. There was a man with her whom I had never seen before, short and thickset with a heavy dark moustache, and I wondered who he was, but just then the lights went down, the overture was in full swing and I who had been to the theatre so seldom was quite carried away by the splendid singing and the gorgeous costumes.

In the interval we were besieged by visitors. One of the young men who came to Madame's drawing room presented me with a box of expensive sweets. In gay mood I opened it and drew off my glove to select one for myself.

'What an unusual ring,' said a cool voice which I knew only too well. The last person I had expected to see was Jean Reynard. As he bent to kiss my hand, he murmured, 'Surely I have seen that lion somewhere before.'

'Possibly,' I said quickly. 'I wear it occasionally,' and wished I had not been so rash.

'I had not expected to see you in Petersburg, Mademoiselle Sophie. I always understood Andrei liked to enjoy the hunting before he came to town for the winter.'

'I am staying with Madame Lubova.'

'You will be attending the races of course. Rumour says that

Leon has acquired a matchless horse from somewhere, but is taking care to keep it secret even from Prince Astrov.'

'I am afraid I know nothing of such matters.' Deliberately I turned away from him and across the crowded stalls under the blazing chandeliers I saw that Leon had entered the box opposite. He was standing behind Olga. He bowed slightly and raised his opera glasses. I looked quickly away, feeling sure that everyone's eyes must have followed his gaze.

'Well, look who has arrived,' whispered Madame Lubova behind her lace fan. 'The young hero himself, and looking sour as a lemon too. No doubt he feels he must put in an appearance now that Olga has a protector at her side.'

'Do you mean the gentleman with her?'

'Her brother, my dear, years older of course, holds some government post in the Ukraine. No doubt he is here for the wedding.'

I could not concentrate on the next act. All I could think of was what I would say to him when he came to our box. I needn't have worried. Through the applause and the encores I saw that he had gone and he did not appear again.

It was all very well for Aunt Vera to say 'fight for a man,' but what could I do ... a young woman alone in Petersburg? I called at the Astrov house but Irina was away, staying with friends in the country, said the footman. More likely banished by her grandfather, I thought, to keep her safe from Michael Federov. It was frustration that drove me into an indiscretion.

Madame had been talking for some days about a visit to the Strelnya restaurant one evening. It was famous for its gypsy dancers and one of the favourite haunts of the young officers. Rilla had told me about it once and I was wild to go, but for the first time Madame Lubova hesitated.

'I don't know, *ma petite*, it's not quite the thing, you know, for an unmarried girl. The Countess Kuragina would not approve.'

'She won't know,' I objected. 'Besides I shall be with you, dear Madame, surely that will make it quite proper.'

'*Mon Dieu*, how you have changed!' she said, laughing. 'Last February when you came from England, you were a little mouse, and now you are bold as a lion.' She wagged her finger at me. 'Which of the young men has caught your fancy, eh? There's something behind all this, I'll be bound.'

I blushed and shook my head, but she was good-natured and easy-going, so it was all arranged, Madame Lubova and myself with Jean Reynard who had always been her favourite and an elderly General, one of her old admirers. Then when the day came, she was laid up with a raging toothache and the party was called off. Messages were sent but somehow must have missed Jean Reynard. Later that evening he was shown into the drawing room where I was sitting at my needlework, elegant as always in his black evening coat.

'What a pity,' he said when I told him of Madame's indisposition. 'Tonight of all nights too. They have a new singer who is said to be quite remarkable.' He looked me over. 'Would you care to trust yourself to my protection? I should be delighted to escort you, Mademoiselle.'

I knew perfectly well that to go with him alone was quite improper. I did not like him. I did not trust him, but from him I might learn something of Leon. When I still hesitated, he gave me his half teasing, half contemptuous smile.

'Are you afraid of me, Mademoiselle Sophie?'

'Is there any reason why I should be?'

'That is for you to judge.'

It was foolish, I knew, but something in his manner annoyed me. I said, 'If you will wait, Monsieur, I promise I will not keep you waiting long.'

It was a cool September evening, but the restaurant blazed with light and warmth. Giant palm trees flanked the entrance. Jean led me to a table in an alcove opening out into the main room and it was a brilliant spectacle, the candlelight gleaming on jewels and satins and splendid uniforms, on silver, sparkling glass and exotic flowers.

I knew at a glance that I should not have come, but I didn't care. This was Russia. It was the society in which Leon moved and I wanted to know everything about him. A magyar orchestra in embroidered blouses, black breeches and soft leather boots was playing haunting music.

We drank champagne but I scarcely noticed what I was eating. It was the Tzigane who took my eyes. Never had I seen such strikingly beautiful women with their long black silken hair, flashing eyes and exquisite slender bodies. They danced with an abandon that both shocked and fascinated me. I stole a glance at Jean. He leaned back in his chair, eyes half closed, a contemptuous twist to the thin lips so that I wondered why he had invited me to accompany him.

Once our eyes met across the table and I lowered mine quickly. He laughed softly.

'Don't disturb yourself, Mademoiselle. I am well aware that you dislike me.'

I did not know how to answer and he went on, one hand playing with the stem of his wine glass.

'I'm not a fool. Your sister will have told you who and what I am, and it is easy to condemn, is it not?'

'I ... I don't know. ...' I stammered.

'Don't trouble to lie, but it is not everything ... not by a long way. What can you know of the dark forces that can drive a man beyond himself?'

I don't know what made him speak as he did, but I saw the fingers grip the slender stem of his glass until it snapped and the golden wine spilled across the table. A waiter sprang forward with a napkin and he looked down at the blood on his hand almost with surprise.

'It is I who play the madman,' he said with such an intense bitterness that I felt a momentary pity for him. He must have read it in my eyes for he rejected it instantly. 'Don't be sorry for me. I share the Kuragin blood. I have my pride too, you know.' He leaned forward, the blood-stained handkerchief round his hand, the strange light eyes fixed on me. 'Andrei thinks he can buy me with our father's money, but gold is not everything. I want him to suffer too and I shall wait my opportunity. It wo'ʻ. be difficult, Mademoiselle, believe me.'

I looked at him, afraid, and did not know what to say. Later I was to remember and wonder if in any way he had been trying to warn me.

Then I forgot it almost at once because the orchestra had started up again and one of the gypsies, vividly lovely in a poppy-red gown, began to sing. The tune, wild and melancholy, had a harsh stirring rhythm. She began to thread her way through the tables, pausing here and there, until she came to a halt by a group of officers sitting together in one of the alcoves. Still singing, she snatched up a glass of champagne and leaned towards one of them offering it to him with a provocative gesture. He hesitated a moment, then took it, drank it off and tossed the glass over his shoulder. She laughed exultantly, clapping her hands, and he leaped to his feet, caught her in his arms, swung her round and kissed her to the laughter and cheers of his comrades. With a sickening clutch at the heart, I saw that it was Leon.

I knew that it meant nothing, just a party of young men drinking and amusing themselves, but quite suddenly the heat, the music, the smell of food and wine, nauseated me. I half rose to my feet.

'I think it is time for me to leave.'

'Does it shock you?'

'No, of course not, only. . . .'

'As you wish, Mademoiselle.'

But before we could go, Leon had seen me. He thrust aside the girl who still clung to him and came purposefully across the floor. He gripped my bare arm.

'What in God's name are you doing here?'

'Don't touch me,' I exclaimed fiercely. 'You're drunk.'

'Not too drunk to know you shouldn't be in a place like this. What is Andrei doing to allow such a thing?'

'He is not my keeper,' I said, stung to anger. 'Besides I am staying with Madame Lubova.'

'That old devil!'

'Leon please . . . you are hurting me.'

'If you will forgive me, I am escorting Mademoiselle Sophie,' intervened Jean Reynard smoothly. 'You really do not need to concern yourself.'

'And what the devil do you mean by bringing her to the Strelnya?'

Jean had risen. The two men faced one another angrily.

'Listen, both of you,' I broke in, exasperated because people around us were beginning to stare curiously. 'I came because I wanted to come. Nobody tells me what to do.'

'Oh yes, they do,' said Leon violently. 'I am taking you home this instant. As for you, Monsieur Reynard, you can go to the devil for all I care.'

'Your grandfather shall hear of this,' Jean was white with rage.

'Tell him what you please.'

Before I could even take breath, Leon had picked up my wrap, thrown it round my shoulders and hustled me out of the restaurant. The fresh night air was cool on our hot faces. It took the doorman a few minutes to bring up the carriage and I stood beside him in the porch, trembling with anger and mortification.

He handed me into the troika and we sat in unfriendly silence while the coachman threaded his way through the busy traffic. Then Leon suddenly put out a hand and clasped mine.

'You are not wearing my ring.'

'Why should I?' I tried to pull my fingers away but he only gripped them more firmly.

'You wore it at the opera.'

'And I wish I hadn't. You can have it back just whenever you wish.'

'Are you very angry with me?' And when I didn't answer, he leaned forward to peer into my face with that charming grin that was so difficult to resist. 'Sophie darling, look at me.'

This was what I had longed for and somehow it was all going wrong. I said faintly, 'Why did you behave as you did just now? Everyone was looking at us. It will be all over Petersburg by tomorrow.'

'I know, but why did you go there? With Jean of all people?'

'Why are you so concerned?' I said perversely. 'Are you ashamed of the company you keep?'

'God damn it, Sophie, why are you wilfully misunderstanding me?'

'You shouldn't have spoken to Jean as you did.'

'To hell with Jean!' The carriage had come to a halt outside Madame Lubova's door and I made a movement to alight. He held me back. 'I must talk to you, Sophie, but not here, not in Madame's drawing room. There are too many probing eyes and bitter tongues. Will you meet me tomorrow?'

'No. . . .'

'Eleven o'clock . . . on the Troitsky Bridge?'

'I don't know if I want to come.'

'I shall be waiting for you.'

He stepped down and handed me out of the carriage. Phillips had already opened the door. Leon bowed and leaped back into the carriage. I hurried into the house. Mercifully Madame Lubova was asleep. She had taken an opiate to ease the pain of her tooth, otherwise I should have had to tell her where I had been. In the morning when I went into her room to ask her how she felt, she was still drowsy and it was easy to evade questions.

Should I meet Leon or not? All night I had debated with myself knowing quite well what the answer would be. Just

167

before eleven, I left the house leading Togo and Mitzi on their double leash and with Katya demurely accompanying me. At the corner of the Nevsky Prospect, I sent her off to make some purchases for me. She gave me a quick look from her black eyes and said saucily, 'Shall I meet you here, Mademoiselle, when you come back from your walk?'

I smiled at her and nodded. Katya and I were good friends. I knew she had guessed I was meeting someone, but she was a loyal soul. She would not say a word.

The day was crisp and cool and a September haze half veiled the white and green splendour of the Winter Palace as I hurried past. I glimpsed Leon long before he saw me. He was leaning on the parapet of the bridge gazing up the long stretch of the river.

He turned as I came up to him, reached out for my hand and drew me to his side.

'Look,' he said. 'Do you see?'

On the further bank a slender golden spire rose out of the mist topped by a gilded angel holding a cross above the grey-pink walls. It looked as fragile and fantastic as a castle in a fairy tale.

'Do you know what that is? It's the Peter and Paul prison.'

'But it's beautiful. . . .'

'Yes, it's like Russia, so lovely and yet hiding savage and unspeakable cruelties.'

Then he threw off his sombre mood. He tucked my arm in his and we walked on together. Where we went, I hardly knew except that we sat for a time in a little park and while the dogs went scampering after fat pigeons, he told me all that had happened.

'You were angry with me because I didn't write, but it is worse, far worse than I thought, Sophie. Grandfather has borrowed heavily from Madame Leskova so that now we are deeply in her debt and for what,' he said bitterly, 'just so that we can continue this stupid senseless life of luxury that the Astrovs have lived for centuries. I faced him with it one day and he laughed at me. "In a few weeks," he said, "you'll be her husband and can command her fortune. Why are you worrying about a few paltry debts?" I'm in prison, Sophie, a worse one than a rat-ridden cell in the Peter and Paul, but I swear I'll not stay in it. Like the Prince in the barrel, I'll burst it even if I drown.'

He frightened me with his violence. 'Don't say such things even in jest.'

'Why, Sophie darling, what are you afraid of?'

'I don't know, only that if I were Olga I would never let you go.'

He smiled. 'Not everyone thinks as you do.' He had drawn off my glove and with a tender gesture raised my hand to his lips, kissing each separate finger. Then he said casually, 'You said she spoke to you at Valdaya. What was it she told you?'

But I could not say it. I no longer believed it. Afterwards I regretted my silence. It might have warned him of what was to come.

That morning was the first of many such meetings. In the three weeks before the races, I found all kind of excuses to escape out of the house and never once thought of anyone seeing us together or of the wagging tongues. I doubt if it would have made any difference if I had. I was drowned fathoms deep in love. All my doubts had vanished.

Petersburg is a city of the sea built on a hundred and one little islands with more bridges than any other city in the world. Palaces, domes and spires rose out of the mists of autumn. It seemed to me a magical place when I explored it with Leon during those golden days.

In the English Garden the bushes were thick with berries, golden, scarlet and black, and there by the stone fountain Leon drew me into his arms and kissed me, his lips cool as the running water, and I knew that whatever happened and whatever he did, I loved him utterly and for ever.

In the last week before the races I only saw him once and he talked of nothing but Varenka and how splendidly she was shaping.

'I shall win,' he said confidently, 'and after that nothing can go wrong. Olga cares nothing for me. She will be as glad to be released as I shall be.'

I wished I felt so sure. No woman likes to be scorned even if she loathes the man who scorns her. In a broken engagement it is not the man who suffers. To be pitied by the society you move in is the most galling thing in the world.

I tried to say something of this but Leon would not listen. All he could think of was winning his freedom in a final act of defiance against his grandfather, and neither he nor I remembered the malice of Jean Reynard.

Only a couple of days before the races I had an unexpected visitor. It was after luncheon and I was in my room when Phillips knocked at the door.

'Madame would be glad if you would go to the drawing room, Miss. Prince Astrov is asking to see you,' he said and my mind immediately flew to Leon. Something must have happened to bring him to the house when I had only seen him the day before. I ran down the stairs, but when I opened the door, it was not Leon but his grandfather who was standing by the window, leaning on his ebony stick, while Madame Lubova hovered uncertainly in the middle of the room. She came hurrying to meet me, greatly flustered at such a distinguished visitor.

'The Prince wishes to have a few words alone with you, Sophie,' she whispered, and I wondered what he had said to make her so unusually flustered.

'Here is my little protégée, your excellency,' she said. 'I will leave her with you,' and she snatched up Togo and almost ran out of the room with an agitated swirl of her silk skirts.

I was afraid but I was determined not to show it. I walked boldly forward and stood waiting. 'You wished to say something to me, sir.'

The old hooded eyes beneath the thick grey eyebrows looked me over searchingly, then he said abruptly, 'Yes, Mademoiselle, I do. I am here for one purpose only, to ask you to leave my grandson alone.'

The suddenness of his attack took me aback. I said, 'I don't understand you.'

'Don't pretend to look surprised. You know perfectly well what I mean.' He made an impatient movement. 'I am making no excuses for Leon. He has behaved irresponsibly as he has done so often before but if you were to refuse to see him, it would mean that this scandalous nonsense would come to an end once and for all.'

'What nonsense?'

'Oh come, don't play with me. I know quite well you are meeting him here in Petersburg. No doubt you came from Ryvlach for that very purpose and I tell you it must stop here and now before it goes any further.'

170

'And why should I do any such thing?'

'Surely you do not need me to tell you that. Leon will shortly be married. This . . . this liaison between you is causing pain and distress to Olga Leskova and I will not permit it.'

I was trembling all over but I was not going to let this old man stand there and reprimand me as if I were a kitchen maid caught kissing the footman. He had had his own way for far too long.

'I am not aware of any . . . liaison as you call it,' I answered with dignity. 'And I refuse to give up an innocent friendship with your grandson simply because certain malicious people are making something out of nothing.'

'Friendship,' he repeated disdainfully, 'is that what you call it?' He took a step towards me. 'Mademoiselle Weston, you force me to be frank with you. Leon has no fortune of his own. Don't think for a moment that you will be making a wealthy match for yourself just as your sister did. I have no intention of allowing Leon to make a fool of himself like Andrei Kuragin.'

The slur cast upon Rilla angered me more than the attack on myself. 'Please do not bring my sister into this,' I retorted.

'You oblige me to do so since I can only believe she has encouraged you in this folly. But let me tell you this,' he went on with scalding contempt. 'If Leon breaks with Olga and makes you the Princess Astrov, you will live in beggary together.'

'Money, money, money,' I flung back at him. 'It is all you think of. Well, I am not concerned with such matters. Leon must do as he thinks fit, but if it so happens that he is free and still wants me, I will marry him whenever he wishes.'

'Love in a peasant's hut! I thought the English had more good sense. You are, I fear, a romantic, Mademoiselle, if you think such a life would satisfy my grandson. I see I have been wasting my time in making this extremely distasteful call.'

He moved towards the door but I stood in his way. I could not let him go. I had to say something of what had been burning inside me ever since the summer.

'Why do you always force Leon to do what you want? Why will you never try to understand his point of view?'

He looked at me as if I had taken leave of my senses. Then he said icily, 'Are you trying to be impertinent?'

'No, I am not, believe me,' I said earnestly. 'Please don't think that. But sometimes an outsider sees things more clearly.

171

Leon has talked to me. Don't you see if you force him beyond himself, he may well do something crazy, something you and he will both regret.'

He gave a short bark of laughter. 'My dear Mademoiselle, are you trying to teach me how to behave to my own grandson whom I have brought up since a boy? Do you really believe you know more about him than I do? It would be amusing if it were not so ridiculous. I see no point in continuing this useless discussion. I bid you good afternoon.'

He brushed past me into the hall and I heard Phillips open the door. I was appalled at what I had said and yet glad too. My knees were shaking and I would have been happy to escape to my room but Madame Lubova prevented me. She came hurrying through the door and I knew at once she was in one of her tantrums. She went in to the attack immediately.

'I take you into my house, I take you everywhere, I treat you as a daughter, and how do you repay me?' she burst out. 'By meeting this young man in secret and making my name a by-word all through Petersburg. I would never have believed it of you, Sophie.'

'But it's not like that at all,' I broke in, but she would have none of it.

'Do you know what Prince Astrov accused me of? Of encouraging you, of allowing you to meet in this house, my house ... of permitting ... unspeakable things. . . .' on and on she went ranting and raving so that if I had not been so upset, I might have found it amusing. She must have been remembering every speech from every old melodrama in which she had played a leading part. At last when she had exhausted herself, I managed to make myself heard.

'I am sorry if I've caused you so much distress, Madame Lubova. If you feel like that about it, then I will leave your house. I will go now if you like. . . .'

'And where would you go?' she exclaimed. 'A young girl like you alone in the city and what would Count Kuragin have to say to me if I allowed you to do such a thing, tell me that ... and what about Togo and Mitzi,' she wailed, 'what will they do without you? You know how attached they have become to you.'

The absurdity of that on top of everything else was too much for me. I began to laugh half hysterically and Madame, after a moment of furious indignation, began to laugh too and went on laughing. She threw herself back in a chair, rocking backwards and forwards, and wiping the tears from her eyes.

'Oh Sophie, Sophie, what an old fool I am! As if I ever cared a button what other people say! Let them talk their silly heads off! You sly puss,' she said, tapping my cheek, 'capturing the most talked of young man in Petersburg and never saying a word about it. And what is he going to do, eh? Come now, tell me all about it. I think you owe me that anyway.'

It was an hour before I could escape from her. I had told her as little as I could but she was delighted at being as she thought at the very heart of what promised to be the most exciting scandal of the season.

Upstairs in my own room I sat on the bed, sick with reaction, and worried to death lest I had only made things worse for Leon. His grandfather could not be lightly dismissed. He was still formidable, though one thing struck me very forcibly. For the first time he must have realized that Leon meant what he said and he feared what he might do.

I had an intense longing for my sister. She had written to say she and Andrei would be at Peterhof for the races and that afterwards I should go back with them to their house in Petersburg. They would have to know everything and Rilla would reproach me, I knew, but Andrei might be on my side and for all my brave show of independence, there was comfort in the thought.

Chapter 16

A thick white mist hung over everything when we set out for the races and Madame Lubova was so nervous I trembled in case she should turn back, but by the time we reached the course, the morning had cleared and the sun was golden and surprisingly warm. I wore my pink bonnet and carried the muff of silver fox. Under my glove I could feel Leon's ring and it comforted me to know it was there like a talisman.

We had seats in the front row of the pavilion and a fashionable crowd were strolling up and down in front of it. I caught a glimpse of Irina with Prince Astrov and she waved to me. I could not see Rilla or Andrei but I felt sure they had gone to speak with Leon and inspect Varenka. There were a number of races before the steeplechase in which he was to ride. The horses were already being led out by the grooms and Michael Federov came hurrying up to me. He was bubbling over with enthusiasm.

'Every man in the regiment has put his last kopeck on Leon,' he said.

'Aren't you riding yourself?' I asked him. I felt quite unable to talk about Leon's chances. Too much depended on whether he won or lost.

'Yes, I am . . . in the first race, but that is nothing. I am not in the same class as Leon. May I come and sit with you afterwards?'

'What about Irina?'

He nodded ruefully towards Prince Astrov and I knew how he felt. He hurried away to where his groom waited with his horse.

The Grand Duke Nicholas drove up with the Grand Duchess and a brilliant party from the court. I saw that Olga with her mother and brother were seated further along from us and beyond them, Prince Astrov with Irina.

I watched the first races in a dream, all my thoughts were concentrated on Leon. Michael came in second to great applause from his friends and after he had received his prize from the Grand Duke, he came to sit beside me.

In between the races he insisted on describing every dangerous detail of the steeplechase until I longed for him to keep silent.

'The course is four miles,' he explained, 'and there are nine jumps as well as a river, two ditches and one hazard which is the very devil, a brushwood fence and beyond a wide stretch of water which the horse can't see, you understand, until he has already jumped. He has to change his mind in mid-air and it takes an intelligent beast and a skilful rider to clear the water. That's where most of them come to grief.'

He sounded quite unconcerned while I could only think of Aunt Vera's tragic tale and inwardly pray that Leon would go carefully and take no reckless chances.

There were fifteen officers in the race. My hands trembled so much that I could scarcely adjust my racing glasses and at first I could see nothing. Then quite suddenly Leon swam into view. As he came past the pavilion, he took off his cap bowing towards the royal party and the sun glinted on the tawny hair. He was having difficulty in holding Varenka still at the starting line. She danced and fretted. I thought she looked beautiful, but far too slender and elegant against the powerful horses who were her rivals. Then the signal went up and they were off.

Michael Federov was giving me a running commentary, but I hardly heard him. There was a singing in my ears and my throat was dry. I kept losing sight of Leon and then finding him again. At first he was obviously holding Varenka back, then she seemed to shoot forward, going over the fences light as a bird. To my eyes horse and rider seemed one, like the centaurs of ancient legend, half beast, half man. They were two lengths ahead as they came up to that last terrifying hazard. Up until then there had been a buzz of conversation, then suddenly there was silence, as though like me, the spectators held their breath. Varenka cleared the brushwood fence and then literally seemed to fly, poised in the air before stretching herself for the long jump. As she came down, her hind legs hit the water, sending up a fountain of mud and slush. Madame Lubova screamed. Someone shouted, 'My God, he's done for!' and I could not bear to look. I buried my face in my hands so that I should not see him fall. Then Michael was gripping my arm so fiercely that I cried out. He was shouting in an absolute frenzy.

'It's all right, Sophie, he's up . . . he's still ahead. Look! You must look! He is magnificent, he's passed the winning post.'

Leon was popular with his men. They went mad, cheering and shouting and streaming on to the course. No one seemed to be taking any notice of the other riders as they came in, only seven out of the fifteen starters. Then Leon was riding back, laughing and waving. I saw Andrei go down to him. He was shaking his hand. He flung his arm round the neck of the horse.

For a few moments I sat in a daze too happy and relieved even to speak while Leon went up to the pavilion. The Grand Duke clapped him on the shoulder. The ladies were congratulating him. Then he came slowly back. His white breeches were filthy, his face splashed with mud, but he looked exultant. I saw Olga half rise from her seat, but he rode past her without a glance, reined in just in front of me and looked down, grinning and triumphant as a schoolboy.

'I've done it,' he said, 'I've done it. It's yours, Sophie,' and he leaned down and dropped the silver trophy into my lap.

It was a gesture of defiance towards his grandfather, a declaration before everyone that he had made his own choice. It was wonderfully sweet and it thrilled me through and through, but all the same he should not have done it. It was an insult that Olga would find unforgivable and it had an immediate result.

Her brother rose to his feet. He strode after Leon and caught at Varenka's bridle. I could not hear what he said, but I saw the anger plain on his face. Leon threw up his head and his haughty reply reached us quite clearly.

'You are mistaken, my dear sir, the trophy is mine and I can give it to whom I please.'

'You have slighted my sister. For behaviour such as yours there is only one answer,' retorted Fyodor Leskov furiously.

Leon jerked himself free. 'Time enough for that later,' he said and cantered away towards the horse boxes, leaving the other man standing. He went back to Olga and I saw them for a moment together with Prince Astrov. Jean Reynard was there too, a little apart, his eyes on Andrei who, with Rilla on his arm, was surrounded by a group congratulating him on the success of his horse. Jean swung round and caught my glance. His smile reminded me of the evening at the Strelnya though at that time I had not the faintest inkling of how he would seek his revenge.

I went back to Petersburg with Rilla and Andrei after a tearful farewell from Madame Lubova, who made me promise faithfully that I would not forget her or the little dogs. All that evening friends and acquaintances dropped in, eager to hear the very latest news and there were a good many knowing smiles directed at me. It was very late before we were left alone and I braced myself to answer the inevitable questions.

Rilla condemned Leon at once. 'Really, he is quite irresponsible,' she said. 'It is just the sort of foolish thing he would do and it's so unfair to Sophie when everyone knows he is engaged to Olga.'

'I think there is more behind it than that, my dear.' Andrei was pouring himself a last measure of brandy. He stood for a moment looking down at the glass cupped in his hands, then he glanced at me. 'Isn't that so, Sophie? Don't you think you should tell us a little more of what you've been doing in this last month?'

I wanted to confess everything, but I felt it was not fair to Leon. I must let him free himself in his own way. Then it would be different. Then we could say openly and proudly that we loved one another.

'I have met him once or twice since I have been in Petersburg,' I said carefully.

'Sophie, you should have told me,' exclaimed Rilla.

'Why? There was nothing wrong in it and after all he was riding Andrei's horse. It was quite natural he should want to tell me about it. Besides you know how he feels about Olga . . . he thinks only of breaking his engagement.'

'Well, now's the time,' remarked Andrei cheerfully. 'He must have won a small fortune today, thanks to Varenka. He can snap his fingers at his grandfather.'

'Andrei, how can you say such a thing! They have been betrothed for six months. Think how Olga will feel.'

'I am thinking of her, my dear. I can't imagine a more unpleasant fate than to be tied to a man who dislikes you, especially a man like Leon. He will lead her a devil of a life. I know you don't think as I do, Rilla, but maybe this is the very spur he needs to show his independence, make something of himself. It is high time.'

I don't think Rilla was at all satisfied, but for the moment she did not press me further and events moved very swiftly in the next few weeks. I heard the news first from Irina, then it was

177

all over Petersburg. Leon had lost no time in calling on his betrothed and her mother, formally withdrawing from his engagement and laying on the table a sum far in excess of what Prince Astrov had borrowed.

'I wish I could have seen Olga's face,' said Irina wickedly. She had never liked her or her mother. 'Madame Leskova came storming round to grandfather and said her daughter was prostrated with nervous shock. I don't know what he said to Leon but it drove him out of the house.' She looked at me anxiously. 'I'm worried, Sophie. I never know what Leon will do and Fyodor Leskov has been calling and calling, asking for him.'

I knew Leon was condemned by some and secretly congratulated by others, though very little was said to us. Andrei had a way of freezing scandalmongers. Maybe it was foolish of me to feel so miserable because he did not at once come to me. Maybe he was showing unusual consideration for my reputation, but every morning when Katya brought my tea and I saw the silver trophy standing proudly on my dressing table, hope rose up inside me and each evening I went disappointed to bed.

I never thought of Olga and her humiliation until the day I came face to face with her quite by chance when I came out of a shop on the Nevsky Prospect. I would have passed her with no more than a brief acknowledgement but she stood directly in my path, saying nothing only looking at me with an odd little smile.

Out of sheer nerves I found myself stammering, 'I was so sorry to hear of your illness. . . .' and she cut me short.

'My dear Sophie, don't concern yourself about me. When I buy anything, I expect only the best and if I don't get it, I exact my price . . . to the full. I learned that from my shop-keeping father. You may find it useful to remember,' and with a cool nod, she walked on.

It means nothing; she is speaking out of hurt pride, I thought, and did not know why it disturbed me so much. I tried to put it out of my mind.

Andrei was away for a few days. Varenka had gone back to Ryvlach and he was anxious to make sure that she was well housed and that work on his new stables was progressing satisfactorily.

Rilla was immersed in preparations for the October ball.

'Andrei only half approves,' she said, 'but it used to be his father's custom when the family came to Petersburg for the winter and I have persuaded him to revive it.'

It was wonderful to see my sister so radiant with happiness and one morning that week she told me that she was to have another baby.

'Oh Sophie, I can hardly believe it after all the misery of last winter.' She looked away from me. 'Perhaps it was foolish of me, but there have been times when I felt I was being punished for taking Andrei from Natalya, but now it is different. I feel as if nothing could ever come between us again.'

'Have you told Andrei?'

'No. I wanted to be absolutely sure.'

'I'm so happy for you, dearest.'

To please her, I threw myself enthusiastically into all the preparations.

'Andrei has won so much on Varenka, he says we can be as extravagant as we like,' she said gaily, and insisted on buying me a new ball gown. It was lovely, ivory satin embroidered with gold.

'Une robe pour une jeune mariée!' exclaimed the French dressmaker as she adjusted the last fitting. Only I did not feel like a bride.

It was to be a small intimate party with only about thirty guests, the cream of Petersburg society, and in the white panelled drawing room with its ceiling of pale green and gold, I felt proud of my sister standing beside her husband. She was as poised and elegant as any of the high-born princesses who graced the ballroom. I guessed she had told Andrei about the baby; there was a renewed tenderness in his eyes when he looked at her.

I stood beside them and as I curtseyed and smiled accepting compliments from the young men who kissed my hand and clamoured for the favour of a dance, I thought of only one person. Leon had been invited, but would he come? That was what tormented me.

I had almost given up hope. The musicians were playing a dreamy waltz. Rilla was dancing and Andrei had come to take my hand when quite suddenly Leon was there, standing in the doorway, a little flushed, the tawny hair falling across his forehead, but looking so splendid in his white uniform that my heart leaped. The grey eyes went all round the room, then he was coming straight to me, taking both my hands.

He said half apologetically, 'Andrei, do you mind?'

'It seems I have no choice,' Andrei looked from me to Leon with his ironical smile. 'Enjoy yourselves, my children,' and he left us together. Floating round the ballroom in his arms, there seemed no need for words, all that could come afterwards. Once I murmured, 'We should not dance together all evening, people will talk.'

'Let them,' he answered savagely. 'They've been doing nothing else for the past weeks. We will give them something to talk about.'

He released me when Michael Federov came to claim me, but he did not dance with anyone else. I saw him leaning against the wall, a champagne glass in his hand, until the music stopped when he came to my side again.

It was after supper when it happened and I never knew how Fyodor Leskov got into the house. Somehow he must have got past the footman in the hall. It was long past midnight. We had been dancing together and then Leon whispered in my ear and we slipped out of the door, across the hall and into the deserted dining room. There was only one candelabrum still burning and he drew me into his arms and kissed me until I felt drowned in bliss.

'Oh Sophie, it's been agony waiting and waiting, but I felt I should not come too soon. Tomorrow I will speak to Andrei. You do feel the same?' he held me at arm's length, looking anxiously into my face. 'You don't regret anything?'

'I don't know,' I said just for the pleasure of teasing him. 'Your grandfather was very insistent that to marry you would be to live like a beggar.'

'It might be true,' he said ruefully, 'there will be little enough. He's furious with me. It will not be at all like this,' and he waved his hand round the room. 'Will you mind?'

'Why should I? I can cook and sew, I can bake and brew. I have all kinds of useful accomplishments,' I said demurely.

He burst out laughing. 'Oh Sophie, I've never known a girl like you before,' and then we were kissing again so that we did not notice the door opening.

'So here you are. You've been very clever at hiding yourself, but I have found you at last.'

Fyodor Leskov stood in the doorway, his cloak soaked by the rain, his boots splashed with mud. He took a step into the room, his head thrust forward like a bull making a charge, and it was then that I saw the riding crop in his hand.

'I am not aware that I have been hiding from anyone,' said Leon haughtily.

'You refused my challenge, but you shall not escape, neither you nor the young woman for whom you jilted my sister,' said Leskov, making a threatening gesture.

'You will leave Sophie out of this,' retorted Leon fiercely.

It was horrible. Through the open door I could see the faces in the hall as more guests piled out of the ballroom, staring, greedily listening. Fyodor Leskov deliberately raised his voice.

'She can go to the devil for all I care. It is you I am concerned with. Men who dishonour a woman and then abandon her for another should be whipped out of society and that is precisely what I have come here to do.'

Leon had gone white. He said thickly, 'I refused your challenge because I would not kill Olga's brother. I've done her enough harm already, but don't try me too far.'

They were glaring at one another. In another moment, I thought, they will be at each other's throats and I did not know what to do. Then to my intense relief Andrei was there. He had thrust his way into the room through the gaping guests. He shut the door firmly behind him and leaned back against it.

'What is all this?' he said quietly and when no one answered, he looked coldly at Leskov. 'Since you have forced your way into my house, sir, kindly behave decently while you are in it.'

'It is not I you should charge with indecent behaviour but the man whom you call friend. You had better take care, Count Kuragin. He has ruined Olga, he may do the same to your wife's sister.'

'I do not need you to teach me how to protect those under my care,' replied Andrei with an icy edge to his voice. 'I would be obliged if you would leave my house.'

'Not until I have done what I came here to do,' and before anyone could prevent him, Fyodor Leskov had taken a step forward and slashed his riding crop twice across Leon's face.

For an instant he did not move, the weals standing out lividly across his cheek. Then he whispered furiously, 'Very well, if that's what you want, I will meet you when and where you like. And now go, or I might be tempted to give you back some of your own medicine.'

'I'll go, but don't fail me this time or by God, I'll have you publicly horse-whipped if I have to do it myself,' and Leskov turned and went out, brushing past Andrei and slamming the door behind him.

'The fool, the damned fool,' muttered Leon. 'I did my best to avoid this and now he has forced it on me.'

Andrei's face was sterner than I had ever seen it. He said, 'How much truth is there in his accusation?'

'None, I swear it.' Leon looked wildly at Andrei and then at me. 'You cannot believe that of me, you cannot. I have never touched her, never . . . never. . . . Whoever says such a thing is a filthy liar!'

'All right, all right, that's enough. I believe you . . . but you will have to go through with it or he will blacken your name from here to Moscow.'

'It seems he has done that already, God damn him. But why? Why? I've done nothing to him.'

'He's an ambitious man. Your grandfather still has influence. He might have won promotion if you had made his sister the Princess Astrov.'

'I never thought of that.' Leon made a restless movement. 'Andrei, will you act for me?'

'It's a crazy business, but someone has got to see you through it, I suppose.'

'I would be grateful.'

I think they had forgotten about me. They were both so calm about it. I burst out indignantly, 'You cannot mean what you say. You cannot be intending to kill one another all for nothing.'

'I am afraid so,' said Andrei grimly. 'Sophie, my dear, this is no place for you. You had better go to Rilla. Tell her to keep the party going for heaven's sake. I will be with her in a moment. Leon and I have one or two details to discuss.'

'I am not going. This concerns me just as much as you.'

'Oh God,' said Leon despairingly, 'why does everything go wrong for me?' He lifted his head proudly. 'I had intended coming to see you tomorrow, Andrei. I have been wanting to say it for a long time, but I had to wait . . . I love Sophie . . . I think I have loved her since the first moment I saw her . . . I want to marry her.'

Andrei looked from him to me. 'And you, Sophie, do you feel the same?'

'Oh yes, yes,' I answered. 'More than anything in the world.'

There was silence for a moment, then Andrei said firmly, 'No. No, I couldn't possibly allow it.'

'But why? Why? There's no possible reason.'

'There is every reason. Oh-I'm not forbidding it for ever. In a year perhaps when you have both had time to think. . . .'

'I don't want to think,' I interrupted fiercely. 'I know . . . now and for ever.'

'You think you do, my dear, but you're very young, you still have a lot to learn and I know Petersburg society. After tonight and what comes from it, every door will be closed against you. You are the stranger, the foreigner, and Olga is one of them. They would ostracize you, destroy you. . . .'

'I don't care. . . .'

'You very soon would. Do you think I want that to happen to Rilla's sister?'

'You cannot stop me,' I said wildly.

'Indeed I can. While you are here in Russia, you are in my care.'

But I would not give in so easily. I turned to Leon. 'Why don't you say something? Tell him it is not so.'

But Leon did not respond as I had hoped.

'No, Sophie, I hate to say it but Andrei is right. I had not thought of it before but it will be all the harder for you because you are not one of us.'

The strain of all that had happened caught up with me. 'Coward!' I cried out at him. 'Coward. It's all words, words, words. What about all those things you said at Valdaya? Did they mean nothing? You are still afraid, afraid to stand up for yourself, afraid of your grandfather. . . .'

'Sophie, don't, please. . . .' but I would not listen to him. The dry sobs choked in my throat and I ran out of the room.

It seemed incredible, but they were still dancing. I could see the couples whirling round, hear the gay lively music, the laughter, and I could not endure it. I ran up the stairs and threw myself on the bed, beating my fists into the pillows, refusing to acknowledge the truth of what Andrei had said, tortured with anxiety when I thought of what could so easily happen to Leon when he faced that madman, Fyodor Leskov.

It must have been four o'clock in the morning when Rilla opened my door. 'Sophie, are you awake?' she whispered.

'Yes.'

She came in and sat on the bed, looking down at me. The candlelight glinted on the jewels round her neck and in her red-gold hair and I felt guilty. She had gone through such a hard struggle to establish herself as Andrei's wife and now I was making it all so difficult for her.

'Andrei has told me everything,' she said. I lay there silently expecting her to load me with reproaches, but she didn't. Instead she said, 'Why didn't you tell me, darling? Did you think I wouldn't understand?'

'You never liked Leon ... besides at first I hardly knew myself. . . .'

'Oh Sophie dearest. . . .' and she leaned forward to kiss me and in a moment I was in her arms, letting the tears come while she murmured soothing words just as she had done when I was very young and had hurt myself or done something foolish and been punished for it.

It was a comfort to feel all barriers gone between us, to tell her everything even though she agreed with Andrei that we must be patient and wait until it had all blown over.

'After all, Leon has brought it on himself, Sophie, you must see that. Try to sleep now,' and she tucked me in and smiled down at me before she blew out the candle. 'Are you sorry that I persuaded you to come to Russia?'

'Oh no, no, never!' I said fervently and meant it with all my heart.

Chapter 17

I don't know what I would have done without Rilla. I would never have been able to face it without her. It is horrible to feel yourself pointed at, to enter a room and feel all eyes turned to you, to hear the whispers and realize it is you that they are talking about, though in the few days before the duel I could think of nothing else but what might come of it. All kinds of crazy ideas went through my mind. I would go to Olga, I would beg her to speak to her brother, I would plead with Prince Astrov. They were all useless, I knew that. Inevitably the day would come and there was nothing any of us could do to prevent it.

Andrei had made the arrangements. He was sterner and more silent than usual these days and it was from Rilla I learned that Jean Reynard was acting as Leskov's second. It distressed me to realize how unpleasant it must have been for him to deal with the man he disliked and how Jean must have enjoyed it. It struck me that it might well be he who had roused Leskov's anger and kept it at boiling point. He had a subtle way of getting under the skin. I knew that.

On the morning they were to meet, the first snow fell. I could not sleep. I tossed restlessly all night and a little after six, I was up, huddled in my dressing gown. Outside, a light blanket of white was laid over everything, pure and sparkling in the first dazzling streaks of sun. At seven I saw Stefan bring up the carriage and Andrei come out of the house, his long black cloak sweeping away the snow, the mahogany case with the pistols under his arm.

I stood in front of the little icon of St George slaying the dragon and tried to pray, but the right words would not come. I thought back to that morning in the Petrovsky Park when Leon and Andrei had faced one another, only I knew instinctively that this time it was deadly serious. There would be no relenting, no firing into the air, no last-minute reconciliation. I could see it all so clearly ... the stretch of grass, the two dark figures, the crisp carpet of snow soon to be stained crimson.

I was letting my imagination run away with me. I plunged my face in icy water and dressed quickly. Downstairs I found Rilla in the dining room pretending to eat and as anxious as myself. We talked of ordinary everyday matters and kept breaking off, our thoughts distracted. The hands of the clock never seemed to move, the minutes went by so slowly. Katya brought in fresh coffee and Rilla poured it. 'Try and drink some, Sophie, while it is hot.' Obediently I lifted the cup to my lips and then put it down again untasted.

It was ten o'clock when we heard the carriage drive up. I was trembling so much I could scarcely speak when Andrei came into the room.

'Leon. . . .' I said and my voice came out in a croak.

'Wounded, but not seriously.'

I got up, hardly knowing what I was doing. 'I must go to him.'

'No.' Andrei stopped me, his hand firmly on my arm when I would have run to the door. 'No, my child, you must not. He will be all right. I have seen to that.'

Rilla said, 'What about Fyodor Leskov?'

Andrei shook his head.

'You can't mean he is dead.'

'Not yet, but it's a bad business. The surgeon holds out little hope.'

'Oh no,' exclaimed Rilla. 'How could Leon do such a thing? They will call it murder.'

'You don't understand. It was his own fault.' In a few graphic words Andrei sketched the whole picture of that morning. 'By his own wish they tossed for first shot and he won. He fired, badly as it turned out. Leon was hit in the left shoulder, but he was still able to take his turn. It takes a particular kind of courage to stand and wait facing a loaded pistol and Leskov is not a soldier, he is not trained to it. I honestly don't think Leon meant to kill, but Leskov's nerves betrayed him, he walked into it.'

'What will happen now?'

'God knows, Sophie, we can only wait and see.'

It was not long before we knew. While Fyodor Leskov hovered between life and death, the Grand Duke took action. He had

186

always been a stickler for morality and the good name of his officers. He had been greatly offended when Leon had broken his engagement, now he sent to have him arrested and Leon had disappeared. He was not at the Astrov palace, not at his army lodgings, not at Valdaya. He had simply vanished.

When I begged Andrei to make some endeavour to find him, he shook his head. 'He's done the wisest thing, Sophie. All this agitation will die down in time. The Grand Duke has suspended him from the regiment. All he will do is to banish him from Petersburg for a while and what does that matter?'

'You don't know how he feels, Andrei,' I said frantically. 'He had pinned every hope on this. He wanted to free himself once and for all and now if Leskov dies, he will feel guilty, he will feel he has failed. He could do something desperate.'

'Listen, Sophie, I think I understand Leon better than you. He was distressed at what he had done. He needs time to find out about himself. Have patience. Time heals a number of things. A few months and this will all be forgotten.'

But there was one thing that Andrei had not calculated on nor I nor anyone. I had never thought that outside events could affect one's life so completely but I was to learn differently.

It was three weeks after the duel when a rumour trickled through from the south that the Tsar had been taken seriously ill. It meant nothing to me. I had never seen Alexander, had hardly even heard him mentioned. He was in Petersburg when I came to Russia and ever since had been in the remote town of Taganrog with the ailing Empress. Everyone believed that it was she who was dying, not the Tsar. Then quite suddenly with a shocking swiftness we heard that he was dead, and the whole city was plunged into the deepest mourning.

Theatres and restaurants were closed, requiem masses were being sung in all the churches, bells tolled from morning to night. But there was more than that. There was no direct heir to the throne. There was no proclamation: 'The Emperor is dead. Long live the Emperor.' It was as if Russia had suddenly become masterless, without direction or leadership. People stood about in the streets muttering and crossing themselves. In the markets the peasants were grumbling to one another, 'We're like sheep. They will sell us in the end.'

It was Andrei who explained the situation to me. One evening when he came from a day spent at the Winter Palace, he said cynically, 'They are offering the crown around like a cup of tea and no one wants it.'

'But that is ridiculous,' I exclaimed.

'You're right, my dear. I agree and so do a number of ministers of state. Such a thing could happen only in Russia. You see, Alexander has no son, no legitimate child, so his next brother should be the heir. But Constantine has never wanted the crown, we all know that. He lives in Warsaw happily married to his unsuitable wife. Only his refusal has never been made public. So Nicholas is between two stools. Should he seize the crown or will he be condemned for it? He has never been popular with the army like Constantine.'

All this controversy seemed rather absurd and quite remote from me until the day I called on Madame Lubova. I don't know what drove me there. The weeks had dragged by on leaden feet. No word had come from Leon and I had a faint hope that in her drawing room I might hear something that would provide a clue as to where he was.

She welcomed me with all her usual exuberance but I did not stay long. There were not so many people as usual in her drawing room and all the talk was of the death of the Tsar and what Nicholas would or would not do until I was weary of it. I was just about to leave when I overheard a few words between Anatol Ryelev and another young man. They were arranging to meet and I heard the poet say, 'He has a flat on Vasilievsky Island. You know it surely, the students' quarter.' And quite suddenly I remembered walking with Andrei at Ryvlach and what he had said about Leon keeping a studio in the city and making sure it was a secret from everyone. I had completely forgotten it until this very moment when it struck me that perhaps this was where he had gone, a place far from fashionable Petersburg, where no one would think of looking for him, where he would be unknown.

It was a chance I was determined to take. I said nothing to Rilla and Andrei, but the next morning I set out, threading my way through the streets, not quite certain of my way and forced to ask the direction in my few words of Russian.

It was a district of tall wooden houses, painted in faded pink and blue, all divided up into rooms and flats, dirty, crowded and colourful. Despite the raw damp morning and the bleak wind blowing off the Neva, children played in the narrow road-ways and women and old men stood in doorways.

I looked round me helplessly, realizing my stupidity in think-ing that I could find him in this warren of buildings when I didn't even know if he might have rented rooms under an assumed name. I spoke to one or two of the women, but it was difficult to make myself understood and they stared and shook their heads. I walked up one street and down another, and had almost given up in despair when I saw a young man come out of a house carrying a pile of books under his arm and took a chance on his speaking French.

'Leonid Karlovitch,' he repeated in answer to my question. 'Yes, I know him. Second house on the right, first floor up. Can't say whether he's there or not. He comes and goes. He's rich, not like us.' He grinned and ran his eye over my fur jacket. 'If you'll pardon my saying so, Mademoiselle, you don't look much like a revolutionary.'

'Revolutionary?'

'Never mind,' he laughed, 'just a joke of mine. Good hunting to you, Mademoiselle.'

It was easy to guess what was in his mind, but it was not that which troubled me. Why revolutionary? And involuntarily I thought of Ryelev and all I had heard in Madame Lubova's drawing room.

The house the student had indicated was painted blue, rather better kept than the others. I ran up the wooden stairs and then stood on the landing, my heart beating painfully. I knocked and waited. I knocked again and a voice said, 'Come in, Marfa, the door is only on the latch.'

So there was someone else . . . I nearly turned and fled, but I braced myself and pushed the door open. It was a large room; canvases, books and papers were scattered everywhere, but it was clean and unexpectedly comfortable with one or two fine pieces of furniture and a Persian rug on the floor. These things I noticed afterwards. All I saw at first was Leon in a high-necked Russian blouse belted round the waist, a smear of paint on one cheek, the tawny hair ruffled and untidy where he had run his fingers through it. He was standing at an easel, brush in hand and he did not look round.

He said irritably, 'Shut the door, can't you? There's a hell of a draught.'

189

I slammed it and he looked up. I saw his eyes widen in surprise. 'Sophie! What in the name of God are you doing here?'

'I came to find you.'

'But how did you know? Who told you?'

'No one. I guessed. Do you want me to go?

'No, of course not. You took me by surprise, that's all.' He threw down his brush. 'When you knocked just now, I thought it was Marfa.'

'Marfa?' I repeated, feeling stifled.

'She's the woman downstairs. She comes to clean for me. Does Andrei know you are here?'

I shook my head. A cold feeling was creeping through me that it was all a terrible mistake. I shouldn't have come. He didn't want me there. I was right, but for the wrong reason, only that was something I did not understand at once. As he came towards me, I noticed he carried his left arm awkwardly and had tucked his hand into his belt and I remembered the wound Andrei had spoken of. It was a month ago now. Surely it should have healed.

'Does your shoulder pain you?'

'Sometimes. I did something foolish and opened it up again.'

'Has a doctor seen it?'

'Not since the beginning. It's not necessary.'

'How do you know? It could be dangerous.'

He laughed. 'It's all right, I tell you. Come and sit down.'

We were talking like strangers with a barrier of ice between us that I could not break down.

'What are you working at?'

'Nothing of importance. It helps to keep me occupied, and while I paint, I can think.'

'What about?'

He took an uncertain step or two and then swung round to face me. 'Sophie, do you remember what you said to me that night after Leskov had gone?'

'I was upset. I said all kinds of foolish things.'

'No, they were not foolish. You called me a coward. You said that all my life I had been afraid and it made me angry. When I faced Leskov in the Alexandrovsky Park, all I wanted to do was to kill him to prove something to myself. Then when I saw him, shaking, nerving himself to await my fire, I despised myself for it and I would have avoided it if I could.'

'He's not going to die,' I said quickly. 'The doctors say now he may pull through.'

'Lucky for me if he does,' he said sombrely. 'But don't you see, I had to have time to think, time to see myself clearly.'

Looking round the room, I had a sudden intuition that this was the real Leon, the man whom Andrei had always known and whom I had only glimpsed occasionally in the hut at Valdaya, with the dogs, with Yakov, the real person behind the irresponsible careless mask of the young aristocratic waster which he had worn for so long.

He came and sat beside me. 'Do you understand, Sophie? Or do you still despise me for it?'

'I shall fall in love with you all over again.'

He smiled and kissed me gently on the lips. 'Now you must go.'

'I shall come back.'

'Better not. Soon I shall come to you. And now I'll walk with you to the bridge and find a droshky to take you home.'

But I did go back, just a week later. I knew it was not the right thing to do. To visit a young man alone in his apartment was enough to blast one's reputation for ever, but I no longer cared. I had a feeling that there was something he was hiding from me and I had to know what it was.

It was a cold crisp morning. The trees in the gardens in front of the Admiralty building were etched in black against a pale sky when I walked across the bridge. The Neva was frozen already from bank to bank and some bold spirits were walking across it. I did not dare. The thought of being sucked under the black waters was too frightening. The streets in the students' quarter were deserted. It was too bleak. The wind bit my face and I was glad of my sheepskin boots and fur hood.

The door to the flat was open but when I went in, I thought at first the room was empty. Then there was a stir on the couch in the corner and Leon half sat up. He looked flushed, his eyes clouded and he said irritably, 'I thought I told you not to come again.'

'What's the matter? Are you ill?'

'I'm all right.' He swung his legs to the floor and got up. 'It's just this cursed shoulder of mine.'

'Let me see.'

I was no expert in these matters, but at home in England with no money to spare for expensive doctors and two young brothers always in trouble, we had all been brought up to know something about treating cuts and bruises.

Leon protested, but I made him pull aside his dressing gown and turn back the shirt. The bandage was blood-caked and had slipped so that it was chafing the raw place. He winced as I tried gently to pull it away. The wound looked red and inflamed, but it was not swollen and I did not think it infected. I fetched water from the tiny kitchen on the landing to cleanse it and since there was no fresh bandage, I folded my own clean linen handkerchief into a pad and fixed it firmly in place.

'Is that better?'

'Marvellous.' He caught at my hand and kissed it. 'My guardian angel.'

'Don't make fun of me. Have you had any breakfast?'

He shrugged his shoulders. 'Marfa seems to have forgotten me this morning.'

Leon might be making a valiant attempt to live the simple life of an artist but he had no idea whatsoever how to look after himself. The cupboard-like kitchen was crammed with dirty cups, half-eaten food, empty wine bottles and stained glasses.

I found some coffee already made and heated it. Then I carried it back to him.

'Where the devil did you find this?'

'Never mind. Drink it.'

'Only if you will stop looking all round you with such a disapproving eye and come and sit beside me.'

There is something inexpressibly sweet about caring for the man you love. I had been fascinated, dazzled, drawn to him almost in spite of myself. Now suddenly Leon had entered my world. I think the hour we spent together, intimate, warm, close, was the happiest I had ever known with him until I made the frightening discovery.

I had taken his cup to the kitchen and while he dressed, I tried to introduce a little order into the chaos. As I piled bottles into an empty box, some papers on the table fell on the floor and I picked them up. I glanced at them before throwing them in the waste bucket. The top sheet was obviously a rough draft with a great many crossings-out and as I stared at it, phrase after phrase leaped out at me.

192

'The basic drive in Russia is fear and fear destroys all life, all intelligence, all generous movements of the soul. . . .'

'The passion for destruction is creative . . . we must tear down in order to rebuild. . . .'

'We must look for abolition of the government, abolition of serfdom, equality for all . . . it is the Tsar who has strangled our liberty in the past, who has raised our hopes and killed them . . . let him die the death of all tyrants. . . .'

Terror clutched at me. I went back to the living room. Leon was struggling into his coat. I took it from him and eased it over his wounded shoulder. Then I held out the paper.

'Leon, what is this?'

He looked startled, then snatched it from me and tore it up. 'Nothing. Just ideas we put down on paper one night when a few friends were here.'

'What friends?'

'No one you know, some of my comrades in the regiment.'

'Revolutionaries?'

He laughed. 'Whatever put that idea in your head?'

But I persisted. 'Is it because of the trouble over the succession? Is something being planned?'

'What could be planned?' He came to me, cupping my face in his two hands. 'Listen, Sophie, your coming here so bravely, the certainty that you care, means more to me than anything in the world, but you must not come to this place again. Do you understand?'

'Why?'

'Never mind why. I don't want any harm to come to you.'

'Leon, what are you going to do?'

'You must trust me. You remember what I said to you once, that we Russians talk and talk but do nothing. Well now, for once, we shall prove that wrong. We shall stir ourselves, we shall act.'

'Who are "we"?'

'You must not ask me that.'

'Does Andrei know about it?'

'Andrei was with us once, but now he thinks differently. Don't worry, Sophie. There's no danger, but this is something I must do or live a coward in my own eyes for the rest of my life. After it's all over, I shall come to you and everything will be different.'

He would not tell me more however much I begged him.

There was about him a resolution, a firmness of purpose that I had never seen before and he would not be shaken. All the way home it tormented me. He had made me promise to say nothing to anyone, but as the unrest in the city grew, I was terribly tempted to break my word.

December came and winter held Petersburg in a hard grip. Snow lay everywhere under grey sullen skies. A bitter wind and showers of freezing sleet blew in my face the morning I crossed the Neva again. I could stand it no longer. Something Andrei had told us the evening before had terrified me.

'It is settled at last,' he had said. 'Constantine has written renouncing the crown and Nicholas has overcome his scruples. He has summoned the State Council for the day after tomorrow. On 14 December, the oath of allegiance will be taken at the Winter Palace and most important of all, the troops will be sworn in.'

'Do you think there will be any trouble?' asked Rilla.

'I doubt it, though there have been rumours. Nicholas is a hard man and not liked by the army, but when it comes to it, they're like sheep. They will do as they are told. The time has not yet come.'

I thought Andrei sounded regretful though he spoke cynically and was wise in the ways of men. But I could only see the light in Leon's eyes, hear the fervour with which he had once said, 'The tree of freedom must be watered with blood.' It thrilled me and it frightened me. I had to go back to the flat. I had to find out what was being planned.

It was midday when I reached the house with the blue shutters and ran up the stairs. On the landing I stopped. The door was half open and the room seemed crowded. I heard someone speaking and recognized the voice of Ryelev.

'It is now, gentlemen, now that we must make our stand. Alexander deceived Russia. He deceived Europe. After we defeated Napoleon and our dead lay scattered on the battle-field, he promised us liberty, but the golden chains wreathed in laurels have been taken off and left only the bare rusty iron that fetters our people.'

There was a murmur of agreement and the poet went on, his voice rising, high-pitched with excitement. 'It is for us to restore the image of man in all its splendour and beauty. Shame and grief and beggary will vanish and be transformed into perfect joy. Freedom for all, this is our aim and there is none greater on this earth. And if we fail, if they strike us down, what does it matter? Someone must point the way. Our martyrdom will teach others, it will awaken Russia, it will never be forgotten.'

The exultation in his voice was madness, yet it was inspiring too, and the young men in the room were carried away by it. They were all talking at once. It might have been a wedding party instead of a conspiracy. I saw Leon leap on a chair. He raised his glass.

'In the Senate Square tomorrow, we shall show Nicholas we mean what we say ... to liberty ... to freedom!' and they cheered him, drinking the champagne and smashing the glasses with a joyful abandon that was both unbearably moving and sheer insanity.

I felt sick. When I thought of the power of Russia, it seemed doomed to failure and yet there was nothing I could do. Even to reveal myself was impossible. Leon would never forgive me. I had grown up in a hard practical world, but he was living in a dream, caught up in something beyond me, something which I could scarcely understand. Hopelessly I went down the stairs and slowly retraced my steps through the thickening snow.

Chapter 18

There are some days in your life that you never remember without an inward shudder. Even in the midst of happiness the horror will flash across your memory and for an instant you are once more caught up in it before it vanishes again into the limbo of forgotten things.

There was a thick white fog curling round houses and rooftops when I looked from my window that morning in December. It had snowed all night and every bare twig in the garden was frozen stiff in a hard frost. I had said nothing to my sister of what I had seen and heard the previous afternoon and, lying in bed sleepless, it had seemed fantastic that the young men whom I knew, who paid me compliments and danced with me, could be concerned with such a desperate plan. It must all come to nothing, I said to myself, it could not really happen, but I was wrong.

The first rumours reached us as we sat at breakfast. Stefan, who had been sent on an errand, came rushing into the dining room, still in his padded overcoat, snow encrusting his boots, forgetting to snatch off his fur cap.

'They are marching, your honour,' he exclaimed breathlessly, 'the regiments, hundreds of them. They are massing in the Senate Square, shouting for Constantine.'

'What are you talking about?' said Andrei. 'It is not Constantine, it is the Grand Duke Nicholas who will be Tsar. You must be mistaken.'

'No, sir, believe me. I speak the truth. I called out to some of them. They have refused to take the oath, they are defying their officers.' He crossed himself hurriedly. 'God protect us, your honour, but what is to become of our country? We shall all be murdered before the day is out.'

'Nonsense. Pull yourself together, Stefan. Is this the way to behave? Go back to the servants and tell them there is nothing to fear.'

'Yes, sir, yes, of course.' He bowed himself out of the room. When the door had closed behind him, Andrei pushed aside his plate and stood up.

'I am going out to see what truth there is in all this.'

'No, Andrei, please.'

'I must, my dear. If there is some disturbance, I want to know how serious it is.'

'But don't you see?' urged Rilla. 'It has happened at last . . . what you have been afraid of . . . what you advised them not to do again and again. If you go out now, they will believe you have changed your mind, that you are prepared to march with them and what good will it do? How can anyone stand against the Tsar?'

I realized then with a shattering certainty that this was something Rilla and Andrei had talked of a hundred times without my knowledge. Even back in the spring they must have argued about it.

'They are my friends,' said Andrei stubbornly. 'I owe it to them. This shout for Constantine is only a blind. What they will be demanding is reform, freedom for the serfs, freedom for the press, a constitutional government and Nicholas will never agree. They misjudge his strength and his will. I may be able to do something, persuade them to see reason, prevent unnecessary bloodshed.'

'They are not all your friends,' said Rilla quickly. 'You know that. Isn't Jean Reynard one of them? You have said so all along and if things go wrong, he will not hesitate to turn his coat. He will betray them and you too.'

I could not keep it in any longer. I said, 'Leon is with them. He will be out there too.'

'Leon? What are you talking about, Sophie? You are dreaming. He is not in Petersburg.'

'He is. I have seen him, spoken with him.'

'Sophie, how could you keep it from us?' exclaimed Rilla reproachfully.

'I wanted to tell you, but he made me promise. . . .'

Andrei interrupted me. 'This is no time for childish promises. When have you seen him? Where? Don't you realize what this could mean? This is not a game. It's deadly serious. Now quickly, what is it you know?'

'It was at his flat in the students' quarter. I heard them

yesterday. I think they have been meeting in many places.' I told them about Ryelev, about what Leon had said. It was little enough, but it brought Andrei to a decision.

'The fool! The damned young fool! I warned him of this months ago. I'm going out. I may be able to reach him and bring him back.'

'But where will you find him?'

'At the barracks if he is not already in the square. His men will be only too ready to listen. Already they resent the way Nicholas has treated him.' Rilla tried to protest, but he put a hand on her shoulder. 'Now listen to me, both of you. Stay in the house and don't worry. This won't affect us. I will take Stefan with me and try to send him back with news when I can. It's more than likely the whole affair will come to nothing and to-night we shall be laughing at it, but it is as well to be prepared.'

We did not believe that any more than he did himself, and it was hard to remain quietly indoors carrying on with ordinary household tasks when so much was at stake. One of the servants who had been to the market came back with a garbled story of having heard shots fired.

'You imagined it,' said Rilla firmly. 'It could have been anything.'

'No, Barina, I heard them, I swear it,' she gabbled. 'And afterwards I saw him, galloping away from the square, all covered in blood he was and his horse too.'

Rilla calmed them down in the kitchens as best she could, but when we came back to the dining room, she looked grave.

'If that is true, it's just the kind of thing that will set them off. One such incident, someone is hurt, and they will all go fighting mad.'

Stefan returned at midday and confirmed our worst fears. One of the generals who had tried to persuade the men to turn back had been shot at and was believed dying, another had been dragged from his horse and was lucky to escape with his life. The Grand Duke himself had come out of the palace, riding round the square, appealing to them to go quietly back to their barracks and no harm would come to them but though no one had yet raised a hand against him, they still would not move.

Luncheon was served and we made a pretence of swallowing some of it. Then quite suddenly Rilla laid down her knife and fork.

'I can't stay here and wait,' she said. 'I'm going out to see for myself.'

'I'll come with you.'

'No, Sophie. You don't know these people and if we get separated. . . .'

'Don't argue, Rilla. I'm just as afraid for Leon as you are for Andrei. I'm coming with you.'

We dressed ourselves in the thickest darkest clothes we had and tied woollen scarves tightly over our heads. It was three o'clock when we left the house and an early dusk was already creeping along the streets and darkening the sky. We were not more than ten minutes' walk from the square, but the streets were so full of people, some bewildered, some just curious, that it took us a long time to push our way through.

I don't think I shall ever forget my first sight of the square, that dense mass of men standing quietly in their ranks and behind them the towering snow-covered Admiralty building with its slender golden spire. All work had ceased on the gaunt structure of the half-built Cathedral of St Isaac. Men and boys were perched on the iron girders like birds on a tree. It was strangely quiet. Throughout that packed mob there was only the occasional burst of laughter, the jingle of spurs and the crackling of one or two fires burning against the biting cold.

For an instant we stood there helplessly. How were we ever to find anyone in that huge silent crowd? Then Rilla pointed.

'Do you see, Sophie? Over to the left—there is Leon's regiment,' and I saw the green uniforms with the gold oak leaves.

We began to edge our way round the side of the square. At one spot we were forced to climb a flight of stone steps and at the top, Rilla gripped my arm.

'The Grand Duke has come out again. He is there—on a white horse. . . .'

'What is he saying?'

The voice reached us, thin and distant, but quite clear in the hush. 'He is saying this is their last chance. If they do not disperse now, he will have to use force.'

'What force?'

'The guns have already been brought out. They are turned on them. He has only to give the order to fire.'

'Oh no !' The horror of it strangled my breath in my throat,

199

but the threat was ignored. No one stirred, no one moved a muscle.

Rilla said urgently, 'Come on. We must find them if we can.'

We had begun to realize how foolish we had been. We had to fight every step of the way round two sides of the square. I was the first to see them. I grabbed at Rilla's hand and pointed, and at that very moment the guns fired, a volley so deafening and thunderous, it shook us where we stood. We threw our arms round each other in terror. A shudder seemed to run across the square, but still they did not break.

Then as the smoke cleared a little, Rilla exclaimed shakily, 'They have fired into the air. They have refused to shoot down their comrades.'

Men, women, even children, had come out to join the insurgents. Some of them had brought food and wine, sharing it with the soldiers. A few of them were drunk. One of the men was laughing. He put his arm round my waist.

'Looking for your lover, pretty one, eh? Give him a kiss for me when you find him,' and I felt his rough beard tickle my cheek.

The second volley came while we were still struggling to reach them. This time the orders must have been more strictly enforced. The shells mowed a bloody path through the silent crowd. I was too frightened to move. For a few seconds as the thick smoke drifted and eddied, there was no sound, no movement, the soldiers still held their ground. Someone beside me choked and fell to his knees. I saw the blood stain the trampled snow and I wanted to scream, but my throat seemed to close up with horror. Then with a sort of groan of anguish, they broke and began to flee.

I cannot describe the next few minutes. It was a crazy inferno. What had been a silent demonstration, almost a picnic, had become a massacre lit by the lurid glare of exploding shells and yellow bursts of musket fire, a pandemonium of shattering glass, falling bricks, of screams and groans and horses slithering in panic on the icy cobblestones. I think Rilla and I were possessed by the same madness. In absolute terror we thought only of reaching the men we loved and dying with them.

Nicholas must have called out those regiments still loyal to him. After the guns came the cavalry charging into the crowds with drawn sabres driving them back and back. Everywhere they were fighting. The light had faded by now. It was difficult to see anyone clearly or to know friend from enemy.

I had lost Rilla in the stampede. I was crushed against a railing only a few paces from Leon and Andrei but I could not reach them. I climbed up a couple of steps clinging to an iron post to prevent myself being trampled by the plunging horses. I could not move, but as the crowd shifted in front of me, I could see that Leon had drawn his sword. He was making an heroic attempt to rally the few men left to him, but their spirit had been crushed.

Then quite suddenly out of the shadows and confusion I thought I saw the tall dark figure, the white face of Jean Reynard. Andrei had his back to him. He had gripped Leon by the arm. I think he was arguing with him, urging him to come away. Jean had a pistol in his hand. He raised it slowly. I knew now what he had meant. His chance had come. He had only to take Andrei prisoner, denounce him to the Tsar, and Leon too, and his revenge would be complete. Nothing could save them. I wanted to cry out and couldn't. I had to watch like in a nightmare where you are paralysed and cannot move. What happened next none of us ever knew for certain. More cavalry had come charging across the square. One of them was shouting in a kind of frenzy swinging his sabre above his head. He was riding straight towards Andrei. Jean seemed to leap forward. I saw Andrei stumble and fall, but it was not he but Jean who went down under those cruel hooves.

Rilla reached them before I did. I made a supreme effort and fought my way through. The horseman had passed. Andrei was staring down dazedly at the man at his feet.

'He saved my life,' he said, 'but for him. . . .' He went down on his knees beside the twisted broken body.

In the midst of turmoil and confusion, the issue between them had come to a sudden and horrible finish. I could guess how he felt but there was no time to think of that now. No mercy was being shown anywhere. The loyal troops were taking a savage revenge. They were killing and taking prisoners. Anyone wearing the uniform of the rebel regiments was in deadly danger. I could think only of Leon. I realized with terror that he had been hurt. He was struggling to find a footing on the slippery ice and I could see the soldiers rounding up the stragglers. I did the only thing I could think of. I threw myself on my knees beside him, putting my arms round him so that my dark cloak covered us both.

A rough voice said, 'Best get your sweetheart out of this, Mademoiselle, quick as you can or he'll go the way of the rest.'

My gloves were covered with blood. Leon groaned and slid away from me when I tried to help him. Then Andrei was beside me. He hoisted Leon to his feet.

'Hold on to me,' he said, and drew Leon's arm round his shoulders. Then half carrying, half supporting him, with Rilla and I helping as much as we could, we made our slow difficult way across the shambles of the square where men, women and even children lay dead or dying, the blood already turning to ice and cracking under our feet.

It was a nightmare journey. Leon was only half conscious and we were haunted by the fear that we might be stopped at any moment, but we reached the house at last. Between them Andrei and Stefan carried Leon up the stairs and laid him on the bed. They stripped off his coat. The sabre cut had bitten deep into his shoulder and slashed across his breast and he had lost a great deal of blood. His shirt was caked with it.

Rilla said anxiously, 'We should fetch Dr Sorin, Andrei. The wound needs to be stitched.'

'We dare not risk it, not until we know what reprisals Nicholas will take for this day's work. If Dr Sorin talks, then it could be all over for Leon. The only way we can save him is to keep him here and, if necessary, swear that he has been sick for days in this house and never stirred out of it.'

'But if the leaders are arrested, they have ways of making them talk . . . and what about you?' said Rilla. 'What will they do to you?'

Andrei shrugged his shoulders. 'That's a risk we must take. Staunch the wound. Do the best you can for him, Rilla. It is all we can do.'

I held the bowl of water while my sister sponged away the blood. Leon had recovered consciousness. The grey eyes turned frantically to Andrei.

'What happened? How did I get here? I was trying to rally the men. . . .'

'Lie back, my dear fellow. You'll only start the bleeding again. It's all over. There's nothing anyone can do now.'

Rilla said, 'I'm sorry, Leon, I'm going to hurt you,' and I saw

202

his face contract with pain while she firmly pressed the wound together and placed the pad over it. Andrei raised him while she wound the bandage in place. Leon's eyes were on him again.

'I remember now ... I saw Jean Reynard ... he had a pistol in his hand ... I thought he was going to kill you. ...'

'On the contrary he saved my life. If he had not thrust me out of the way, I would not be here now.'

Leon's face was flushed. 'We were betrayed. We knew that this morning before we even set out from the barracks. Someone had warned Nicholas. Was it he, Andrei? Was it Jean?'

'That is something we shall never know,' replied Andrei sombrely. 'He is dead. It is finished.'

'And the others? What has happened to the others?'

'Now don't excite yourself.' Andrei pressed him gently back against the pillows. 'Keep quiet. As soon as we know anything, I promise you shall hear of it.'

It was a long evening and a still longer night. Leon was in great pain and so restless that we took it in turns to sit beside him. He kept asking for news and we could give him none. It was as if a hush had settled over the city, a conspiracy of silence. The streets were empty. Everyone had barricaded themselves inside their own homes and Andrei judged it wise to forbid any of the servants to leave the house until he was able to find out more of what was happening.

Towards morning Leon fell into an uneasy feverish sleep and I left Katya sitting with him. I came down the stairs intending to fetch myself some hot tea and met Andrei in the hall, booted and cloaked, and after the weariness and anxiety of the night I had a tremendous longing to be free of the house even if only for a few minutes, to feel the fresh icy touch of snow, breathe the cold clean air.

I said, 'Where are you going?'

'I don't know. Perhaps to the palace. Tell Rilla, will you? She is sleeping and I don't want to disturb her.'

'May I walk with you?'

He smiled and touched my cheek. 'You ought to go and rest, little one, you look exhausted.'

'I'd rather go out even if only to the end of the road.'

'Very well, but wrap yourself up. It will be bitterly cold and you had better bring Malika with you.'

A few minutes later we were outside the house, the Borzoi

pacing beside me on his leash. Except for tradesmen and a few men and women hurrying to their daily work, the streets were empty. Andrei drew my arm through his and we walked quickly towards the Senate Square. Yesterday's tragedy was still so vivid in my mind, I don't know what I expected to see—a battlefield perhaps strewn with wreckage—certainly not the uncanny spectacle that met our eyes.

An army of workmen must have laboured all night. It was swept, no trace of blood, no dead, no guns, not a stone or brick or pane of glass out of place, and everywhere a carpet of fresh clean snow though none had fallen since the previous morning.

'So that is it,' said Andrei with bitter irony. 'The slate is to be wiped clean. It is not to be forgotten—oh no—it never happened.'

'But it did happen,' I insisted, 'you cannot wipe a massacre out of men's memories.'

'That remains to be seen. Go back now, Sophie. Take Malika with you. I am going to the Winter Palace. I have acquaintances there. I shall be able to find out the truth.'

I did as he told me and I was with Leon later in the morning when he returned. As soon as he came into the room, Leon forced himself up in the bed despite my protests.

'Thank God, you are here at last. Tell me quickly—what is Nicholas going to do?'

Andrei did not mince his words. He said grimly, 'It is bad, very bad. There have been more than a hundred arrests already.'

'Ryelev?'

'Yes, others too. They are being interrogated now by the Tsar himself.'

'Oh God, and I am not there with them. We did not intend bloodshed, Andrei, I swear we didn't. It was not we who fired the first shot. We wanted to demonstrate our belief in what we asked. We demanded only the right to speak, to think, to live as free men.'

'Forget it now.'

'How can I forget?' Leon was feverishly excited. 'I am the deserter, lying here safe, and leaving them to pay the penalty.'

'It is small thanks to you that you are,' said Andrei with a sudden gust of anger. 'Do you realize that if it were not for Sophie, you would be dead by now, like so many others, thrust through the ice of the Neva to drown, or on your way to a cell in the Peter and Paul....'

'Andrei, don't! He is sick. He doesn't know what he is saying.'

But Andrei firmly put me aside. 'Sick or not, he is going to hear what I have to say.' He stood looking down at Leon, more angry than I had ever seen him. 'I have put my wife, my unborn child, my household, to say nothing of myself, in danger for your sake and all you can do is to lie here babbling heroic nonsense about wanting to be out there, dying with them. Isn't it time you stopped being obsessed with yourself, pulled yourself together, tried to do something useful with your life, instead of talking?'

'Andrei, stop! You're being unfair to him.'

'Be quiet, Sophie. I've been wanting to say this for a long time. Isn't it high time you grew up, accepted your responsibilities? It is not Russia you have been fighting for. It is just another excuse to defy your grandfather.'

'That's not true. Damn you, Andrei, you know that. It was you who first showed me the way.'

'Yes, and regretted it ever since. Oh don't think I don't grieve over yesterday's tragedy just as much as you. Don't think there haven't been moments when I too wanted to stand up on the barricades, wave my sword and shout defiance at the Tsar, at all the injustices, all the persecutions, all the restrictions under which we live, but it's no good. It's got to take time. I have realized that the moment has not yet come to tear out the evil by the roots. One has to be content with cutting off the rotten branches. And if you want to marry Sophie ... and I suppose you do ... or are you going to break her heart too...?'

'By God, Andrei, this is too much. If I wasn't tied to this damnable bed, I'd ... I'd....'

'Call me out, I suppose, and shoot me as you tried to shoot Leskov, and a lot of good that would do!' Andrei's rage blew itself out as quickly as it had arisen. 'Oh for heaven's sake, grow up, Leon, and don't look so furious. You will work yourself into a fever and then Rilla will blame me for it. You had better take things quietly and regain your strength. We are not out of the wood yet, not by a long way. Now I'm going to take Sophie away. She is worn out with taking care of you.'

Leon was leaning back against his pillows, looking so white

and stricken that I wanted to stay with him, but Andrei took my arm and pushed me out of the room in front of him.

Outside I said indignantly, 'You shouldn't have done that. It was unfair, it was cruel.'

'It was nothing of the kind. It was the best thing for him. It shocked him into reality which is what I intended. You mustn't be too kind to him, my dear. A sharp wind can be bracing. Now go and lie down.' When I still hesitated, he smiled and gave me a little push towards my own room. 'Go on now and don't fret. I'll see that he doesn't die while your back is turned!'

Chapter 19

We were living on a knife edge of insecurity. At any moment during that brutal interrogation at the Winter Palace, someone driven to despair and hoping to save himself might well denounce Leon and even Andrei too. Rilla never said a word of reproach, but every time I thought of their happiness at the coming child, I felt guilty that, because of me, their whole life might be destroyed. To add to our anxiety, as the hours went slowly by, Leon grew steadily worse.

Rilla had tried every remedy she could think of but still the fever mounted. The sabre cut had slashed across the partly healed wound. She was gravely worried about infection. Late one night she said, 'I dare not take the responsibility. We must call the doctor.'

Andrei nodded. We had been forced to call upon his help. Hardly knowing what he was doing, Leon had been struggling to get out of bed, saying wildly that he must leave the house, must give himself up.

'If they find me here,' he kept muttering, 'it is you who will suffer. I have done enough harm already.'

Andrei was kind but firm, persuading him, soothing him, until he lay back exhausted and while I wrung out towels in ice-cold water and laid them on his burning forehead, Andrei said, 'Maybe I was too harsh with him. I should have remembered the pressure he has been living under these last months. I will send Stefan for Dr Sorin.'

It was nearly midnight when the doctor came. He was not homely and comfortable like Dr Arnoud, but a fashionable physician, elegant and self-assured, who wasted no words and had a cool sarcastic manner. He examined the wound and commended Rilla briefly for what she had done.

'It will heal well enough,' he said, 'he is young and has clean healthy flesh. How did it happen?'

'A carriage accident,' said Andrei shortly.

'Indeed.' The doctor raised thin ironic eyebrows. 'A strange accident that threw him forward on to a naked blade. Is he in the habit of travelling with an unsheathed sabre? What was he afraid of?'

'These are dangerous times.'

'Dangerous indeed, Count Kuragin, in more ways than one. I suggest you keep him very quiet, no worry, no anxiety, no visitors,' he smiled thinly. 'I imagine you realize that already.' And we knew that he had guessed the truth and all we could do was to rely on his professional integrity not to run with the story all over Petersburg.

He went out with Andrei and Rilla and I remained sitting by the bed. After a moment Leon opened his eyes, lucid, not clouded with fever as they had been all day.

'What did that old fool say? Am I going to die?'

'No, of course not. If you'll only be sensible and lie quietly, you'll soon be better.'

'Sensible? That's something I've never been. Maybe it would be better if I did die. Andrei is right. A popinjay soldier, a failed revolutionary. . . .'

'Sometimes it is good to fail,' I said firmly, 'for then you can go on trying.'

'Oh Sophie, Sophie!' He laughed weakly. 'I'm not even going to be allowed to die in peace. . . .' but though he turned his head away wearily, the hand on the coverlet groped towards me and I clasped it in mine.

When Rilla came back, he was asleep, the first restful sleep since we had brought him back from the square. A few days later he was insisting on getting out of bed though the doctor was against it. It was that afternoon that Prince Astrov called.

I was in the morning room, my needlework on my lap, and Andrei was writing at his desk, when he was shown in and I got up at once to leave them together. Andrei stopped me.

'Don't go, Sophie.'

'I would be obliged if I could speak with you alone,' said the old man stiffly. He stood just inside the door, small, erect as ever, in his old-fashioned dark blue coat, the white jewelled cross for valour in battle at his neck.

I looked at Andrei but he gestured to me to stay so I sat down again, picking up my embroidery and pretending to hunt for silks to thread my needle.

'If you have something to say concerning your grandson, my dear Prince,' said Andrei, 'I think perhaps you should know that Leon has informed me that he wishes to marry Sophie.'

The Prince frowned. 'When did he make this outrageous proposal?'

'Some little time ago,' went on Andrei smoothly. 'I have not yet given my consent, but since it concerns Sophie, I think she should hear what you have to say.'

Prince Astrov was clearly taken aback. 'You have not given your consent,' he began.

'Certainly not. I do not consider Leon a fit husband. . . .'

'Not fit,' he repeated with proud indignation, 'an Astrov . . . and a little English miss. . . .'

'I would beg you to remember that the little English miss is the sister of the Countess Kuragina,' replied Andrei calmly. 'But it is not the question of birth that troubles me, it is the question of character.'

'Character? What are you implying? I did not come here to hear my grandson insulted,' said the Prince with dignity.

'I intend no insult. I was simply explaining the situation. I am surprised you should take offence. I understood that you disapproved of Leon as much if not more than I.'

I had a suspicion that Andrei was enjoying himself and if I had not been so anxious, I think I too would have been amused at the neat way he had turned the tables on the old man who was struggling between family pride and his anger with Leon, but I could not help feeling there was something more serious behind his coming and we were soon to know what it was.

The fierce grey eyes under the jutting eyebrows gave me a withering look, then he took a step towards Andrei, leaning on his stick. 'What I think or do not think is beside the point,' he said curtly. 'What I want . . . what I demand from you is the whereabouts of my grandson at this moment?'

I saw Andrei hesitate before he said quietly, 'He is here . . . in this house.'

'Ah, I thought as much. Do you realize what you are doing, harbouring a traitor, a renegade, a revolutionary?' He spat out the words with a cold anger.

'I really don't understand to what you refer. You are quite mistaken. Leon came back secretly to Petersburg some days ago, rashly, I thought, in the circumstances, but he had suffered quite

209

a serious accident and though I do not care for the way in which he has behaved, it is not my custom to turn a friend from my door.'

'Tscha,' snorted Prince Astrov contemptuously. 'If you think that flimsy story will stand up under interrogation, then you are more of a fool than I thought. Don't imagine that I don't know perfectly well what has happened. For two hundred years an Astrov has served the throne loyally. How do you think I feel when the last of them in his madness destroys a long and honourable tradition?'

'Without admitting that Leon has done anything of the kind, has it never occurred to you, Prince, that it sometimes requires more courage to fly in the face of tradition than to follow meekly in the easy path laid down for you since babyhood.'

Prince Astrov stared at him for a moment, then he said abruptly, 'I am not concerned with your opinion, nor did I come here to bandy words with you. I would be glad of an opportunity to speak with my grandson.'

'I suppose I cannot prevent you, but I would beg you to remember that he has been ill and is still scarcely recovered. I should be sorry to see my wife's hours of devoted care destroyed in one afternoon. Sophie, go and see if Leon will consent to receive his grandfather.'

I preceded Prince Astrov up the stairs and left him standing outside while I went into the bedroom. It was late afternoon and the short winter day was already drawing in. Leon was lying on the sofa half asleep. I lit the lamp on the table and touched his hand.

'Dearest, your grandfather is here to see you.'

He opened his eyes and I saw a curious look, half anger, half dismay, cross his face. Then he put aside the rug and pulled himself to his feet as Prince Astrov came into the room.

I had no intention of leaving them alone together, but I moved away to draw the heavy velvet curtains. Outside it was snowing, the flakes swirling down in a white cloud out of a bleak grey sky. When I turned back, I saw them in the mellow light of the lamp, Leon, a little unsteady but tall in the long dark dressing gown, and it struck me suddenly how very frail and old his grandfather looked.

They stood facing one another in silence, then the Prince said irritably, 'Sit down, sit down. You should not be standing when you are only just out of your bed.'

But Leon did not sit. I think he feared to show even the slightest weakness. He looked his grandfather straight in the eyes and said, 'You know, don't you?'

'Oh yes, I know, though your friend downstairs tried hard to make me believe otherwise. Do you know what I was tempted to do when the news came to me? I was tempted to go to the Tsar, to say to him, "There is one missing out of your bunch of traitors ... my grandson, Leonid Astrov, son of a man who died for you at Borodino, grandson and great grandson of men who've given their whole lives to Russia. Take him, do what you like with him ... a treacherous dog deserves to die the death of a dog!" '

'And did you?'

'No, fool that I am.'

'Why?'

'Why? Why? God knows. Because in the end it is hard to see one's own flesh and blood die on the gallows or be buried alive in Siberia. But I could still do it,' the old man's eyes flamed with sudden fire. 'I could still do it even if it means tearing the heart out of my body.' He took a step towards Leon, watching him. 'Suppose I give you a choice. Give up all this nonsense,' and the wave of his hand included me, 'come home with me now or tomorrow the Emperor has proof of your treachery.'

For the space of a heart beat they measured one another, then Leon said quietly, 'There's no question of choice. If that's what you want, I'll save you the trouble. I'll go to the palace now tonight.'

I trembled because I knew he would do it. He would give himself up rather than bring harm to Andrei and I watched the old man with my heart in my mouth.

'No,' he said at last with a weary gesture. 'No. By some miracle or other you have escaped and who am I to question the intervention of God ... or is it the devil?'

'Neither as it happens. If it had not been for Sophie, I should not be here now.'

'Running away, eh? Is that it? Hiding behind a woman's skirts?'

I saw Leon flush but he held back the anger. 'You're a hard man, grandfather. You know well enough that if it comes to it,

211

I am as willing to die for my Russia as my father did. I would not fail him.'

'Your Russia,' repeated the old man with contempt. 'And what is that? An anarchy, a country with no law, no decency, no authority. You would knock away the prop that supports the state. Do you think you can uproot the tree of sovereignty which has stood since the first Prince of Muscovy wore the crown of Holy Russia?'

'Perhaps not, but I can do as Andrei says, I can begin by cutting back the branches.'

'Well, well, you must go your own way, I suppose. I tried to give you back your heritage, the Astrovs were princes before the Romanovs came to the throne, but you have rejected it. You will paint your pictures, till your soil, hobnob with your serfs like your friend, Andrei Kuragin. I want no part in it.'

He moved slowly towards the door. As he reached it, Leon took a step towards him. 'Grandfather, I am sorry, truly I am.'

The old man stopped and looked back, his face stern, no softening, no relenting in the harsh features, yet I could have sworn there was the glitter of tears in the bright eyes, but he only said gruffly, 'Irina was asking to come with me today and I forbade it. I shall send her to you tomorrow.'

When he had gone, Leon let himself drop on the sofa. 'He despises me,' he said dully.

'No, he doesn't, not in his heart. It's just that it's hard for him to see things as you do. He lives in the past.'

'Maybe.' He looked up at me, smiling ruefully. 'I'm like the prince in the fairy tale. I've burst the barrel, Sophie, but the question is: am I going to drown?' He held out his hand and I went to sit beside him. 'Valdaya will be mine at any rate,' he went on. 'Grandfather can't deny me that. Will you like living there, Sophie?'

The thought of the great gloomy house frightened me, but I knew his love for it. 'Why not?' I said. 'We can change it.'

He began to talk of what he would do, impossible dreams most of them, but it was as if he had shed a burden. For the first time he would be free to do as he pleased and, as we planned our future, we forgot that it is not always so easy to escape the consequences of the past.

Irina came very early the next morning and with her came Michael Federov. We were all there in the room. She flung her arms round her brother's neck, but after the first moment of joyful reunion, she drew away.

'Michael has something to tell you. It was grandfather who said he should come. You must listen, Leon.'

'What is it?'

I knew that Michael had held different views. He had refused to join in the march to the Senate Square. He had remained loyal to Nicholas. He said a little awkwardly, 'I have been on duty all night at the palace and one cannot help hearing what is going on. Your name was mentioned.'

'By whom?'

'Does it matter? The Tsar dismissed it.'

'What did he say?'

'You won't like it.'

'Oh for God's sake, Michael,' said Leon impatiently.

'He said, "Leonid Karlovitch has never had a thought in his head for anyone but himself. Besides he is not even in Petersburg." '

I saw Leon flush at the Tsar's contempt, but Michael went on urgently. 'This is what is important. If it should come to his ears that you are here in this house and wounded ... and it could so very easily ... it is happening to others ... he is going to think again.'

We looked at one another with a cold touch of fear, then Andrei said briskly, 'In that case you must not be in Petersburg. You must be miles away from here, the further away the better. I suggest England.'

'England?' I exclaimed.

'England,' he said firmly. 'And we will make the first move now. The sooner all of us are out of the city, the less chance of someone carrying tales to Nicholas.'

That very evening the sleighs carried us out of Petersburg.

There was a reception at the Winter Palace and as we swept past, we saw the light streaming from the windows, the carriages drawing up and the guests in their diamonds and furs going up the steps. Leon sat in silence and I knew he was thinking of the days and nights of questioning and of the friends who already lay in chains in the dungeons of the Peter and Paul. The roads had frozen hard and we were travelling swiftly over the packed ice. We reached Ryvlach in the early morning. The journey had told on Leon. He was deathly pale, but he would not let Andrei help him from the sleigh. When he had gone in, Rilla looked after him anxiously.

'He cannot possibly travel yet. The wound will reopen. It needs constant care.'

'He has a couple of days to rest and regain his strength,' said Andrei. 'It will take that time to make arrangements.'

No one had said a word about me and in that time I made up my mind. It was the evening of the next day when we were all in the drawing room that I dropped my bombshell.

Andrei had been out all day and when he came back he said, 'It is all fixed. I suggest you leave tomorrow, Leon. With post horses you will soon be out of Russia.'

'You have all forgotten one thing,' I said loudly so that they all turned to look at me. 'Leon is sick. He cannot possibly travel alone. I shall go with him.'

'No, Sophie, I will not allow it,' exclaimed Rilla.

'You cannot stop me.'

'Sophie dearest, you must not.' Leon was more forcible and more urgent. 'In a few months, this will be all over and I shall come back.'

'A few months may be too late. Who knows what is going to happen? I am going with you now.'

'Andrei, you do something,' said Rilla. 'Tell her it is impossible, quite unthinkable to do such a foolish thing.'

Andrei was leaning back in his chair. He said dryly, 'I can tell her all that. I can even lock her in her room, but is it going to stop her? I've been married into your family for more than four years, my dear. I am beginning to know when I am beaten.'

I had made the bold move, I had proved my courage, and now suddenly I was overwhelmed with doubt. Not of myself, but of Leon. I said in a small voice, 'If you don't really want me. . . .'

'Of course he wants you and he will marry you too, properly and decently, instead of running off like a pair of eloping lovers.'

The sharp voice startled us and we all gasped at the sight of Aunt Vera coming downstairs for the first time in years, leaning on Katya's arm and brandishing her stick at us.

'Not one of you thought to tell me what was going on. I'd not have heard a word of it but for this sensible girl here. Andrei, lend me your arm,' she commanded imperiously. 'It's a long time since I've done any running up and down stairs.'

He assisted her to a chair where she sat bolt upright, bright blue eyes looking from me to Leon.

'Don't all sit there staring at one another like a lot of boobies. Do I have to do all the thinking for you? What could be more natural than a wedding trip to England to visit the bride's family?'

'She's right, you know,' said Andrei slowly. 'It's an excellent idea. It will have the ring of truth even if it comes to the Tsar's ears.'

'Of course I'm right,' replied the old lady acidly. 'I haven't quite lost all my wits.'

'No,' said Leon. 'It is kind of you, Vera Andreyevitch, to take so much thought for me, but you don't quite understand. Sophie could be marrying a hunted man. The Tsar has a long arm. I could still be arrested.'

'And what if you are? My dear boy, you may think yourself very worldly wise, but you don't know one thing about women. Do you imagine that Sophie would not prefer those few months with you to years and years with nothing. But do as I say and nothing will happen,' and she beamed round at us triumphantly.

So that was how I came to be married in the village church by a nervous priest in deadly fear of Dmitri's wrath if he refused to perform the ceremony. I went up the aisle on Andrei's arm and Simon stood by Leon and there was no music, no singing, no ritual and not even a wedding ring, only that plain old-fashioned gold band that had once belonged to Leon's grand-mother.

There was no wedding feast. Outside the church Rilla hugged me with tears in her eyes and Andrei lifted me into the sleigh beside Leon.

'We will see you at our son's christening,' he whispered and kissed me lightly. 'Take care of her, Leon, or you will answer to me for it.'

Miles and miles of snow and dark pine forests with the rugs piled round us and Leon's hand in mine. I thought of last spring. Ten months since I had come to Russia, sore and unhappy, hating every mile that took me from England. Now I was going back there with my husband and it was home no longer. I wondered what Mamma would say, faced with another Russian son-in-law, and what Leon would make of the shabby little house in Fulham.

He turned to look at me, his gloved fingers touching my cheek tenderly. 'Scared?'

'Yes.'

'So am I.'

He leaned forward to kiss me, his lips cold as ice, but a deep warm joy ran all through me. The future was uncertain, difficulties might loom ahead, but we were together and we would come back. In my baggage somewhere was the icon Andrei had bought for me on the day of the fair.

'Pray with faith and simplicity and the saint will give you your heart's desire.' He had already given me Leon, he would give us our future too.